I could have no greater joy
than to hear that my children live in the truth.[1]

---

[1] 3 John 1:4, New Living Translation

The Butler Did It

By Susan McGeown

Faith Inspired Books

Published by Faith Inspired Books

Published by Faith Inspired Books
3 Kathleen Place, Bridgewater, New Jersey 08807
www.FaithInspiredBooks.com

ISBN: 978-0-6151-4877-9

Magnificent Cover Art courtesy of Laury Vaden
magentaswan@patmedia.net

<u>Just in case you're wondering:</u>
All characters in this book have no existence outside the imagination of the author and have no relation whatsoever to anyone bearing the same name or names. They are not even distantly inspired by any individual known or unknown to the author, and all incidents are pure invention.**

**However, that doesn't mean I haven't put some of you in some of my other books! Ha.

<u>To My Boys:</u>

My Sons
- ❖ Ian
- ❖ Luke

My Nephews
- ❖ Matthew
- ❖ Jack
- ❖ Joseph
- ❖ Dominic
- ❖ Samuel

Table of Contents

He attacked everything in life with a mix of extraordinary genius and naïve
incompetence,
and it was often difficult to tell which was which.[2]

Chapter One

Profile on Computer
Industry Executive Adam LeGrande

The world according to Adam LeGrande –
the youngest person ever to head a Fortune 500 firm.

Business Today, May: When Adam LeGrande graduated from MIT with a doctorate in computational research, he was still unable to drive a car, cast a vote, or even enter one of the many local college bars. That's because he was only sixteen. By the time he revolutionized the worldwide computer banking industry at twenty-five, he was old enough

---

2 Douglas Adams, 1952-2001

to consider any and all adult pursuits but far too busy. LeGrande Inc. has skyrocketed onto the business scene making LeGrande, at twenty-eight, the youngest person ever to head a Fortune 500 company. With a net worth estimated at over $13 billion dollars, LeGrande surpasses Bill Gates' estimated net worth at the same age and has earned the distinction of being number five on the Forbes 400 list of wealthiest Americans. Certainly he has earned the right to the title 'Computer Whiz and Financial Genius' …

"Sir, your eleven fifteen is here. And, if I might be so bold as to suggest, you should run a comb through your hair and straighten your tie."

Adam looked up at Miles standing in the doorway of the study. His *butler*. How ridiculous was such a thing in this day and age? Personal assistant: yes. Executive secretary: yes. Senior aide: yes. But *butler*? NO. Were he carved from, marble Miles' appearance could not have been more precise and perfect: tall and thin, gray hair precisely combed, black butler suit absolutely lint free, and an expression completely void of emotion. At Adam's nonresponsive gaze, Miles reached up a white-gloved hand and gestured to the top of his head letting Adam know just exactly where the offending hair was.

Glancing at his Blackberry, Adam read, *Kathryn McFadden, Advancement Corporation, 11:15.* He looked up at his butler/personal assistant/chauffer/chef … and sighed. What Adam wouldn't give for a few, brief moments of normalcy in his miserable life. Miles was still waiting. Miles would wait, unperturbed, probably for hours. In the battle of wills, Adam always lost the daily waiting games they played. Something he was willing to concede – at least for this moment – however, he would go out fighting. "What's she look like, Miles? Is she hot?"

"Sir, it would be highly inappropriate for me to respond to that question." And they both knew it. In the end, both knew that the question was not asked so much for the gleaning of information as for the annoyance factor.

It had been a long, boring morning and there was every sign of it being a long, boring afternoon and night. Everyone was always trying to grab a piece of the pie that was Adam LeGrande: family, friends, colleagues, enemies, and even strangers. As Miles would probably never say, one must take one's opportunities to enjoy one's self when one can. "Why's that, Miles? What's the harm in letting me know what I've got to face for the next hour? Is she a dog with a capital 'D'? So ugly even her own mother doesn't acknowledge her? Or maybe she's middle of the road, so if I had a few stiff drinks in me I might even manage to entertain something more than just a professional encounter." Adam threw down his pen, put his feet up on the desk and laced his hands behind his head, suddenly enjoying himself immensely. "Or, now here's the dream scenario: she walks in with a skirt up to here and a neckline down to there, with drop-dead gorgeous legs and a mouth to die for. She saunters over to my desk, leans over, and says, 'Honey, I'll do anything to get you to buy into this deal.'"

Adam gave Miles a wolfish grin. Who the hell cared if he was too stiff to join in the fun? "Come on, Miles, why can't you just play along for once and have a bit of fun? What's so inappropriate about that?"

Miles never rose to the bait. Ever. But Adam was a competitive man as well as eternally optimistic. Plus, sometimes Miles had a quick comeback. As he did today. "It would be inappropriate, Sir, because Ms. McFadden is directly behind me and can hear every word we're saying." Without an ounce of condescension, he inclined his head, turned, and walked out of the doorway. Leaving one very annoyed young woman standing in the doorway. A very attractive and annoyed young woman: long, dark brown hair carefully twisted up to look businesslike, dark brown expressive eyes narrowed with blazing anger, and a figure that was absolutely and completely wasted as it currently was wrapped up in a boring dark blue suit. She was much closer to dream scenario than Adam ever could have hoped.

Crap.

Adam hastily stood up, adjusted his tie and made quick efforts to smooth down his ever-uncooperative hair. Walking from behind his desk he turned on his 'sincerely apologetic' smile (he had a million of them) and extended his hand to the furious woman glaring at him from across the room. "Ms. McFadden, please forgive me. It's been a long morning and there seems to be no end in sight. I'm so terribly sorry for my inappropriate behavior." He stopped, hand extended, and waited.

He knew she had to accept his apology even if she didn't mean it. It was a known fact that people's tolerance factors were significantly higher with the wealthy and powerful. And that was he: Adam LeGrande, also known as 'Boy Wonder of the Computer Industry' or something like that. Whether she needed his wealth, his power, or probably both, she was going to have to suck it up big time and get over his admittedly atrocious behavior. It was definitely not the first time Adam had behaved appallingly and people had had to get over it and for sure it wouldn't be the last. He mentally shrugged; might as well get some benefit out of the mind-numbing expanse of his life.

But Ms. Kathryn McFadden surprised Adam by looking him directly in the eye, ignoring his outstretched hand, and saying, "So, what category do I fit into? I'd like to hear, since your … butler … was too polite to say and we both know that you have no such qualms."

That was another thing about being rich and powerful, you didn't have to apologize more than once. Nor did you have to continue to be polite if that didn't seem to be working. "Well now, Ms. McFadden," Adam said, as he pretended to study her intently, "you've put me on the spot. Normally, I don't share that opinion, but since you've asked me …" He took a step back and brought his hand up to his chin, frowning intently. This might be fun. He motioned that he wanted to walk around her. "Do you mind?"

If it were possible for steam to come out of her ears, it would have. She was speechless with fury as he leisurely walked around her, checking her out from head to toe. Stopping in front of her with his hands on his hips Adam shrugged, "You're definitely not in the dog category. But I must admit, you're not in the dream scenario either." He gestured with his chin. "Skirt length, etcetera. The suit's abysmal. Does nothing to compliment what I suspect to be a sumptuous figure. But you are clean, tidy, well put together …" He sighed and shook his head in mock disappointment for opportunities lost.

"So I'd just better make sure you don't get near any alcohol and we always stay in professional settings," she ground out through gritted teeth.

Adam nodded and smiled an insincere smile. He had to give it to her, she was quick on the uptake. "Yeah, exactly."

Kathryn shook her head, turned, and walked out of the office. What?!

"Hey!" Adam followed her out into the hallway. "Where are you going? Didn't you want to meet with me?"

She stopped, paused, and then turned and walked slowly back towards him. A nice package, he thought. Very nice. Kathryn studied him for a moment, her brown eyes attempting to perhaps read his mind. Fat chance. "Yes, I wanted to meet with you," she said quietly and Adam realized that he liked the smooth sound of her voice. A little bit husky, a little bit sultry. Of course it could be the blazing fury that was still simmering just below the surface that made it sound so interesting. "I heard that although you are ruthless with your competitors, very recently you've been open-minded and interested in new business ideas. I understand that within the last year, on at least four occasions, you provided venture capital funds for start up companies that banks refused to back. I had hoped that you would listen to my presentation and recognize the potential opportunities for both yourself and the people I represent. I wanted to find someone with the same enthusiasm I have for taking nothing and making it into something. Lastly," she took one step closer and lowered her voice, as if she were going to share something vastly important. Intrigued, Adam leaned forward. In a husky whisper she said, "I prayed, that for once, I would encounter a businessman who thought more with his heart rather than his …" Kathryn seemed to catch herself, cleared her throat and took a step back. With a deep sigh filled with regret, she smiled sadly and said, "I must be slipping. It's been a long time since I've been so incredibly wrong about someone. At least I always learn from my mistakes. Goodbye, Mr. LeGrande."

Adam was still standing in the empty hallway looking at the closed front door when Miles spoke from behind him. "Sir, I've brought you some iced tea and a turkey sandwich."

Adam turned and looked into Miles' expressionless face. "I really blew that one, didn't I?"

"I'd say so, Sir. That's why I've brought you the wet cloth."

Sure enough, carefully folded next to his glass of iced tea was a damp cloth. While Miles did not partake in verbal exchanges it did not mean he kept his opinions to himself. Far from it. Miles was a master at getting his complete, unabridged message across in the face of sometimes stunning adversity. Sighing, Adam looked directly at his accursed butler, "Okay, I'll bite. Why do I need the wet cloth, Miles?"

"For the egg on your face, Sir."

Adam gave him a pointed look. "You could have clued me in. Given me a high sign. Done something. *Anything.*"

"I don't *do* 'high signs,' Sir. Perhaps, in the future, you will strive to remember that you are a professional and, as such, you should strive to maintain a higher standard for yourself in all aspects of your life."

"As you do, Miles?"

Miles gave him his standard bland look. *"The superior man is modest in his speech but exceeds in his actions."*[3] When all else failed, Miles had a million and one absolutely infuriating quotes to throw when the time was just right.

Adam took the tray with more force than was required, unwilling to enter into a battle he knew he could not win. "What's next on the schedule?"

"I will have the car out front for you at twelve-thirty. You have a one o'clock at Capital Investments' headquarters to discuss the Dylander merger, followed by a four o'clock meeting with John Mercantele. That meeting must be over by five-thirty so that you can return home and get dressed for the black tie affair at the Wickfield Country Club. Cocktails are at seven o'clock and you must be there promptly so you can meet Mayor

---

[3] Confucius, 551-479 BC, The Confucian Analects

Willoughby and discuss the new computer system that has just been approved by the town council."

"So let me get this straight, Miles. I'm Fortune 500's number five wealthiest American and by their very words a "computer whiz and financial genius" but you've got me scheduled to personally help to set up a no-nothing town's computer system? Isn't there something very wrong with this picture? Don't I have a company - called LeGrande Inc. - that employs hundreds of people to do just this? Aren't I supposed to be resting on my stunning collection of laurels now, in the twilight of my amazing life, instead of doing things I did *before I finished junior high school?*"

Miles meticulously removed the food, drink, and damp cloth from the tray Adam held, initiating the waiting game once again. Adam felt a wave a hatred for the man so strong he could almost taste it. "It is a worthy cause that you should be proud to be involved in, Sir. Just like the other small venture capital opportunities that you backed recently."

"That you nagged me ceaselessly to take on." Miles made no response. As usual. "That's what brought Ms. Kathryn McFadden to my door you know. Heard I was turning into some goody-goody save the world kind of guy."

"She impressed me as a stunning judge of character, Sir. I don't believe she would be so horribly mistaken."

"I've got a capable staff to handle the mayor's little computer project, Miles. I'll tell Mayor Willoughby that tonight at cocktails."

"She is depending on you to select, advise, and direct said new system. It was a significant victory for her that she was able to get this new budget passed. She wants her first year in the mayor's office to be stellar and is smart enough to recognize the key roll you will be able to play in that. Your willingness to *personally* assist her would be another noteworthy success on her part."

Adam grinned, his mood taking an upswing. "Was there a compliment for me in that last sentence, Miles? Ready to acknowledge my clout and substance out there in the world?"

As Miles walked sedately away, Adam heard him say, *"Conceit is God's gift to little men.*[4]*"*

At precisely seven o'clock p.m., Adam stood in the main entrance of the cocktail area at the Wickfield Country Club. When was the last time he had worn comfortable clothes? It was particularly cruel that the more successful he became in business the more often he was forced to wear uncomfortable clothes, like this tuxedo with its bow tie and cummerbund. Adam shifted in the dress shoes and resisted the urge to stick his finger into his collar and pull.

"Adam! On time as always!" Adam turned and looked into the smiling eyes of Mayor June Willoughby. She barely came up to his shoulder, but every square inch of her was always busy, always moving, and always planning. With a conspiratorial wink she said under her breath, "I'm so glad you're willing to do this, Adam! Thank goodness for Miles, huh? You know, I've tried unsuccessfully to steal him away from you on more than one occasion. His loyalty is phenomenal."

She was only half-kidding. Adam knew that she'd offered Miles an astronomical salary to come work for her. When Miles had told him, Adam had enthusiastically offered to pack Miles' bags and drive him over to her office personally, but no such luck. "It has nothing to do with loyalty, June. He's found the perfect prey to torture. He's just got me well trained and is loath to have to start on a new victim."

The Mayor laughed, thinking he was kidding. "You must pay him tremendously well."

Adam shrugged. Far be it for him to go into the boring details of his life that included one annoying butler of whom he was unable to rid himself. He hated this polite conversation crap he was always required to dish out at business functions. Politeness was so not part of his structural make-up. Why not just get on with what needed to be done, okay? "Sometimes it's not about the money," Adam murmured under his breath. Sometimes it was more about making a point.

---

[4] Bruce Barton, 1886-1967

June laughed as if Adam had just told the most hysterically funny joke. "What a sense of humor you have!" Helping herself to a glass of white wine from a waiter, she launched into business mode, tucking a lock of short gray hair behind her ear. Gold hoop earrings dangled in her ears and her blue eyes were bright with eagerness. "I'm riding on a high right now with the budget passing by such a wide margin. I really want to show everyone that I know what I'm doing, or that I know the right people to help me when I don't. Everyone's watching: those who love me want to keep smiling like proud parents and those who hate me can't wait to yell, 'See! I told you she'd screw up!' That's where you come in. We have a tremendous opportunity to revamp the entire computer system throughout the township - do you know that there are at least five secretaries still typing on IBM Selectrics? I don't know what's more frightening, that or the fact that the people using them don't want to change." She shuddered and then rolled her eyes. "Here's how I see it. You know what's out there and how much things are going to cost, you understand budgets and politics, and Miles assures me you're comfortable working with small, start-up organizations. I figure with you taking the lead on this, even if the company we've hired is without any kind of reputation - good or bad - that you'll be able to keep a handle on everything -"

Completely perplexed, Adam stopped her mid-sentence. "Wait, June. I'm sorry to interrupt you, but I suddenly have no clue what you're going on about. I know about the new computer system and I think I understand my role in all of this. But I don't understand what company you are referring to, and I am confused with your reference about me being comfortable working with small, start-up organizations. Can you back up a bit and fill in the blanks?"

The Mayor gave Adam a puzzled look. "I explained this quite thoroughly with Miles. You see, I'd like to kill two birds with one stone. So, in redoing the computer system, I thought I'd also grab some extra political points and use a new, woman-run, start up company here in town to do the grunt work. The fact that the company is an unknown is where you come in. Any risk will be nullified with your expertise and supervision."

He couldn't believe what he was hearing and it was impossible to keep incredulity out of his voice, "June, I've got my own company to do the work you're describing! That's what started all of this for me. I've got well-qualified people working for me now with experience in consulting, financial planning, and business development. Above and beyond the fact that you're asking me to assist a competitor, why would you think I'd be in anyway interested in assuming such menial responsibilities?"

June laughed again uproariously. "Why Miles and I discussed all this! First off, this small company is in no way a competitor with your organization! It is so small, so new, so untried that this opportunity within the township is its first major job opportunity. Miles and I talked about how it would almost be a mentoring situation where you could help, advise, and encourage this new company." She lowered her voice and stepped closer, "While at the same time gathering your own collection of political points to be stowed away for the future. Miles said that lately you've been interested in "helping out the little guy" for want of a better term. You've done it a few times before in the past year, so I thought this would just be another golden opportunity for you. Don't you see? Big, bad, business guy goes out of his way to help small, struggling, woman-owned business through its first major job. It's a win-win situation for both of us all around." June gave him a big, slow wink.

Finally. At long last. Now it all made sense to Adam. So that's where Miles was headed. Always looking out for the underdog, just so long as in the end it benefited the primary objective: LeGrande, Inc. Adam took a sip of his wine and gazed out at the collection of elegantly clad people. So Miles had political aspirations for him now. It wasn't enough that at sixteen he'd graduated with highest honors from MIT with a doctorate in computational research in economics and management science. Nor was it enough that at twenty-five he turned the entire economic community on its head when he developed a computer system that revolutionized the financial structure of every banking organization in the world. Or enough when at twenty-eight he had brought LeGrande Inc. into Fortune 500's 'Top 100 Fastest Growing Tech Companies'.

It was never, ever enough. More power, more money, more influence. More, more, more ... It was so not fun anymore. He snorted to himself. Who was he kidding? It had *never* been fun, but for a period of time it had been ... challenging. Now it was ... a hamster wheel he couldn't get off. Keep running, Adam. Keep impressing, Adam. Keep going, Adam ...

So, here Adam was at thirty-two: bored and jaded. He'd been there, done that, and (eye roll) was so not interested anymore. Lately, Miles had been encouraging him to get involved in civic duties, charitable organizations, and venture capital opportunities. That must be what June meant about "comfortable working with small, start-up organizations." Hence the disastrous meeting with Ms. Kathryn McFadden of Advancement Corporation this morning and this "win-win situation" now between him and Mayor Willoughby. What had Miles said? *Make all you can, save all you can, give all you can.*[5] Yeah, that was it. Apparently, making it into the political arena was where they were headed now. Jeeze. He'd really become complacent. He hadn't seen any of this coming.

"Well, Adam? What do you say?" June took a sip of her white wine, smiled, and waved to a group across the room.

God, he was tired. He looked down into June Willoughby's blue eyes and sighed. "I'm going to pass, Mayor. I've got a lot on my plate right now and just don't have the energy or, quite frankly, the desire to do this right now - the whole babysitting, hand-holding thing. If you want the job done - quickly and efficiently - without fuss or bother - you know where I am and my company can be in and out in no time. But, otherwise ..." He broke eye contact and looked out across the room again and right into the stunned big, brown eyes of Ms. Kathryn McFadden.   Looking extraordinarily lovely, too, in a long-sleeved black velvet gown with her brown hair curled and clipped back off her face. Yes, quite lovely, indeed.

The Mayor was talking to him and he'd missed most of what she'd said, "... answer just yet. I'll give Miles a call tomorrow and maybe we can sit down and talk about this in more detail."

---

5 John Wesley, 1703-1791

Oh yeah, that's a great idea. Give Miles a chance to come up with some quotes about political suicide and lack of initiative. Don't think he's heard all of those quotes yet. June had stopped talking and followed Adam's obviously preoccupied gaze across the room. "Why, what a coincidence, Adam! That's Kathryn McFadden! She's the one that sold me on using Computer Dynamics when we redo the township's computer system. She's head of a company called Advancement Corporation whose sole purpose is to help women succeed in business. She's quite a dynamo — sold me inside of thirty minutes. Her reputation is excellent — puts her money and her time where her mouth is, stays visible and available throughout every project and is quite, er, well, what's the best way to say it? Honest, no," she shook her head, frowning, struggling to find the right word, "principled, no, reliable, no ..."

Adam broke his sustained eye contact with Kathryn to turn and look at the Mayor. "What are you trying to say, June? You're making her sound like she's a saint or something."

June chuckled. "Oh, no, she's not a saint. She's just one of those," she leaned forward and raised her wine glass so that no international spy ring could read her lips, "born-again Christians."

Kathryn stood and watched Adam walk toward her. The look on her face would have discouraged a lesser man. So, let's bat for 1,000 here on this miserable day to top all miserable days, his head said. "Hey, Ms. Kathryn McFadden. Imagine meeting you here."

"You'll have to pardon me if I seem rude, Mr. LeGrande, but you're standing next to me drinking alcohol and this is a decidedly unprofessional situation. For my own safety and the sensibility of all the others I must end this ... conversation." Kathryn turned and began to walk away.

Before he could think it through Adam grabbed her arm, halting her departure and spilling her drink down the front of her dress. Absolutely perfect. "Oh, damn, I'm sorry Kat-, Ms. McFadden." He reached into his pocket. "Here, take my handkerchief."

Kathryn stared at him for brief moments, looking at his one hand still clutching her arm and his other extending his handkerchief. "Look,

Mr. LeGrande, if it makes you feel any better, I'm over this morning's …
catastrophe, okay? I'm willing to move on and forget about you and
LeGrande Incorporated, so you can relax. You owe me nothing
whatsoever, and I'll do my best to stay out of your way from now until the
end of time. If you'll let go of my arm, you can keep your handkerchief
and, hopefully, we can both go ahead with a relatively disaster free
evening."

Adam was exceptionally good at many, many things, but
conversing personally with a woman had never been one of them. If he
couldn't dazzle with math facts, business ideas, or computer innovations he
was pretty much at a complete loss. And in cases in which being human
was required, Miles usually did a thorough job of initial prepping. Tonight
had been business, not pleasure: do his business song and dance with the
Mayor, have a sustained period of visibility, and then split. But here, trying
to talk to the beautiful Ms. McFadden in her luscious black velvet gown —
stain or no stain — it suddenly seemed as if pleasure should be first on the
agenda. The catastrophe train was screaming downhill ready for its second
grand stop of the day. Quick, think.

He pocketed his handkerchief and released her arm, but before she
could turn and walk away he said quickly, "Tell me about Computer
Dynamics. I hear you're hoping to do the new township computer
system."

Kathryn stopped a waiter walking by, put her drink on his tray and
helped herself to a napkin. "Why?" she said as she wiped her hand and the
front of her dress. She avoided making eye contact with him, scanning the
room, probably for an escape route. But at least she was still standing there
talking to him.

"June Willoughby says you're a dynamo. Says you sold her in less
than thirty minutes on Computer Dynamics. You were scheduled for an
hour with me this morning. I'm intrigued about what you could have sold
me in double the time."

Kathryn sighed and turned to glance at him briefly. It seemed to
cause her physical pain. "June Willoughby operates on a different plain
than you do. I'm not so sure comparisons are possible."

"Different meaning she's a woman and I'm a Neanderthal."

That got him a slight smile, but still no eye contact. "You said it. I didn't."

"She spoke very highly of you."

Kathryn nodded, seemingly pleased. "That's good. I work hard at the image I project and the impression I give. A lot of people depend on me to be successful in what I do."

"So, since I missed the full length tour this morning – my mistake entirely – give me the fifty cent tour and tell me, in a nutshell, what you do."

"In a nutshell?" At last. She turned and gave him her full attention. Great mouth …

He smiled his "I'm really, honestly, completely sincere" smile at her and nodded.

She narrowed her eyes slightly, not in the least fooled. "I help make people's dreams come true," she said with an absolutely straight face and then turned and walked away.

I know God will not give me anything I can't handle.
I just wish that He didn't trust me so much.[6]

Chapter Two

(Voice filled with panic.) "I can't do this, Gran. I just can't. They already think I'm odd because I'm two years younger than everyone else."

"Why of course you can, Kathryn! You've researched, prepared, and rehearsed until you know your information backwards and forwards."

"I don't think I can stand up in front of the whole school."

(Spoken with calm and patience.) "Tell me why you chose this topic for the debate in the first place."

(Frustrated sigh.) "You know why, Gran. I'm a product of parental neglect and foster care success. It's a subject I feel ... passionate ... about."

"Now tell me why you were chosen to stand in front of the whole school stating your position instead of some other high school student."

(Louder frustrated sigh.) "Because Mr. Benjamin said that no one else came close to presenting all the salient points in such a cohesive, yet captivating manner."

---

[6] Mother Theresa, 1910-1997

"Did you just hear yourself? No one else came close. God has given each and everyone of us a purpose, Kathryn McFadden. No one can do the job but we ourselves. Your goal in life should be to make God smile. Think of all the people you will educate today with your presentation."

Her ringing cell phone woke her out of a restless sleep. As Kathryn fumbled in the darkness to find it on her bedside table, her brain registered the time on her alarm clock: 2:54 a.m. Great. That meant she'd had maybe forty-five minutes of sleep, none of it quality. "Hello?"

"The shop's flooded."

It was Lydia's voice, breathless and near hysteria.

Kathryn sat up, pushing her hair out of her eyes. "Flooded? How? What? Where are you? Are you there?"

"Yeah, I'm here." Lydia's voice broke with the edge of a sob. "Mrs. Murphy upstairs called. Wanted me to know that she'd had a little overflow in her washing machine upstairs and wanted to let me know that the ceiling in the shop might have a 'bit of a wet spot' I think was how she put it. Something made me come down here and check. It's up to my ankles."

"Oh no …"

"What should I do? I can't believe this! We broke even, what, two months in a row? And now this! I've got two new art classes starting tomorrow! What? Do I call and tell them to bring umbrellas and boots with their paint sets?!" Again Lydia's voice caught on a sob.

Kathryn was up, digging through her drawers looking for clothes. "I'll be there in twenty minutes. Hang in there. I'm coming!"

She tripped over the velvet gown she'd taken off two hours earlier. Why bother hanging it up when it was going to have to be dry-cleaned to get a soda stain out of it? She pulled on jeans, sneakers, a tee shirt, and a sweatshirt. It might be May but night times and early mornings were still cool.

The building that housed Lydia's shop was in a part of town that was fighting its way back to life. Interspersed among the signs that said

"Property For Sale" and "10,000 Sq. Ft. Available" were some charmingly unique shops that made Lydia's Art Studio fit right in. Parking in front of Attic Treasures, a consignment shop, Kathryn rushed to the front door of Lydia's shop and knocked.

Lydia opened the door, hazel eyes red rimmed from crying, curly blonde hair doing the riot dance on top of her head and light blue sweat pants wet up to her knees. "Welcome to the pool," she said and swung the door open wide. She was standing in two inches of water.

Kathryn immediately went into damage control, stepping into the shop and gasping as the cold water seeped into her sneakers. "Is it like this everywhere? Where did it all start?"

"The back is dry. Initial entry had to be right there." Pointing to the front left corner of the shop as Kathryn waded over to look at the damage. "Four paintings are ruined and it looks like the wall will have to be replaced."

Kathryn bent down and picked up one of the ruined paintings. "This was my favorite," she murmured. "I almost bought it myself." It was a beautiful watercolor, a beach scene done with pale blues, light greens and soft yellows. What had intrigued her most about the painting was the shape of it: a very long rectangle. Matted and framed it was no more than six inches high by twenty-four inches wide. The picture was different and unique, just like Kathryn.

"Yeah, I particularly liked that one, too."

Putting the painting down, Kathryn pushed up the sleeves of her sweatshirt, formulating a mental 'to do' list. "So, I see new carpeting, a new south wall at least up to here, and," she looked up and counted, "fifteen ceiling tiles." She looked at Lydia. "What are the boys doing?"

Lydia looked at her like she was crazy and rolled her eyes. "Sleeping."

Flipping open her cell phone, Kathryn looked at Lydia, "Are you calling them or should I?"

Lydia was a single mom with three boys. In Kathryn's opinion, three huge, strapping, tremendously lazy boys. Boys who liked to eat and sleep, and have their mom do their laundry for them so they could watch the game – any game! Boys who were fifteen, sixteen, and eighteen and, if Lydia wasn't careful, were still going to be home letting her do their laundry in ten years.

The two women had originally met at church. It had been summer, and the church was in high gear getting ready for the annual weekly Vacation Bible School extravaganza. Over two hundred children from the neighborhood converged on the church for a fun filled week of songs, stories, crafts, and games. Kathryn had been unable to devote a full week to teach due to her work schedule, but had volunteered to help with the setup on Sunday. It was the time when each of the classrooms in the church's educational wing were transformed into magical places meant to capture the children's interest and imagination. That year's theme 'Adventures in Living in God's World' involved a jungle, a desert, an underwater world, a garden, and a city. Dragging chairs and tables, craft supplies, and other necessary items to each room, Kathryn had had fun watching the gradual transformation of the sites. But when she got to the garden room, all she could do was stop and stare.

It was absolutely magical with flowers and vines, trees and bushes, birds and bugs covering every available space. Bending over to examine a particularly amazing butterfly, Kathryn realized that it had been hand painted.

It was exquisite.

"That was the first one I did. The others are better. I think."

Kathryn had turned to find a petite young woman, probably in her late thirties, standing hesitantly in the door. Straightening up, Kathryn said with wonder in her voice and her arms outstretched, "Did you do all this?"

The woman blushed with pleasure and nodded.

Kathryn walked toward the woman with her hand extended. "My name is Kathryn McFadden and I don't think I've ever seen such beautiful work."

The woman walked into the room and dumped a pile of colorful flowers and leaves on the floor. Hesitantly, she shook Kathryn's hand. "Lydia Mercer. And it's nothing special. I've always been able to draw and paint. It's not like it's ever helped pay the bills or anything."

"Wow, some hobby! How do you pay the bills?"

Lydia laughed and rolled her eyes. "With tremendous difficulty. Since my husband died, I've been struggling big time. I collect Social Security and work as a bus driver. I've got three boys, so it's hard."

Kathryn bent down and picked up a rose. It was pink, and although she could feel it was painted on paper her eyes told her that the petals should be soft and supple. "Have you ever tried to make money doing this?"

Lydia had had lots of excuses: not enough time, lack of business know-how, no money to buy adequate supplies - and the big one - the boys needed her too much. The way Lydia talked about her sons, Kathryn had pictured them all as rambunctious toddlers. She'd been stunned to find out that all three of them were teenagers. Teenagers who wanted to be cared for like they were still toddlers. Kathryn had helped Lydia finish setting up her room that day and they had laughed and talked. Although Kathryn was almost ten years younger than Lydia, Kathryn felt worldlier and more mature. Finally, Kathryn had asked her new friend, "What's your dream?"

Lydia had stopped and looked Kathryn right in the eye and said, "I've always wanted to have an art shop. You know, where I could sell my work and maybe have a classroom out in the back where I could teach, too. Nothing big. Nothing fancy. Just something that would pay the bills. Nothing seems more magical than the thought of getting paid to do," she held up a big, green grasshopper, "this."

Lydia had become Kathryn's big project. Oh, the boys were still lazy lugs who took advantage of their softhearted mother, and Lydia still didn't have enough confidence in herself or her work. But standing in freezing cold water at three a.m. listening to Lydia's phone ring and ring unanswered, Kathryn still felt that all that had been accomplished so far with Lydia's Art Shop was still a success. "They're not picking up," Kathryn said in frustration.

Lydia shook her head and chuckled at Kathryn's naiveté. "Kathryn, they don't answer the phone when they're awake and sitting right next to it. I'm the only one who answers the phone in our house."

"Then are you going to go over and wake them or am I? If we all get working on this, we could have the water gone, the rug pulled up, the wet wall draped and covered, and be ready for your first class. It's at ten, right?"

For the first time that evening Lydia smiled. "I knew you'd be able to fix things. Yes, it's at ten. I'll go wake the boys. I've got brooms and mops, too, that I can bring."

"Okay, good. I'm going home to get a pair of boots and see if I can borrow my neighbor's shop vac. He lent it to me last time my basement flooded."

"Are you going to wake him up at," Lydia looked at her watch, "three fifteen in the morning?"

Kathryn grinned at her, enjoying the camaraderie and the challenge. "When do you think I borrowed it last time?"

Lydia had her unenthusiastic work crew sweeping and mopping up the water when Kathryn arrived. It always struck Kathryn as funny that tiny, blonde haired Lydia had given birth to the three hulking behemoths who were her sons. All three were six feet or taller, all with wild, curly, black hair, all built like Mack trucks, and all totally allergic to physical labor. "Mom, you want me to mop up this puddle, too?" Randy was the youngest and, in Kathryn's opinion, the one with the most hope of amounting to something.

"No, Randy," Kathryn said with a laugh as she stepped into 'the pool', "leave that puddle. I'll just soak it up with all these donuts and bagels I've just bought." She placed a huge bag of fresh, warm bagels and a box of a dozen donuts on Lydia's desk.

Randy gave Kathryn a big grin and ambled over to her. "Hey, Kathryn! YEAH! You brought food. I'm starved." He dug into the donut bag and pulled out a cream filled one while at the same time reaching into the bagel bag, selecting a whole wheat bagel and putting it in his back pocket.

"Did you get jelly donuts, Kathryn? I only like jelly, you know." James was the middle son with all the textbook issues that a middle child was supposed to exhibit and then some.

"Yes, James. I got two in fact. Better take them both or you'll be sorry."

"Hey, don't be a hog, man. I like jelly, too." Keith Mercer was the biggest, the oldest, and the laziest of Lydia's three sons.

"I remembered you liked chocolate frosted, Keith. I got you two of those," Kathryn said with a polite smile glued on her face.

Kathryn suspected that Keith was most like his father. Although Lydia had never spoken poorly of her husband, Kathryn suspected that the tone and the atmosphere of the Mercer home had reflected only the opinions of John Mercer, even now, more than three years after his death. Keith looked at Kathryn and said defiantly, "I said I like jelly, too."

Odd as it seemed, Kathryn enjoyed playing psychological mind games and winning with someone over a foot taller than she and outweighing her probably by seventy-five pounds. She shrugged as if she couldn't care less. "Okay, cool. I'll eat both chocolate ones." She reached into the box with two hands.

"Okay, I'll take the chocolate ones."

Kathryn had her hands on both of the chocolate donuts. She looked up at Keith, smiled, and arched her eyebrow.

Keith rolled his eyes, "Please."

The five of them worked through the rest of the night and into the early morning hours. By seven a.m. they were all exhausted but the shop was presentable. "Go home, Kathryn, we can finish up," Lydia said. "I'm guessing you can't go home and sleep away most of the day like the boys, even if it is Saturday."

The boys were dragging out the last of the ruined carpet padding. Kathryn spoke quietly so she wouldn't be overheard. "I'm afraid if I leave you alone, you'll end up doing everything else by yourself."

Lydia put her hands on her hips and grinned. "Kathryn, they're my boys. You may think that I'm not firm enough with them but this shop means everything to me. I want it to succeed. If that means I have to threaten those three I will. And they know that when I do get mad they'd better run for cover. I don't lose my temper often, but when I do, it's impressive."

Kathryn laughed. "Okay, you win. I do have an afternoon meeting. If I can get home and catch a few hours sleep then I should be good to go. After your class is over, go by the carpet remnant place on Third and see if you like something we can put down in the front room, okay? I'm going to call Paul Winston at church and see if he could spare an afternoon to repair the wall and replace the ceiling tiles. But we'd better call the insurance company first and take pictures before we do much else. Will you call the landlord?"

"Yeah, I will. Mrs. Murphy said she was going to call the landlord first thing in the morning so I will, too." Lydia reached over and hugged Kathryn. "Thanks. You're a life saver."

"No, I'm an art shop saver," Kathryn threw over her shoulder as she walked out the front door.

Thanks Lord, for making the damage only minimal, Kathryn prayed as she drove home. She was weary in body but felt so good in spirit. That smile on Lydia's face when she'd said, 'this shop means everything to me' was such a wonderful thrill. With God's help, Kathryn had helped bring about that smile.

Kathryn had come a long way in her spiritual walk to be able to be "thankful for all things." A long way. She had always imagined her life to be a lot like a river. Observed from above, a river had many faces; not all of them pretty. Sometimes, as her life was now, a river can be tame but full of vitality; crowded with boats for business and pleasure. It was organized, orderly, and teaming with laughter and promise. But there were times when a river could be low, confounded by drought. Looking at a river crippled by the lack of sustaining rains, it can be hard to believe that there is any hope of usefulness or productivity in the future. And lastly, a river can be made swollen and destructive by torrential rains. During times like these, a river could take on a desperate, vicious quality. No one could control such a force nor even want to get close enough to try.

A lot of Kathryn's early life had been like that disastrous, overflowing nameless river; filthy, cluttered with garbage and debris, uncontrolled and wild. Her parents had been free spirits, moving when it suited them, following the seasons, or friends, or even a rock band's concert circuit. The life she led now was a determined opposite of all that she remembered: poverty, hunger, homelessness … namelessness. She had been a complete nonentity. Her parents had never thought much of convention of any kind, so names, addresses, possessions, commitments … well … they just didn't exist.

Kathryn vividly remembered the detailed list of possessions that she brought with her when she entered the foster care system at age five: one pair of blue plastic flip flops, her collection of beer bottle caps, and one woman's medium size tee shirt. Her parents, in the chaos and confusion, had left her behind when they had entered the gates of the concert they were attending. The security people would not let her in on her own, and when she couldn't even provide a name, the police had been called. Besides the pitiful list of possessions, Kathryn remembered reading the detailed report about that first day: October 22, 1980, 7:19 p.m. Child recovered, unattended, by security personnel at Radio City Music Hall. Despite numerous announcements over the concert public address system, as well as three specific announcements over the course of the concert from the stage, no information about the child or her parents/guardians could be obtained. Child could volunteer no specific names other than "Vinnie" and "Lexy" regarding her parents. No surname. No address. No phone numbers. Child appears to be uncertain of her own name. No missing child report was ever filed that day nor in subsequent days following the concert matching the child's description. Probable abandonment.

Probable abandonment. Ha. Kathryn had known the truth immediately standing there in her blue flip flops and her 'Go To Heaven' Grateful Dead tee shirt, clutching her paper bag full of bottle caps, even if it had taken a number of weeks for the authorities to come to the same conclusion. It was a scheduled, absolutely intentional abandonment. Why, her parents had been trying to get rid of her for years. Kathryn still remembered the intensity of the need to stay close even after all this time. For years afterwards, even once she was safe and sound at Gran's, that feeling of indescribable panic when she thought she was lost or alone would flash from the pit of her stomach and send shock waves to all her extremities making her heart pound and her breath come in gasps.

She'd ended up in the foster care system for a surprisingly brief period of time and was adopted by a young couple named McFadden. Only vague memories remained of them; a sweet smell of perfume from "Mama McFadden" and a certain distinct male kind of laughter that she still occasionally heard when out in a crowd that reminded her of "Papa McFadden." They had been a family for exactly four months. Four months. Kathryn - that was the name the three of them had decided on when the adoption became official and they had appeared before the judge - had been safely belted in the back seat when the accident occurred. When she awoke in the hospital with absolutely no memory of the accident, Mama and Papa McFadden were gone, but Gran was there.

And Gran had stayed. For a long, long time. Well, at least fifteen years. Gran, as round as she was tall with snapping green eyes and gray hair that she 'styled herself' with her own sewing shears. Papa's mom had filled in all the spaces that needed to be filled for Kathryn. Every single one: unconditional love, a sense of belonging, security, encouragement, hope, laughter, and silliness. Gran had taught Kathryn how to be a child, had delighted in her amazing intellectual abilities, and had encouraged her blossoming into a capable young woman. And most importantly, Gran had given Kathryn her faith.

Now, Kathryn would have been lying were she to say that things were 'happy ever after' once she settled in with Gran. The whole "I'm a nobody, nameless, nothing" was a specter that chased her for years. In addition, Kathryn's incredible intelligence, coupled with her atypical independence from her neglected upbringing made Gran's job .... challenging ... to say the least. But Gran used to say to her – sometimes during Kathryn's biggest and baddest moments, "I love you, young lady, and you can't stop me, no matter what you do!" Gran was Unconditional Love in action.

Faith came slowly, but surely. You couldn't spend much time around Gran without hearing and seeing faith in action. Kathryn loved Gran too much to rebel against the faith that was so important to her. According to Gran, there was nothing in this world that could justify a person separating themselves from the love of God – not lousy childhoods, not poverty or war, not the death of a loved one, not sickness - nothing. Because, according to Gran, God was the only one who could truly get you through those tough times in one piece.   Did you turn away the fire department when your house was burning? Did you lock the door to the police officer when you were in mortal danger? Did you send away the ambulance when you were bleeding to death? Why wouldn't you turn to the creator of the universe when life got too hard to handle?

Kathryn heard it all; God had a purpose and was in control of all times - easy and hard.   God loved unconditionally.   God wanted a relationship that was close and personal.   God wanted to be present in every aspect of a person's life - not just on Sunday mornings. God wanted us to have faith in Him. Through it all Kathryn had heard, repeated, and smiled politely. Not until Gran died, when Kathryn was twenty and already razzling and dazzling on Wall Street, did Kathryn finally, truly understand it all, see the big picture, finally, face the music. At last, she got with the program.

Gran always said that God's greatest gift to her had been Kathryn's arrival in her life and His second greatest gift had been time. They'd had fifteen years together. A lifetime for a five-year-old, but for a twenty-year - old it had been brutally short. Sitting in Gran's house, after her funeral, Kathryn realized that she was at a crossroads of sorts in her life. She could send the ambulance away, lock the door against the policemen, and turn away the fire department ... or ... she could grab on to the Creator of the universe and have a very long, hard cry on His shoulder.

And we know that all things work together for good to them that love God, to them who are the called according to His purpose.[7] Gran had that Bible verse on a plaque over her kitchen sink. Kathryn had made it at summer Bible camp when she was eleven. She said one time to Kathryn, that were it not for that verse and her belief in it, there would have been times over the course of her life when she would have just curled up and died. Kathryn stood in the kitchen looking at that plaque that day and thought, *Do I know that? Do I believe that? Am I one of the called?* Right there in the kitchen at that moment

---

[7] Romans 8:28, King James Version

she decided that she *did* know it; her life had been a testament to it. She decided that she *would* believe it because she would like nothing more than to be exactly like Gran and believing this was the key. Finally, Kathryn decided that she *wanted* to be one of the called and that from then on every aspect of her life would be an example of that.

Things didn't change overnight. *Hardly.* In fact, in retrospect, many things in her river of life during that time tended to look somewhat worse for a time. Professionally, things couldn't seem to go wrong, but repeatedly she failed in her personal life. She was desperately lonely in those early months and years after Gran's death. It wasn't that she was a loner - far from it. Kathryn was vivacious and outgoing, friendly, and fun to be with. Rarely was she without a boyfriend. But the loss of Gran's love brought those old feelings of loneliness and loss screaming back to the forefront. Her life was a muddy river with a country western love song playing in the background. *Looking for love in all the wrong places.*

Kathryn sighed, as she drew the curtains of her bedroom and crawled, exhausted, into bed. She was thirty-one years old and single. Kathryn *needed* to be single because, as successful as she was with her professional life, she was a complete disaster with her personal one. One of these days, she was going to write a book about her past, failed relationships. She already had a title: *If He Has Potential, Run.* She was too loving, too willing to see the good in even the worst of men. Kathryn suspected that she couldn't dismiss a guy because he was unlikable or flawed because Gran hadn't done that with her had she? She had worked her way through the various relationship phases, such as, "I'm Sure I Can Change Him" and "I'll Be The One To Fill The Empty Void in His Life." She'd only briefly tried the "Casual Relationships Are All I Want" phase. That phase had been the briefest but had done the most damage.

After her last relationship had ended, six weeks before the wedding when she backed out, Kathryn really hit a low point in her life. She had taken a good, long, hard look at herself and she realized she *was not* getting this right. Perhaps it was commendable that she was not a repeat offender with the types of losers she hooked herself up with, but the reality was still haunting. On her own, she did just fine with the right kind of person she knew God wanted her to be. But hook her up with a man and Kablam! she became a walking poster woman for dysfunctional relationships and misguided spiritual failures.

Yes, Kathryn wanted to be married! Yes, she wanted a family! Not only did she see nothing wrong with the whole domestic goddess thing, Kathryn actually harbored the whole white picket fence dream. She laughed all by herself lying in bed and shook her head; *take a look at the house she had bought and now currently lived in.* Kathryn sighed and turned over. She was exactly where she was when she had gotten home from the country club reception last evening. Thoughts of Adam LeGrande had robbed her of quality sleep before Lydia had called last night and they had better not keep her awake now. While she had managed to avoid Adam for the remainder of the dinner, she'd been continually aware of exactly where he was and to whom he spoke. He had been a big, *bad* distraction walking around in his designer tux looking too handsome for words. The last thing she needed was his making half hearted attempts to smooth over the morning's disaster and giving her looks that said he had a pile of suggestions on how she could work herself up into his own personal 'dream scenario.' Groaning, Kathryn rolled over on to her stomach trying to quiet her thoughts.

Standing outside Adam LeGrande's office Friday morning, listening to him describe the various scenarios in which she could possibly fit, made her, for the first time in years, think of her completely nonexistent personal life. For one horrifying minute she had wanted to unbutton the top two buttons of her very professional blouse underneath her very professional suit so that she would at least qualify half way for his dream scenario. That had made her angry with herself and then, quickly getting her priorities straight, livid at Adam. By the time Miles, the emotionless butler, had walked away she'd thought she'd gotten herself together. *Thought* being the operative word.

Then, Adam LeGrande had stood up and walked toward her, all six feet four gorgeous inches of him, oozing charm and smarmy confidence, and trying valiantly to pour sincerity out of those beautiful, big green eyes. Kathryn vividly remembered him smoothing down his highly uncooperative dark auburn hair that was sticking up and curling all around his handsome face, straightening his tie and smiling a grin that could melt bone matter while he held out his hand offering his *sincerest* of apologies. Yeah. Right.

God in heaven help her. If he had potential, *run*.

Oh, he had potential all right. Potential to set her back, personally and emotionally, *for years*. He was irreverent, Neanderthalic, cocky and smug. A self-made man who was dynamic, intelligent, and confident. Despite all the glaringly bad points, reality was that he was the most handsome, most intriguing man she had come across in *forever*. She couldn't remember the last time she had looked at a man and wanted ... Kathryn sighed again. What did she want? White picket fences? Two point five children? Meatloaf cooking in the oven?

Kathryn McFadden was no slouch herself. She was a force to be reckoned with and had the King Midas touch professionally. Pretty much anything she'd tried had gone outstandingly well: a master's degree in business from Columbia University by age twenty, financial independence through success as a stock broker on Wall Street by age twenty-five, and now a very satisfying job running her own business that helped and encouraged others. So what that her personal life was as promising as a burned out forest? Look at her professional side. For the past five years she had happily devoted one hundred percent of her time toward her business and had, surprisingly, not missed a personal life at all. Until ...

For the first time in forever Kathryn felt alone. Lost. Abandoned. No longer did the panic attacks overwhelm her and keep her from being able to breathe and talk and function ... But there was still the fear of them. She missed Gran. She missed the comfort and protectiveness that a loving relationship could give. She missed ... being *loved, sought after, treasured, and desired* ...

God in heaven help her.

Faith is, at one and the same, absolutely necessary and altogether impossible.[8]

Chapter Three

"How come my last name is 'LeGrande'?"

(Thoughtful silence followed by a casual shrug.) "I liked the sound of it."

"It's not my father's last name?"

"Hardly."

(Feigned casual expression, remembering appearances are everything.) "Why ... not?"

"Why would I go through all the pain and torture to give birth to you only to give you the name of some worthless fool?"

"So ... what is my father's name?"

(Sudden, intense fury.) "You listen to me, little Mr. Curiosity, and remember every word I tell you. Your father (said with heavy loathing) didn't want you. You were an unplanned complication that interfered with his perfect life. You've got only me, darling (chilling Adam with her sarcasm) and you better be grateful for all the pain and sorrow I've put up with as a result. Don't forget to give me an appreciative thank-you."

(Wearing a 'Show No Emotion' expression.) Thank – you, Mother.

---

[8] Stanislaw Lem, 1921-

Adam Googled "born again Christian" Saturday morning and took the time reading through a number of sites that wanted to save his soul from eternal damnation. Most of it was boring mumbo-jumbo that tended to make his eyes cross. Finally, Wikipedia, the free online encyclopedia, offered a rather concise, don't-care-if-you-want-to-buy-into-it-or-not definition that he was able to read from beginning to end: *'Born again is a term used primarily in the Fundamentalist, Evangelical, and Pentecostal branches of Protestant Christianity, where it is associated with salvation, conversion, and spiritual rebirth. Outside of these circles, the term is often applied by extension to other phenomena, including a transcending personal experience - or the experience of being spiritually reborn as a "new" human being.*[9]

"Hey Miles, do you know if I was ever baptized?"

Miles, delivering Adam's morning cup of coffee, straightened up and stared at him for a moment or two. "To the best of my knowledge, Sir, no."

"I've got a real Biblical name, though. Adam and Eve and all that. Don't you think that there had to be some kind of God-related agenda when I was a baby?" At Miles' continued silence, Adam persisted. "Come on, Miles, you supposedly knew my mother. Did she ever say anything about the origin of my name?"

Miles collected an empty coffee cup that Adam had left on the mantle. "Your mother, if I remember correctly, was quite a fan of Douglas Adams, Sir. The gentleman who wrote *Hitchhiker's Guide To The Galaxy.* Perhaps instead of wondering what the origin of your name is, you should be thankful that she chose not to name you Zaphod or Marvin."

Adam sighed, recognizing a dead end when he was looking at one. "Okay, so you don't know. Or you don't wish to tell me. Just say that, okay? Why do you always have to take the long route? Let your hair down, man. And cut the "Sir", crap. I've told you that before. How can you be stiffer now than when you first started working for me? And, while we're at

---

[9] http://en.wikipedia.org/wiki/Born-again_Christian

it, can you explain how you ended up as my *butler*? I never wanted, needed, advertised for, or hired you to be a butler. What's your point? Why can't you just loosen up a bit? How is it that I command a multi-million dollar corporation and can't get rid of your annoying presence?"

"I've explained to you on more than one occasion why the title 'Sir' is critical in my dialogue with you, Sir." He bowed slightly as he said the word and Adam was absolutely positive that it was expressly to annoy him. "As to why I am currently serving as your butler, you specifically told me that it was the only position available when we initially spoke. You went to great pains to dismiss any and all other -"

"Yeah, yeah. Spare me the historical recap."

"I've scheduled a meeting with Mayor Willoughby for Monday morning at nine o'clock. Please add that to your schedule. I understand that you further wish to discuss the terms and conditions of this upcoming business endeavor."

Adam blew out a burst of frustrated air. Oh, yeah. That reminded him. "Listen carefully, Miles. I have no political aspirations. Do you hear me? Are you listening? I don't want to run for political office. Cross it off your list. Go work for someone else if that's what you really want to do. Be a butler for a Mayor or a Senator or a President for all I care. But it's not going to happen here with me."

Miles just stood there wearing his white gloves and holding a dirty coffee cup. "Will that be all, Sir?"

"Miles, I'm warning you. I know you're much more than my butler and my chauffer and my personal assistant and my chef," Adam pinched the bridge of his nose, "but I do have my limits. I won't do this. I've tolerated your interference in 'giving back to the community' as you've so blithely put it, but I do not and will never embrace a political goal." Adam was shouting by the time he was finished speaking.

"Lunch is at noon, Sir. Turkey curry." Miles exited Adam's office to the steady thump, thump, thump of Adam's head pounding on the desktop.

Okay, so Mayor June Willoughby talked a good talk. Monday afternoon, despite Adam's best intentions to back out of the babysitting assignment with Computer Dynamics, found him scheduling a meeting with the woman who ran the small start up company, Maria Gonzalez. What had made him pick-up the phone finally and call had been June's promise that Adam had the final word on how the entire operation would go, right down to his ability to decide that Computer Dynamics was not the organization to use for this very important venture. So, how could a five-minute phone call hurt, right? He'd call this Ms. Gonzalez, determine within moments that all of his instincts were absolutely correct, and then set this job up exactly the way it should be set up: his way with his company. Not that he was conceited but hey he was a computer genius, his company was internationally recognized and traded on Wall Street, and he regularly did jobs like this in his sleep, so ... Okay, so he was conceited. But it was all based on fact.

On the phone, Ms. Gonzalez sounded very professional, highly qualified, and to his immense frustration, didn't give him one reason not to use her. She was articulate, enthusiastic, and more than willing to listen to any and all advice he implied that he wanted to throw her way. Finally, she invited him to take a look at all of her plans and then decide if he thought her company could handle the job. After all, she'd said in her quiet, slightly Hispanic accent that he was the expert here, wasn't he? How could Adam argue with that?

What intrigued him in the end, was her insistence that they meet at his office on his turf. His gut told him that this was something to pursue. What, was she working out of her bedroom? Or worse yet, her car? No, he firmly pushed back and insisted he'd be more than happy to come to her. In the end, she reluctantly agreed (she really had no choice), and they'd set up a meeting for the first thing Friday morning. The address she gave was in a residential part of town. He just hoped he wasn't going to be sitting in her bedroom.

The house he pulled up to Friday morning was a big, rambling old Victorian. It had a neat yard, brilliantly waking up in all its spring glory and a profusion of daffodils, crocuses, and grape hyacinths added haphazard color to the otherwise still slumbering garden. Maria Gonzalez greeted him with a firm handshake and a confident smile as she invited him in.

It was a home and a business in one. The living room was warm and welcoming, eclectically furnished with old and new pieces. Ms. Gonzalez led him through the living room into the formal dining room, which was obviously the base of operations. There was a computer and a desk in the far corner and spread out on the dining room table's shiny surface was an assortment of papers, as well as a pot of coffee and two mugs.

Maria Gonzalez was a study in contrasts: some things that Adam had expected and many things that he had not. Though she spoke with a Hispanic accent and bore a Hispanic name, she was an attractive black woman with snapping dark eyes, shiny black hair and a quick wit. The cynic in him realized that Mayor Jane Willoughby, in using Computer Dynamics, was killing far more than two birds with one stone. In one fell swoop, she was going to please women, blacks, and Hispanics … it couldn't get much better. Adam, should he choose not to use this company, had better have very solid reasons why.

And he found absolutely none. Maria, as she insisted he call her, was open and interested. Her ideas were good and her plans were solid. She simply was stuck in the lose-lose situation of having no references, no experience, and no businesses willing to take a chance on her. Which was why this opportunity was so very critical to her future. She knew it and he knew it.

"Look, Mr. LeGrande, I know you weren't keen on taking on this project with me involved. Even if Mayor Willoughby hadn't clued me in on your reluctance, I would have known. I just want a chance to prove myself. I don't want any favors, and I don't want anyone to accept anything less than a first class job. I'm hoping you'll watch me walk through this step-by-step and I won't let anyone down, most importantly myself. But," she shrugged and gave him a small smile, "if it happens, then you'll be a perfect safety net to keep the township from suffering."

In the end, that was what hooked him. Right up until the last sentence he was still on the fence, leaning heavily in favor of saying no. But when he realized that her bottom line was the township, not herself and her reputation, he felt himself mentally give in. "Okay, Maria. I'll bite. I'll give you this opportunity to prove yourself and make Mayor Willoughby happy all at once. But I've got a few conditions that you'll have to agree to."

"All right." She didn't shout 'yippee!' and do a little jig, or worse yet, throw her arms around him and give him a big kiss on the cheek. Maria just stood there intent and sincere.

"You keep this open, honest bit going. You have a question, you ask it without hesitation. I don't want your pride or concern for how your company will be perceived to take precedence over what's the best way to get this job done." As she nodded in agreement, Adam continued. "And if, when I make suggestions, I don't want any arguments."

"Can I at least ask you to explain your reasoning if that happens? I don't think I'd do too well in a dictatorship."

Adam smiled wryly. No one had ever dared call him a dictator to his face but he was sure there were many who thought along those lines. "I may have trouble with that."

Maria chuckled and put her hands on her hips. "How about I won't argue in the heat of the moment, but in the cool of the evening, will you at least make sure you explain yourself? I won't learn if you don't take the time to teach me."

"Deal."

Adam declined a second cup of coffee as he was eager to get on with his day. Making his way out of the neighborhood, he was lost in thought considering Maria's plans and any anticipated complications. He was drawn back into the present by the sight of a trim, athletic, young woman jogging alongside the road. His personal life might be nonexistent but it didn't mean he didn't appreciate an opportunity when it presented itself. He had a nice view. A very nice view from behind, and, as he passed the woman he checked out the front view from his rear view mirror. Adam was stunned to see the face of Kathryn McFadden.

Kathryn McFadden. What was she doing jogging in this neighborhood? Never one to believe in coincidences, Adam turned the corner and parked the car at the side of the road. Fishing his cell phone out of his jacket pocket, he dialed.

"LeGrande Incorporated."

"Miles, what's Kathryn McFadden's home address?"

After a few moments of silence, Miles answered. "1271 Claire Drive is the address listed on her business card. Right here in town."

The very same address where Adam had just met Maria Gonzalez of Computer Dynamics.

"What's your first impression when I tell you that Computer Dynamics has that very same address?"

Miles didn't answer immediately, but then finally said, "Did Ms. Gonzalez offer disclosure of this information? That in and of itself lessens the negativity factor."

Adam sighed. "No, she said nothing about her "roommate" or "friend" or whatever. I've just finished a very impressive meeting with Ms. Gonzalez and drove past Ms. McFadden out for a jog. I'm putting two and two together here. Obviously, Ms. McFadden has a lot more personally invested in Computer Dynamics if the woman is sharing a home with her. It can't be nepotism, but it looks pretty damn close. I'd bet that Kathryn McFadden is going to get a lot more out of this deal financially than just the opportunity to help Ms. Gonzalez's," sarcasm just dripped from his words, "dreams come true."

Miles sighed over the phone. "I might caution you, Sir, that things are not always as they seem. You know that better than most people." When Adam remained silent, Miles asked, "What are your intentions, Sir?"

"I think I might have to drive back and have one more chat with Ms. Gonzalez."

Miles sighed. "I'll reschedule your one o'clock, Sir."

"You do that, Miles."

Adam had parked his car and gotten as far as the front porch before he caught sight of Kathryn rounding the corner and heading right toward him. He opted to sit down on one of the big wicker chairs and wait rather than ring the bell.

In the final five hundred feet of her run, rather than slow down, Kathryn pushed herself into a fast sprint. Stopping at the bottom of the driveway, she made herself walk in slow, steady paces, hands on her hips, breathing heavily. She was drenched in sweat. It took almost ten minutes for her to cool down sufficiently then to make her way up the driveway and then the front path. It was only when she had one foot on the front step that she realized she had an audience. And she did not look happy.

When he made no move to speak to her, Kathryn volunteered, "Well, Mr. LeGrande, I guess it's your turn to appear unexpectedly. I thought your meeting with Maria would have been long over by now."

"I'm sure you did," Adam said sarcastically.

She arched her eyebrow questioningly and used the back of her hand to wipe a trickle of sweat off her forehead. Narrowing her eyes at him she said, "What's that supposed to mean?"

"Exactly as it sounds," Adam said, standing to add superior physical height to his moral indignation. "How long did you think you could hide the fact that the owner of Computer Dynamics is a close enough personal friend that she lives with you?"

Kathryn walked the five steps up to the porch so that she only had to look up to compensate for their height differences. "What?" she said incredulously. Adam recognized the fury that seemed to roll off of Kathryn. Unfortunately, he'd been here, done this, and annoyed before.

"You heard me. It's called 'preferential treatment' one step away from nepotism, and as appealing as it is for Mayor Willoughby to help women, blacks, and Hispanics I don't think this is what she had in mind."

"How dare you! You insufferable, egotistical, self-absorbed, idiot!" Kathryn turned her back on him, ripped open the front door and slammed into the house.

How dare he? How dare she! Just as furious, Adam followed her inside without invitation, trailing behind her down the hall where it finally opened up into a bright, airy kitchen. Walking over to the sink she grabbed a glass, filled it with water, and drained it with angry gulps. Whirling around, she said low, "Get out of my house."

He crossed his arms and leaned against the door jam matching her fury. "Gee, I thought this was a place of business. I was just in your dining room a few minutes ago discussing a business deal with your roommate, Maria Gonzalez."

"What's going on here? Kathryn?" Maria walked in from the back door carrying an empty trash can. When Kathryn didn't answer but continued to glare at Adam, Maria gave him a concerned look. "Mr. LeGrande?"

Adam looked at Maria and said, "You neglected to give me a fair and accurate representation of the entire scope of your business connections, Ms. Gonzalez. I had no idea that Ms. McFadden had a vested interest in your business deals."

Maria looked at Kathryn, sweaty and furious, and then at Adam who looked extremely smug. "Kathryn doesn't have -"

But Kathryn cut her off waving her hand. "Don't bother, Maria. Adam here, brilliant man that he is, has it all figured out. He knows. There's nothing we can do about it. The jig is up. The cat is out of the bag. He's figured out that we're part of an insidious plot to take over the entire town's computer system and, in the process become filthy rich. He's figured out that I'm Mr. Big."

"What are you two talking about?!" Maria looked on the verge of tears.

Kathryn pushed herself away from the counter and walked over to the telephone hanging on the wall. Flipping open the address book on the counter she found the number she was looking for and dialed. "Yes, Kathryn McFadden here, from Advancement Corporation. Yes, is Mayor Willoughby in? Yes, it is a bit of an emergency. It's in reference to the new computer system we're trying to get up and running for the township." All the while she talked she stared directly into the angry face of Adam LeGrande. "Hey, June. Sorry to bother you. I've got Adam LeGrande here and he needs to talk with you about Computer Dynamics, can you spare a few minutes? Thanks so much." Kathryn held out the telephone receiver to Adam. "It's all yours."

It had been an extremely long time since Adam had been in the position of doubting himself. Being a child prodigy, a business whiz, and a financial genius tended to foster that in a person. But standing in Kathryn McFadden's kitchen, with Maria Gonzalez fighting back tears, Adam had a moment's pause about all of the conclusions he had so hastily drawn. He had blown the meeting with Kathryn, in which perhaps she would have disclosed some of this vital missing information. Perhaps "preferential treatment" and the strong implications that she was behaving inappropriately was a bit harsh of him in retrospect.

Kathryn waved the phone at him. "Come on, Mr. LeGrande. I can't wait to see you make a complete fool of yourself the second time in two weeks." Dimly, Adam heard Maria gasp.

Taking the phone, Adam spoke to the Mayor, "June, sorry to disturb you. Yes, I'm here meeting with both women. Yes, I know how important this all this is. Look, I do have a few questions, but perhaps it would be better for me to meet with you face-to-face and we can discuss this all at once. Good. Yeah, I'll have Miles call and schedule something. Thanks." He handed the phone back to Kathryn who hung it up.

Kathryn didn't thank him for his forbearance. She had the nerve to look a bit disgusted. "Chicken." She tilted her head, "Or should I say, 'Strike Two'?"

"Will you two please tell me what's going on?" Maria looked like she was ready to pull out her hair.

"The only thing I'm going to do is take a shower. I have a twelve-thirty appointment." Kathryn brushed past Adam without even a glance.

Clean and dressed in a tan business suit, Kathryn knew, from looking out her bedroom window, that Adam LeGrande was still in her house, unless he'd walked home and left his car. She forced herself to stop gritting her teeth, which happened every time she thought of him.

Whenever she had a "difficult" encounter, she always tried to review things once she was in a calmer place, physically and emotionally. The whole *"Don't let the sun go down on your anger"*[10] coupled with *"A gentle answer turns away wrath but harsh words stir up anger"*[11] that her grandmother had drilled into her still had their effect. The fact that she was still fighting not to grit her teeth told her that she had a way to go until she was truly in a calm space. But she couldn't come up with anything she'd done wrong,

---

[10] Ephesians 4:26b, New Living Translation
[11] Proverbs 15:1, New Living Translation

aside from calling him an insufferable, egotistical, self-absorbed, idiot. But those were all true, weren't they? And being a bit self-righteous and in your face rather than appreciative when he'd backed down on his unbelievable accusations.

She had to get going. Kathryn always worked better with a calm frame of mind and a full stomach. Lunch she could manage before this afternoon's meeting but her frame of mind was shaky enough as it was without another encounter with Adam LeGrande. Maria would just have to play the mediator. Kathryn would go about her business of preparing a lunch, keep her mouth shut, and get out of the house as fast as humanly possible.

Things were completely silent when Kathryn came downstairs. If she hadn't known better she would have thought she was alone. Walking down the hallway towards the kitchen, her mind registered an empty living room, an empty dining room, and, sure enough, an empty kitchen. Maybe Adam had finally left. His schedule was certainly as busy, if not more so, than hers. He couldn't just while away the morning waiting, could he?

Just as she was going to take a bite of her peanut butter sandwich, Kathryn saw movement at the front door. "I'll ask if I can come in this time," Adam said through the screen door.

Rats. Where was Maria? Wandering down the hallway toward the front door, sandwich in hand, Kathryn said, "Why don't we cut our losses, huh, Mr. LeGrande? I'm sure Maria explained the situation here. You now know that should you wish to work with Computer Dynamics, you need never deal with me directly. That should make us both very happy." She stopped on the opposite side of the screen door gazing up into his handsome, serious face. She didn't invite him in and made no move to open the door.

"Maria didn't explain anything to me. She had some meeting she couldn't be late for."

Great. Kathryn sighed. "Well, she'll bring you up to speed next time you talk to her. I'm pressed for time, too."

"I don't usually find myself in this type of predicament."

"What type of predicament is that? The kind of predicament where you're not in complete control and dazzling everyone with your brilliance? The kind of situation where everyone is just speechless with wonder at the magnificent Adam LeGrande?" Kathryn took another bite of her sandwich. It had been a long time since someone had exasperated her so completely.

Adam stopped looking at her through the screen door, turned, and leaned back against the house. He had a strong profile. Kathryn noted that he had loosened his tie and unbuttoned the top button of his white dress shirt. He swallowed. "You appear to value many of the same business skills that I do: intelligence, honesty, efficiency. You seem to assume a lot about me. Perhaps we keep clashing because we are so much alike."

How dare he! "I don't think I've ever been so insulted in my life," she ground out.

Adam turned to look at her, hoping that she was making a joke but there wasn't even a hint of a smile. He'd made her mad again. He had done his level best to appear sincere. Honestly sincere. "Would you believe me if I said I meant that to be a compliment?"

"Being as you have such a very high opinion of yourself," Kathryn threw back at him.

He frowned. Wasn't self-confidence a good trait? He certainly knew where he failed abysmally. That's why he was alone. Adam searched her face, trying to get a handle on the conversation, trying to rescue this second major disaster with Kathryn McFadden. "Well, yeah. I know my strengths and I capitalize on them."

"And what about your weaknesses, Mr. LeGrande? Got any of those you're aware of?"

Adam realized at that precise moment that all this was absolutely hopeless and felt his own anger explode. What, did she think she was perfect? He may not have any casual interpersonal skills, but at least all of his mistakes today were sincere misunderstandings. Ms. McFadden, on the other hand, seemed to be determined to draw blood every chance she got. Why was he wasting his time here? He shoved off the side of her house and let the fury run through him unabated. "God, you are such a -," he caught himself.

Now she was standing stiffly, arms straight at her side, one hand still clenching her forgotten sandwich. Through gritted teeth she said, "Go ahead. Say it. Go for strike three."

Adam threw his arms up in exasperation. "You know, I'm a very busy man. I don't even know why I've wasted the better part of my morning here! I really don't! There! That's apparently one of my weaknesses. I don't know when to take the hint and just move the hell on! I've never met such an abrasive, unyielding, holier-than-thou person in all my life! Here's a final insult for you: you may be good at what you do," his voice raised with fury, "but you're not any more likeable than I am!" He turned to walk down the steps of the porch. At the bottom of the stairs, Adam turned to find her still standing there in the doorway watching him through the screen door. "I told Maria Gonzalez at our meeting this morning that everything was a go. I'd be willing to do this mentoring project, provided she abided by my stipulations about the job. If she's concerned, based on what's happened since the meeting between you and me, she shouldn't be. As far as I'm concerned, unless I hear from her and she tells me differently, things are exactly the way we left them. Have a good day, Ms. McFadden."

Watching Adam's car roar away, Kathryn should have been happy that Maria was going to get this fantastic opportunity. In addition, it was another notch of success in her professional King Midas Touch career.

So why was she crying?

Genius may have its limitations, but stupidity is not thus handicapped.[12]

Chapter Four

"But you promised you'd go with me ..."

(Said with impatience.) *"Look, Kat, I promise a lot of things. Haven't you figured that out yet? I promised I'd quit the coke, and I did that, didn't I? Next thing, you'll be bugging me about having a beer now and then. I'm doing the best I can, all right? Get off my back."*

"I just wish you'd show a little more interest and enthusiasm about all of this. How can I make decisions about the wedding if you're not ..."

"Look, I told you I loved you, didn't I? I asked you to marry me. I've agreed to this big, fancy wedding. But that doesn't mean you own me. I am what I am. You better come to terms with that."

Silence.

(Frustrated curse. Crowds in close, speaks emphatically, pounds a clenched fist into an open palm for emphasis.) "This. Is. How. I. Am. Kathryn. I. Am. Not. Going. To. Change. (Spreads arms out in emphasis.) Can you deal with this? You

---

better take a good hard look at me and decide if you love me enough to hang in here and put up with all the good and all the bad."

    Silence.

    "Huh, Kat? It's six weeks until the wedding. Things are getting close so you better decide …"

    In the end, Adam got the whole story about Kathryn McFadden, Advancement Corporation, and Computer Dynamics. He was not the type of man to walk away from an accidental nuclear explosion and not need to understand exactly how everything had gone wrong. Kathryn McFadden was, and this *was* a compliment of the highest order, very similar to him. A child prodigy, just like himself, she'd finished school early (although not quite as early as he) with a master's degree in business from Columbia University. While he had been dazzling the business world in the computer field, she'd been flashing and dancing on Wall Street. Enough so that her personal financial portfolio was so successful that she'd stunned everyone by retiring at age twenty-five, walking away to live off her winnings. She'd kept just a few, *very large, influential* clients whom she still cared for with all the diligence and success that she had employed when she had been doing it full time. But *now,* her grand passion was starting new businesses. Or "helping make dreams come true" as she'd so blithely informed him at the country club that evening.

    To date, she'd found, encouraged, and given significant financial backing to five businesses run by women. All of them, to the best of Adam's investigations, were thriving. There were Lydia's Art Emporium, Financial Innovations, Music Pals, Teach Me, and Computer Dynamics. Three of the four women-run businesses had begun in Kathryn's home, with two of the women actually living with her for a period of time, just as Maria Gonzalez was currently doing. Apparently, Kathryn had an excellent eye for business potential - both ideas and people. She didn't seem to require anything but an idea, a dedicated woman, and the commitment to hard work. Kathryn provided the rest: know-how, connections, financial aid (from herself or others), and encouragement. June Willoughby had been right. Kathryn McFadden was a dynamo.

And Kathryn McFadden had been right. He was an idiot.

Kathryn, on the other hand, had walked away from the disaster known as Adam LeGrande reeling. His heartfelt words, *I've never met such an abrasive, unyielding, holier-than-thou person in all my life,* had literally rocked her right down to her Christian core. For the reality was, she could see how he had that impression. One of Kathryn's greatest assets was her honesty. She prided herself on her integrity and wanted others to recognize that quality in her as well. But being *truly* honest meant you couldn't lie to yourself, either. Somewhere along the line in dealing with Mr. Adam LeGrande when she had thought she was being strong and above reproach, she'd come across as bitchy and holier-than-thou. What a way to win friends and influence people for the Lord.

Grandmother used to say, "Sometimes God speaks in a still small voice. But if you're not listening He *will* use a baseball bat." Or a stick of dynamite. Or Adam LeGrande and his harsh, painful words.

When Kathryn had taken early retirement at age twenty-five, it had been based on a very spiritual and personal recommitment she had made. A recommitment in which she had vowed everything she did from that point on would make God smile. It had been drilled into her by Gran from as early as she could remember that God had blessed her enormously with skills far superior to many. As a result of those skills, at a time when most young adults were still struggling with what they wanted to do, she had amassed a personal fortune that many people never achieved in a lifetime. One morning, in her devotions, she had read, "*All God's people are ordinary people made extraordinary by the matter He has given them.*[13]". It was a baseball bat from God. She *was* extraordinary, but what exactly was she doing with her talents that were pleasing to God?

Not much.

She'd wished long and hard that Gran had still been alive. It was another time when she had felt that horrible, alone feeling. Prayer had

---

[13] Oswald Chambers, *My Utmost For His Highest*, October 25th entry

helped and that's when the idea of Advancement Corporation had been born. The thought that she could please God, use her God given talents, and have a really good time doing it all at once seemed just about perfect.

When she'd quit her job on Wall Street, her boss tried to get her to go into therapy and two of her colleagues suggested some really effective antidepressant medications. She'd sold her co-op in the city, and after careful consideration had chosen a nice suburban town that still had some life and opportunity in it. She'd bought the house in one day. Literally walked into the realtor's office and told her what she'd hope to find. Watching the realtor's face register amazement and hearing her say, "You're not going to believe this but I just listed a house exactly like you're describing not thirty minutes ago," only confirmed for Kathryn that God was validating her decisions. And literally until the moment Adam LeGrande had hit her upside the head with a stick of dynamite - almost seven years running - Kathryn had thought she was doing very well in all aspects of her life. Until now.

Two encounters with Adam LeGrande had left her depressed, sleepless, and distracted. Her confidence had taken a huge hit, too. Had she drifted off the path that she should be on? Were there others out there walking around with the same opinion about her, that Adam LeGrande had, but just been too polite to say so? It was a terrifying thought to think you are in one place and then discover you are in someplace totally different.

Which was her primary problem. If you *think* you are doing well in the way you are handling things in your life, and God sends you a Very Big Black Arrow that you *are not*, where exactly does that leave you? She needed advice, and she needed it fast. Kathryn sighed in resignation. Time to ask the girls.

Whenever people heard that she had been attending a Ladies' Bible Study group for close to three years they invariably got the wrong impression. Even for her, until she'd started attending, Bible study groups just sounded like staid, boring, get-togethers where everyone held hands and prayed the whole time. For all of Kathryn's Christian upbringing, she had always been quite happy showing up at church on Sunday, sitting in the back, and ducking out first chance she got. Even after Gran's death and the personal recommitment she'd made, Kathryn had minimal contact with the whole "God arena." She didn't sing. She didn't do church performances. She instinctively knew that she would be a disaster in teaching. Yes, Kathryn knew what she was good at: giving money in the offering plate, listening attentively to the sermon, applying the salient points to her daily life, and keeping track of her own personal growth and performance. That was certainly a lot more than many people did, right?

But Lydia had refused to take no for an answer. She brought up the subject of Bible study that first day they had met. While Kathryn had thrown around ideas for an art store, Lydia had thrown back the positive aspects of attending Bible study. Kathryn had been a very hard sell. The idea of sitting with a bunch of old ladies for two hours praying and studying the Bible? *Eww.* She would rather go to the dentist, have an IRS audit, or be trapped on the subway *in the summer.* Finally though, after a relentless number of weeks, Lydia had agreed to discuss the idea of opening an art shop, but only if Kathryn would come to her Ladies' Bible Study *just once.* Kathryn had gone *just once* and had been hooked.

A bunch of old ladies praying and studying? How wrong could she have been? It was a group of women who were not just a study group, they were a family. A sisterhood. A group of like-minded Christians who, although they were all at different walks in their life paths, were committed to reaching the same ultimate spiritual goal in the end. That first get-together Kathryn attended had been full of food and laughter, teasing and love, prayer and study, and such a feeling of *belonging* that Kathryn had been stunned when she realized she'd been there for almost three hours. For the first time since Gran's death, she felt the opportunity to be part of a loving group, one that would listen, encourage, and offer sound advice. Every Thursday night, from six o'clock until "whenever you leave" they got together at Gwen's house. And aside from church on Sunday morning, this was the single most important time of her week to keep her spiritually focused and grounded.

What Kathryn liked best about the group was its diversity. No one was knowledgeable about everything but there was invariably someone who'd been there or done that or knew someone who had. There was a wealth of knowledge, support, and tough love. There weren't a lot of things she could rely on in her life, but Kathryn had these six women. God had replaced Gran with a wacky bunch of opinionated, caring women who had welcomed Kathryn with open arms. And while she might not always like hearing what they said to her, she never doubted that they loved her.

So Kathryn sat there on Gwen's enormous couch and told them about her encounters with Adam LeGrande. When she finished telling her tale she finally asked, "Why did what he say upset me so much? I deal with obnoxious, full-of-themselves businessmen all the time, and usually whatever they say to me that I don't agree with I just let roll right off my back. No big deal." She took a deep breath and looked down at her hands clasped tightly in her lap. "But I can't get the look on his face and the sound of his words out of my head. I'm having trouble concentrating and sleeping." She looked up at the faces of her friends and managed a small smile. "This was more than the usual tough business talk. This guy really hit a nerve with me, and I'm hurting. I'm asking you to tell me what you think. Have I missed something here?"

"You're working too hard," Meredith said without hesitation, her dark brown eyes seriously intent. "I know for a fact you work seven days a week. And don't give me that 'my time is my own' garbage just because you're your own boss. It's a known fact that people who own their own businesses work longer hours and take less vacation time than any other professionals. Just tell me this, when was the last time you took a vacation for a *full week*?" She flipped her shoulder length brown hair as she looked around for someone else to back her up. "I think you should get away for a while. Take a break. *Have some fun.* Why don't you go on a cruise? God helps those who help themselves."

Kathryn bit her lip to keep from laughing. That was Meredith, always looking for the simple, surface solution. *Sometimes* she was right, but Kathryn suspected that wasn't the case this time. Meredith's husband, Joe, traveled a lot and there were no children. Responsibility and obligations were sort of *minimum* where Meredith was concerned.

Everyone held their collective breaths and waited for the inevitable. Lots of things bugged Audrey but misquoting or twisting the Bible was at the top of her list. The entire world was black and white for Audrey. You either did or you didn't, you were or your weren't. She was an accountant, which in Kathryn's opinion explained a lot. As far as Audrey was concerned, if your life wasn't the way you wanted it you had no one to blame but yourself for not fixing it. Sure enough, in an exasperated tone Audrey said, "Meredith, that's *not* in the Bible. And you know very well that Kat doesn't have to go all the way to the Caribbean for God to talk to her. Sounds like He's speaking pretty loudly right here. Besides, that's not what Kat's asking us. She's asking us what *we* see in her life that *God* might want her to change. I really don't think He's going to all this trouble so she'll take a week's vacation."

"I appreciate what you're saying, Merry," Kathryn said patiently, "and maybe I do need to reevaluate my personal down time. The fact is though, that I enjoy what I do so much I really don't feel like I work that much. You know what I mean?"

Meredith shrugged, crunching on a peanut. "It's hard for me to fathom enjoying your job so much that it doesn't feel like work." She supplemented working as a cashier at the local mall by selling home products such as makeup, kitchen equipment, and lately, jewelry. But none of what she did was anything more than a way to fill her time and earn some extra cash.

"We're discussing Kat right now, Meredith," Audrey said, standing up to help herself to another cup of strong black coffee. She was one inch shy of six feet and reed thin, with bright red hair that was *always* carefully arranged into a French twist. "But if you want us to discuss you *next*, and your gargantuan fear of change which holds you in a dead end, dreary, never-to-be-challenged, no respect job for over *eight years* ... "

"Audrey, cool it. Remember, you don't need to beat someone bloody to get your point across," Gwen said. Gwen had seniority due to age *and* the impressive ability of often saying the right thing, usually at the right time. She ran her home like a drill sergeant, and both her husband Paul, and her twin daughters, Becky and Terry, treated her with all the respect that a commanding general of one of the major military forces would receive. There wasn't much that flustered Gwen. Gwen looked over at Meredith who was masking her discomfort by fishing out all the almonds in the nut bowl.   Reaching out to touch her so that they would make eye contact, Gwen said, "Mer, point taken. You've noted that Kat doesn't take enough personal down time." Gwen looked at Kathryn pointedly. "I agree with Meredith to some extent, Kat, but I also have to side with Audrey. I don't think that's the main focus of this problem."

April spoke up. She was dressed in a full-length, purple caftan and had Birkenstock sandals on her feet showing off black painted toenails. At twenty-three she was the only one in the group younger than Kathryn. But even though she and Kathryn were the closest in age they were the farthest apart in just about everything else. April lived in an apartment paid for by her stepfather, still hadn't decided what she wanted to do with her life, and right now was house-sitting for a businesswoman who was out of the country for three months. She had no plans further than that nor did she seem to see the need. "What's your gut tell you? When you pray and all? Are you ignoring the issue because you don't want to face it?"

"I don't believe you're the one who's saying that!" Audrey said in an incredulous tone. "Of all the people -,"

"Give us an example, April," Gwen said giving Audrey a sharp look. Audrey rolled her eyes and sipped her coffee.

"Well," April looked down and fiddled with one of the fifteen plastic bracelets on her left wrist, "like, I *know* that making *no* decision *is* a decision." She looked up and made eye contact with Audrey. "And I know that my indecisiveness about my future needs to be faced very soon, okay? But I look at all of you and most of you are all so *driven*. So purposeful. You all seem to know what you want and you just go out and get it." She shrugged and looked around at everyone. "I just don't really want to do anything right now. I'm pretty content with my life the way it is. I'm happy living in my apartment, taking care of my dogs, working odd jobs, hanging out here on Thursday nights for Bible study, and volunteering down at the local food bank each week. I like teaching Church School to the three-year-olds and Pastor Benedict asked me to help with the fifth and sixth grade youth group. You may think I'm lost or unhappy or struggling but *I'm not*. I like my life just the way it is."

April sighed. "But there have been times when I've gotten on the wrong track with things. Like I thought a guy was nice and that I'd like to get to know him better or I thought a job opportunity sounded just fantastic. But my gut got all in a twist." She made eye contact with Kathryn. "I had trouble sleeping and concentrating it was so bad. And I prayed about it, you know, because my life is pretty calm and steady so when I have trouble sleeping and eating I can easily figure out something's wrong. Every time that's happened to me, I've prayed and when *I've listened* I've gotten a pretty clear answer." She shrugged. "'Course then I've got to *make the right decision …*" She shrugged and said matter-of-factly, "Like, it turned out that the guy that I thought was so nice was *married*. I met him and his wife by accident! Can you believe it? And, well, the 'great' job turned out to be," April hesitated and looked around at everyone who were listening intently, "phone sex."

"PHONE SEX!!" Pattilou exploded. She looked around at all the shocked faces. "When was this?!" It took a lot to get Pattilou to talk. She was the quietest of the group, often observing and just asking really profound questions rather than volunteering lengthy opinions or advice. Her life, of all of them, was the most picture –perfect, the most *normal*. Happily married to George for over twenty years they were still, in Kathryn's opinion, the epitome of a couple in love. Factor in their two, good natured, well-adjusted sons, Tyler and Dylan – both gainfully employed and dating girls that Pattilou was crazy about, well, as far as Kathryn was concerned, things didn't get much more perfect than that.

"It was a couple of years ago," April hastily explained. "You know how sometimes you see fliers on telephone poles that says stuff like, 'You can make up to fifty dollars an hour! No experience necessary! Call for details!'?"

"Tell me you called," Audrey said in an incredulous voice, her face still a picture of disbelief.

"Sure I called," April said defensively. "You guys tell me that you've never called about one of those jobs?"

All six women sat there absolutely silently staring at April while she took the time to make eye contact with each of them.

Audrey looked at Gwen. "Maybe she can move back with her stepfather. She needs a curfew. *She needs something.*"

"April," Gwen said gently, ignoring Audrey, "did you take the job?"

April shrugged. "I'll be honest, I thought about it long and hard. It paid *thirty-five dollars an hour* flat rate and then there were bonuses you could earn to get people to sign up for memberships!! I've never been offered money like that to do any kind of job in my life!"

"Thirty-five dollars *an hour?!*" Meredith said in an awestruck voice and got a very sharp look from Audrey. Kathryn bit the inside of her mouth trying not to laugh.

"But like I said," April continued, "my gut got in such a twist about it that I knew God was giving me a clear direction about it. Right after I decided not to take the job, I got a job walking those dogs for the summer. Remember?" She stared off in space for a moment, lost in thought. "The money wasn't as good, but I *do* love dogs and all ..."

Gwen rubbed the back of her neck and sighed. "You made a good choice, April. But we don't need to tell you that, do we?" April shook her head. Gwen looked at Kathryn. "So, are you keeping track of all this, Kathryn? So far, Meredith thinks you need to take a break more often in your professional calendar and April's cautioning you to examine yourself and listen to God's still small voice. And based on the fact that you *are* having trouble sleeping and concentrating, it seems that April is agreeing with you regarding your concern about this. Right April? *April ...*" April was busy answering whispered questions from Meredith about the phone sex job. Meredith looked around with a guilty smile and April nodded in agreement when Gwen repeated her point.

"And avoid married men and jobs involving phone sex," Audrey said pointedly while glancing at Kathryn and glaring at Meredith. Everyone, including April, burst out laughing.

"If you had to pick one aspect of your life," Pattilou said after everyone finished laughing, "that needed improvement, what would it be?" She held her hand up when Kathryn went to answer right away. "And remember, if you can't think of an area, then you are effectively telling all of us you think you're perfect." Kathryn shut her mouth. "I know what area I'd pick." Pattilou looked at the other women.

Lydia smiled and winked at Kathryn. "Me, too."

One by one the women made eye contact with each other and then all finally looked at Kathryn. Frowning, Kathryn said in a frustrated tone, "I don't know! I'm very content with my life as it is! God's blessed all the businesses I've helped get started, the clients whose portfolios I still manage are happy, I've been very active at church, and really feel very contented with my spiritual life …"

Lydia crossed her arms and gave her an *"And?"* look. When everyone continued to stare silently at Kathryn, Lydia finally said, "Okay, I'll ask it. How's the personal life, Kat?"

"Personal life!" Kathryn sputtered. "But you guys, *out of everyone*, know what a disaster I am when it comes to personal relationships. You *agreed* with me, when I told you my sorry history with men, that I should stay out of that arena all together!"

"I certainly didn't mean it should be a life decision," Gwen said shaking her head vigorously and looking at the others for confirmation. "Although you'd look very attractive in a nun's habit. You've got the face for it."

"I hear that not all religious orders wear the whole formal habit now," April began.

Before Audrey could cut her off, Lydia gently laid her hand on April's arm. "Gwen's kidding, love."

"Oh," April said, glancing at Gwen who gave her a smile and a brief nod.

"What did this Adam LeGrande look like?" Meredith asked innocently.

"Maria Gonzalez said he's out of this world handsome," Lydia said. "But that's just say so. I've not seen him."

Kathryn stood up abruptly and went over to the table to pour herself another cup of coffee and grab a piece of carrot cake. "Look you guys, I *am not* going to get into this discussion. *I am not.* I may have shared with you all the poor decisions I've made when I was dating, but you obviously still don't get it. *I am lousy with men.* Really lousy. Horribly lousy. Shockingly lousy. The fact that Adam LeGrande was *so awful in person* and that you are all now picking on my nonexistent personal life is terrifying! Don't you get it? He makes some of the other men *I spent years with* look like dreams come true! It would make *perfect sense* for me to find him handsome and be intrigued by his 'rough' exterior." She was practically shouting when she said, *"But I would not even consider dating him!!"*

Gwen held up her hands in mock surrender. "Whoa, girl! Which one of us said anything about you dating him? *You're the one* who just mentioned how handsome, intriguing, and how much potential for improvement he might have. Why are you so defensive all of a sudden, Kat? Seems like we've hit a nerve. *You asked us* a question. We answered. Now, I guess you'll have to think on it, huh?" Gwen said quietly.

Kathryn turned around to look at Gwen's kind face. Only Kathryn and April had never been married. Lydia was a widow, raising her three teenage sons, and they all knew that while her husband had been alive he'd had ruled his home like a dictator. Love, had there ever been any in her marriage, had been fleeting. Audrey, widowed once, divorced once, and currently married to her third husband, Bill, had plenty of advice on relationships - none of it positive. Out of the rest of them, only Pattilou and Gwen had happy marriages.

"You're thirty-one years old, honey," Pattilou said. "A marriage and a family *were* something you desperately wanted for a long time. *You told us that.* Even though you've avoided the dating scene these past years, can you honestly look at us and tell us you still don't secretly dream of those things?" Kathryn stood there silently while her eyes filled with tears.

Gwen continued gently, *"God is not a God of disorder, but of peace,*[14] Kathryn. You know that. He is not causing this disruption in your life for any other reason than because He loves you. *We know how much God loves us, and we have put our trust in Him.*[15]"

---

[14] I Corinthians 14:33a, New Living Translation
[15] I John 4:16a, New Living Translation

Kathryn came over and sat down on the couch, where April put her arm around her. "How did we get on this topic?" Kathryn said in genuine misery. "Weren't we talking about my crisis with Adam LeGrande and the perceptions that others have of me? *I don't want to start dating again!* How many times do I have to repeat that I am an absolute disaster in that area! You all know that! Although you didn't know me when I was going through most of that time, I've not spared you any of the horrible details." She looked at April. "I *dated* a married man and *had sex* with him for over a year! My gut *told me nothing.*" She looked at the other women all looking at her sympathetically. "I even stopped attending church because the guy I was dating at the time didn't like that I went! I just said, 'Oh, okay. I'll stop!' And I told you about the guy I dated that had such a drinking problem that I don't think I was ever with him when he was sober! That was a *two year* relationship, a*nd he's the one I almost married!!*"

Angrily Kathryn brushed the tears from her face. Looking at Pattilou she said, "I can't tell you that I don't want a marriage and a family *because I do.* But I also like this right relationship I now have with God. Can *you* all honestly say that *you* think I could handle a personal relationship without risking that?"

It was Audrey who finally spoke. "I think you can do absolutely anything with God's help. Without His help I'm not sure I could get across the street. I can honestly say that with God's help I think you could handle a personal relationship without risking your spiritual relationship. I'll make a commitment to pray for you daily." She shrugged. "I do pray already for all of you but I'll get a little bit more specific with you."

"I agree with Audrey," Pattilou said. "Right down to the prayers."

"Me, too," Gwen murmured.

"My prayer life stinks," Meredith said sheepishly. "But I agree with Audrey, too. And I'll try to pray for you every day. And maybe for a new job, too."

Lydia spoke. "It's admirable that you recognize your weakness, Kat. And it's commendable that you have made an effort to avoid putting yourself in situations that will cause you to fall back on old habits. But can't you see that your lack of faith in yourself and God's influence in your life is a significant crack in the whole picture? Think about all of the biblical people we've studied! All of them found their greatest victory in their weakest personal aspect. Moses was shy and stuttered, yet he was chosen to be God's spokesman. Sarah was called the Mother of Israel and yet by all accounts was barren her entire life! Even Deborah, the judge and prophet of Israel, had to have battled her whole life to do what God wanted her to do because she was "only a woman." You've done *a lot* of wonderful things already in your life. But, you can correct me if I'm wrong, I think you've come by all of them pretty easily ... "

Lydia got up and walked over to the couch and Meredith made room so that she could sit down by Kathryn. "I was *never* strong," Lydia said in a soft whisper that everyone could hear. "Never strong in my marriage to speak up against my domineering husband, never strong in my role as a mother to speak up and get my boys to do even the simplest things around the house, and never strong personally to speak up and say what I wanted to do to find personal happiness. *You* helped me do that, Kat. You don't think it was *easy* to say my dreams out loud and then have them put into reality with the very real chance of failure, do you?"

Kathryn was looking at her friend Lydia in a different light. She'd had no idea ... "I never thought about it being hard for you ..."

"It was. It is," Lydia whispered with tears in her eyes. "*It still is.* Anything that matters is always hard. Being successful in your personal life has always been the hardest for you. But it could also be your greatest triumph."

For a few moments, no one spoke. Then, finally, April said, "Well, I'll apologize," in the barest whisper, "but I'm still not sure I need to be sorry." Everyone looked at her in complete confusion. She looked unbelievably uncomfortable, fiddling again with her bracelets and staring intently at Gwen's Lladro collection. Finally she made eye contact with Kathryn. "I didn't mean to cause all of this trouble in your life ..."

"What?" said Kathryn completely perplexed. "*What did you do?*"

"You just seem so alone," April said in a whiny voice. "You know, I've got my stepfather and my dogs, and Pattilou's got George and the girls, and Audrey's got Bill."

"Fat lot of good that does me," Audrey said with a genuine laugh and an eye roll.

"And Gwen's got Paul and the girls and Lydia's got her three boys. Even Meredith's got Joe, even though he travels so much he's hardly ever home, but at least he calls her on the phone." April looked around at the other women looking for support. "I just thought, right after the Christmas and New Year's holidays, that it would be so nice if you had someone special, Kat. So when Gwen said we should all choose something we were going to commit to pray about this year," she looked at Gwen for confirmation, "remember, and you had us write it down and put it in the envelope and keep it secret until the end of the year?" Gwen nodded. "I just decided that I'd pray for you," April said looking back at Kathryn. "And that God would send you someone."

Gwen grinned and then laughed out loud, absolutely delighted. "Oh well, you've got no choice now, Kat! The wheels were put in motion months ago when April started praying. This is going to be so much fun to watch!"

"Actually, my stepbrother is very nice -," April began.

"NO!" every woman, including Kathryn said aloud.

April looked puzzled. "But he seems very nice from what my stepfather has said about him, and I think you two would have a lot in common ..."

"NO," said Audrey working hard not to shudder in horror. "I think you've done enough already, April. Let's just let Kathryn digest all of this stuff we've just thrown at her, okay?"

Everyone looked at Kathryn, who finally nodded in agreement. *Please, someone, change the subject. Move on,* she thought.

"I think that's a good idea, too," Gwen said, grabbing her notebook and pen. "Can we all commit to praying for Kathryn this upcoming week? Specifically that she'll feel God's guidance clearly without any confusion." At everyone's affirmative nod she said, "Good. What else do we have to pray about or praise before we get studying?"

"I think," Lydia said with a grin, "that we all need to start praying that God will show us some *really nice, interesting men* for us to match Kathryn up with."

"Oh, goodie," Kathryn moaned with absolutely no enthusiasm, while everyone burst out laughing.

When the character of a man is not clear to you, look at his friends.[16]

Chapter Five

"Would you stop calling me that? The name's Sheila, I told you. S-H-E-I-L-A. Why can't you say it?"

"I just keep forgetting."

"You've got an IQ so high they weren't able to give me a number and you can't remember my damn name?"

"Why do I have to call you that anyway? No one else calls her mother by her first name."

"How dare you question me?! Haven't I gotten us this apartment, those nice clothes you're wearing, and that fancy computer you're always working on?!

"Yes, but ..."

(Taking threatening steps forward and speaking in a low, angry tone.) "Wrong answer, Adam ..."

(Wearing an 'I'm sorry, you're absolutely right expression'.) "Thanks for everything you've done for me ... Sheila."

---

[16] Japanese Proverb

"Yes, Miles?" Adam looked up from his computer screen.

"Ms. Maria Gonzalez of Computer Dynamics is willing to meet with you tomorrow, Friday, at four o'clock in Mayor Willoughby's office. Since you did not elaborate on how your second meeting went with Ms. McFadden, but given the fact that you're obviously proceeding with Computer Dynamics and the township project, I must assume that your allegations of impropriety were negated."

Adam looked at Miles and rested his chin in his hand. "It's killing you, isn't it? Almost a full week has gone by and you still don't know the whole story, the fact that I haven't told you what happened and your sources are not thorough enough to figure it out. You're just oozing with curiosity."

"I do not need *sources*, as you so ominously put it, to tell me that your encounter with Ms. McFadden was nothing short of a disaster. You have a *history*, shall we say, Sir, of jumping to inaccurate conclusions based on your mistaken belief in your infallibility. I attempted to warn you on the phone, if you recall."

Adam looked back at his computer screen and tried to be glib. "My *history* has something to do with my atrocious childhood. You know, all the neglect, exploitation, abandonment, and lack of love. That warps even the most brilliant of minds. I was left to rely on no one but myself. The fact that I've made it so far and so well is a testament to my abilities and my tenacity. You'll pardon me if I tend to trust myself and my instincts over anyone else's." Adam looked over at Miles standing patiently in the doorway. "That was supposed to be humorous. Ha. Ha."

Miles turned to walk out of Adam's study but not before pointing out, "I would suspect that *my* pardon is not what you should be seeking, but more likely *Ms. McFadden's*."

"You know Miles," Adam said putting his chin in his hand, "we're all a product of our upbringing. What kind of upbringing could you have had that caused you to be what I see before me?"

At first Adam thought that Miles would do what he did so well, which was ignore him. But he turned in the doorway of the study to look at Adam. "What you see before you, Sir, is the product of a lifetime of regret. Nothing more, but perhaps significantly less." Adam closed his eyes and sighed. The guy was absolutely no fun and was *never* going to let him get the last word in. Ever. When he looked up again, Miles was gone.

I don't think I've ever been so insulted in my life. Kathryn McFadden's words kept rattling around in his brain like a loose screw. Perhaps if she had been referring to little Adam LeGrande, the nerdy outcast who was too poor to even own clean clothes or eat cereal *with milk* instead of water, he wouldn't have been so upset. He had never made it a secret about where he'd come from, but only when it was in relation to how dazzling a place he was in *now*. In fact, to the best of his recollection, Adam had never seen anyone offended when compared to the adult Adam LeGrande, boy genius, computer wunderkind, business guru. Most people couldn't get close enough to him, hoping that his dazzling good luck would rub off on them. At least professionally. Personally, it was a different story.

Personally, no one had ever been close to him. He liked it that way, too. People kept at a safe distance had no capacity to hurt. Being hurt was bad: to be avoided at all cost. The best lesson his mother had taught him had been "rely on no one but yourself." Sheila Docherty, the queen of self-absorption. Sheila Docherty, who had never given away *anything* unless she had to or had replaced it with something bigger and better. That even included not giving her name to her own child. Adam had no idea where the name "LeGrande" had come from, and Sheila had never been inclined to elaborate. Perhaps it was his father's name. Perhaps it had been a failed agenda to scam some poor sucker out of some cash. Who knew?

Sheila Docherty had lived, slept, ate, and breathed "rely on no one but your own self." If she couldn't get you to give what she wanted to her willingly, out of the goodness of your heart, then she'd try guilting it out of you. If guilting it out of you wasn't successful (you heartless so-and-so), then she'd steal if from you. No one was immune: not acquaintances (she had no friends), not men (married or otherwise), and certainly not her child. In fact, *especially* not her child. Wasn't a child the greatest drain on any one human being's time, energy, money, and patience? Why, a child owed his mother for all the pain and suffering she'd had to go through from the moment of his birth.

Adam grew up knowing he owed her, big time. And as luck would have it, his opportunity to pay his mother back came about much sooner than either of them had expected. Not a moment before, but as soon as Sheila had realized that her son had something above and beyond the every day trial and tribulation that she expected from him, she'd focused all of her attention on him.

Both Adam and his mother could not have been more delighted with the onset of school. For her, she finally had a place to dump him, and for Adam, he finally had an opportunity to thrive. To explore. To discover. To listen. To learn. To touch. To do. He was like a dried up old sink sponge suddenly submerged into warm, soapy water. The feeling of *at last*, coupled with thoughts like *oh, that's why* and *but how about* made school a magical place to be.

No matter how lousy his life was, learning made it all worth while.

The kids at school hated him. His earliest memories of kindergarten were the palpable dislike of almost every single child in the classroom, a dislike so intense that no one wanted to stand in line next to him and everyone felt compelled to hang their coats in whatever was *not* the closet he had hung his in. The teacher had tried to run interference for him, but the reality was it just made the other children subtler in their ostracism.

Some said he smelled, which was probably very true. The concept of personal hygiene was not something his mother had ever thought to waste her time teaching him: clean clothes, clean body, and clean teeth. *Who cared?* Wake up, get dressed in whatever you could find that covered you, and hope to find some food of some kind in the kitchen (but if not, the school would feed him lunch for free). Quite frankly, the concept of cleanliness never even crossed his mind. There were too many other things to deal with. Just get to school. It was a mantra he would repeat in his head over and over again.

His pants were getting too tight to button.

Just get to school.

His mother's friend was still over. He could hear them in the bedroom laughing.

Just get to school.

Nothing to eat but some dill pickles.

Just get to school.

He had no winter coat that fit and last night it had snowed.

Just get to school.

If he could just get to school, then he would have a bunch of hours (never enough, but light-years better than any other option he had) to get lost in … learning.

He and his mother moved around a lot, depending on jobs, scams, men, and avoidance of trouble, though not necessarily in that order. Everything was relative: cleanliness was way, *way* down on the list after things like avoiding the strap, sating the ever present hunger, and *just getting to school.*

The kids that didn't hate him because he smelled hated him because he was just plain weird. What he couldn't articulate to them was his own puzzlement over the very same dilemma. As odd as *they* thought *he* was, he was absolutely clueless as to what *they* were all about. What was the rush to get to the lunchroom when you could read all those fascinating bulletin boards in the hallway and learn all manner of amazing things? Why run around on the playground during your free time chasing the girls when you could study the pattern and structure of the most amazing spider web under the slide ladder? Why get yourself all worked up over whether a rubber ball had been kicked *in* or *out* of bounds when you could study the pattern of the clouds, lie on your back and feel the motion of the rotation of the earth, and watch the lazy patterns the bumble bees made as they communicated to each other?

His only complete year at public school had been kindergarten. Then 'they' clued into how intelligent he was under all that dirt, grime and neglect. Everything hit the fan when they had done some tests on him and the next thing he knew, he was in third grade for a bit, then sixth, then ninth. He came to hate tests because whenever they were administered it meant that another change was coming.

Seemingly overnight, Sheila Docherty put all of her "people" skills together and turned into Stage Mother of the Millennia. All of a sudden, Adam's "best interests" were her "primary concern." She was the classic example of beauty being only skin deep: blonde, blue eyed, tall. Even as a young child, he was aware of the attention she attracted whenever they went out in public. She could turn on the charm, dazzle you with flattery, and seduce you with a mere look. It even worked on Adam, although she didn't usually bother to expend the effort where he was concerned. There were times when Adam had looked at her and wondered how such a beautiful person could be so … ugly … inside?

He was aware that there was some, albeit brief, scuffle about whether she was caring "suitably" for Adam. He never learned the whole story, but in a flash he was scrubbed literally from the top of his head to the tip of his fingernails and dressed in clothes that were new and the proper size. Along with the accumulated dirt that washed down the drain went his freedom. As soon as his mother knew that he was a potential meal ticket, she became the absolute expert on everything that was Adam. Sheila, the abysmal mother, became Sheila, the nightmare representative of Adam LeGrande, boy genius.

Adam needed a better apartment to study and to have personal space. Adam needed clothes, toys, food, and other things in order for him to be stimulated mentally and physically to the best of his potential. Adam needed private tutors and special schools to channel this tremendous ability that he had been gifted with. Adam needed to be continually evaluated to make sure that the present line of educational study was appropriate.

Sheila's persistence had gotten him into MIT at age thirteen. Two months into the school year she'd been killed in a car accident driving to see him. By that time, their relationship had evolved into more that of a manager and client rather than mother and son. It seemed to suit them both. They both understood the emotionless boundaries of such an association. He had been calling her "Sheila" since he was eight. ("Don't call me Mom, they won't take me seriously. Call me Sheila.") Some at MIT hadn't even known she was his mother when they'd extended their sympathy.

An MIT computer professor had stepped forward and offered to become Adam's guardian. Adam was grateful, but realized it for what it was worth; another person trying to get something from him. It was a suitable arrangement. Professor Freeman and his wife Eloise provided Adam room and board and the necessary signatures that all guardians were required to make. In return, Adam allowed Professor Freeman access to all his own research. It was during Adam's final year at MIT, when he was fifteen, that Professor Alexander Freeman become recognized worldwide for "his" innovative advancement in a new style of computer coded language, language that Adam had written in his spare time. Adam finished his time at MIT at age sixteen and at the same time he received his doctorate from MIT he was granted emancipation making him a legalized adult at age sixteen.

Offers of employment came from all over. Settling in at the computer giant Delmont Graphics at sixteen-years-old had been about as awkward as attending MIT at thirteen. By then, he had numerous coping skills like sarcastic humor and a razor sharp wit. When all else failed, advanced technical jargon always caused major intimidation. He fell into the pattern of his existence: solitary, driven, and cerebral. Everyone avoided him for a variety of reasons and that suited him *just fine*. Stay back, leave him alone, and just make a list of what you needed.

Obtaining financial independence, through the creation of LeGrande Incorporated and the sale of his revolutionary computer system for banking systems worldwide, had allowed Adam to structure a world around himself that suited him and him alone. The need to fit in ceased to exist. Interactions with others were defined within Adam's own comfortable parameters. He no longer needed to worry about pleasing or accommodating others. After all, *they* had always wanted something from *him*, so let them do the approaching. The groveling. Let them be uncertain and insecure. He'd paid his dues.

Working in the corporate offices required him to deal with people daily, something which he absolutely abhorred. So he bought a massive home that doubled as his main office and fed into his desire to remain solitary and aloof. It was an excellent tax shelter as well. Many of his business dealings were electronic, enabling him to keep personal interactions to a bare minimum. He had wealth and solitude. He had a life that suited him and his personality exactly. He had …

The knock on his study door brought him out of his thoughts. "Come in."

Miles stood in the doorway. Adam sighed and rubbed his eyes. He had a butler. How the hell did he end up with a butler? "What's up, Miles?"

"I've brought you some lunch, Sir. Vegetable soup and a ham sandwich."

"Make the soup yourself, Miles?"

"Of course, Sir." He carried over a tray laden with silver cutlery, fine china, and a wonderful aroma.

Adam took a bite of the sandwich and spoke as he chewed, "Did you know when I was a kid I used to eat cereal and water because we couldn't afford milk?"

"I seem to recall your telling me that before, Sir. Do you recall me mentioning what poor manners it is to speak while your mouth is full of food?"

Adam grinned. "No, I don't recall that." He gestured toward a chair. "Take a load off, Miles. Talk to me while I eat. Now's your chance while I'm a captive audience with my mouth full of your delicious food and making a serious attempt at good manners."

"Manners maketh man.[17]" Miles said as he settled into the chair that Adam had indicated.

Adam swallowed and said, "What about women? What makes a woman? Kathryn McFadden better have something else up her sleeve because her manners aren't going to cut it." He tilted his head back and smiled lost in thought. "Then again, she *does* have other attributes that tend to make people forget about her manners, at least momentarily."

---

[17] William of Wykeham, 1324-1404, Motto of Winchester College and New College, Oxford

"Have you ever explored, Sir, your propensity to alienate women?"

Adam looked genuinely surprised. "What are you talking about? Women love me. If I wasn't a bit abrasive, between my money and my good looks, I'd have to beat them back with sticks."

"If that is indeed true, and it would not be my place to disagree, then perhaps I should ask if you have ever explored your propensity to alienate Kathryn McFadden?"

Adam took another bite of his sandwich and chewed. Finally he shrugged. "So, we clash. Big deal. I'm guessing she's one of those man-haters. You know, struggled all her life to get where she is, been constantly beaten back and overlooked by men, has this huge agenda in which she's going to get even with as many men in the population as possible. She's probably a card carrying member of the She-Woman-Man-Haters Club."

"What exactly has she said that leads you to that stunning conclusion, Sir?"

Oh, man. It was always a *big* mistake inviting Miles to sit down and talk. He should have known. Now he was going to have to get into a discussion about Kathryn McFadden *again*. "You know, less than two weeks ago, I had no idea who Kathryn McFadden was. Now, she's been here in my office, she's at parties I've been stuck attending, she's backing a company I'm being forced to mentor, and she regularly comes up in conversations I have with you. This is becoming a rather annoying set of coincidences."

"Sir, Kathryn McFadden has been in business here in town for well over five years. I find it particularly stunning that, in your words, you did not have any 'idea who Kathryn McFadden was' until last week. She tirelessly supported June Willoughby for her mayoral campaign, has sat for more than three years on the town revitalization committee, and on one occasion was directly involved in LeGrande Incorporated - with stellar results I might add. *I* must ask *you*, rather than wasting time puzzling over these "annoying set of coincidences", why you feel compelled to dismiss this very significant business ally?"

"How was she directly involved in LeGrande Incorporated?" Lunch was now forgotten and Adam was leaning forward intently.

Miles looked suitably disgusted. "The mentoring program you currently have working so well at the downtown office? Where the high school students with significant promise are allowed to work alongside various LeGrande employees for a semester? Where said students are able to achieve high school credit as well as experience first hand what it is like in the 'real' professional world? We've got mentoring secretaries, mentoring computer tech assistants," Miles chuckled, a very rare sound, "we've even got mentoring cafeteria staff in the company cantina." At Adam's blank face, Miles shook his head. "Sir, those are all students through the Teach Me tutorial and career training facility. Teach Me is one of Kathryn McFadden's seed companies. I *know* her name was on all the initial paper work when the proposal initially came through. She *always* lends her name and her support when a company is first starting."

"That program's been quite a success," Adam said quietly.

Miles nodded. "Yes, Sir. A stunning success. And it's brought us a lot of positive publicity because we were willing to be one of the first "guinea pig" companies, so to speak. We get points for our willingness, points for our patience, and now we get points for being part of the program's success."

Adam put his head in his hands. "I thought her name was familiar just because it had been in my Blackberry. But now I remember. I must be slipping."

"Well, in all fairness, Sir, she lends her name and her references, but she tries very hard to stay as behind the scenes as possible. She wants the company to succeed on its own merit, not just because of her visible presence. I don't think, until that infamous morning last week, that you had ever been formally introduced to her. You may have been at some of the same functions in the past but you wouldn't have put the name and the face together."

Miles stood. "And we both know how miserable you are with interpersonal relationships. You would never have noticed Ms. Kathryn McFadden, even though she's been at probably all of the meager collection of social functions that you've attended, because you don't do anything but business. She's only come within your scope of recognition because *finally* your business paths have crossed."

Miles collected the tray of cold vegetable soup and a half eaten ham sandwich. "Which leads me back to my two original questions, Sir: *Have you ever explored your propensity to alienate women?* Or, *have you ever explored your propensity to alienate Kathryn McFadden?*"

"Miles," Adam said through gritted teeth, "I *don't* purposely alienate women."

Patiently, as if he were a eight-year-old child, Miles leaned toward Adam, tray in hand and said, "Sir, I am not discussing whether you *do* or you *don't* purposely alienate women. *We both know you do.* I am asking you if you've explored the reason *why.* That's the crux of the matter. *Strong reasons make strong actions.*[18] What are your reasons, Sir?"

As Miles walked out the study door, he could hear the loud thump as Adam's head dropped in frustration to his desk.

Lying with his head on the desk, Adam heard the words he had fired at Kathryn McFadden in anger, *You may be good at what you do but you're not any more likeable than I am!* But, Miles was still wrong. The reality was, Adam didn't purposely alienate women. He purposely alienated *everyone.* He may have worked hard to be different from his mother, but the reality was that he was right where she had been when she had died, absolutely alone with no one to love or care about her once she was gone.

Yippee.

---

[18] William Shakespeare, 1564-1616

Sometimes I've believed as many as six impossible things before breakfast.[19]

Chapter Six

"Kathryn, there's no need for tears."

"But, the doctors just said ..."

"I heard them, Dear. But have you heard what I've been saying? Having you in my life has been a treasure I never thought to possess. At a time of enormous sorrow and grief, He gave me you. I've had cancer diagnoses before, Dear, before you came to live with me. I've had doctors tell me to get my things in order; that I didn't have much time left. The best thing that the Lord ever gave me was you. The second best thing He's ever given me is time. Fifteen years of grace, Sweetheart. Precious years that have allowed me to have love and laughter, joy and discovery. I can only find words of thanks, nothing more."

"What can I do for you, Gran?"

"Keep making God smile, Kathryn. Just keep making God smile."

---

[19] Lewis Carroll, 1832-1898, *Alice In Wonderland*

"These plans look terrific to me," Mayor June Willoughby said to Maria Gonzalez as they wrapped up their four o'clock meeting. Looking over at Adam, she said, "What's your opinion?"

Adam shrugged, "What you've heard and what you've been shown is one hundred percent Computer Dynamics. My company may have done a few things marginally differently, but in general, I think the plan is sound. Don't worry, I'll speak up when I think I should."

As everyone packed up to go and were shaking hands good-bye, June looked at Adam. "A few of us are going over to O'Reilly's for a few beers to celebrate the end of the week. Want to come along?"

Have you ever explored, Sir, your propensity to alienate? "Sure, I'll come along."

June Willoughby looked at Adam as if he'd just stripped naked. She swallowed her surprise and sputtered, "You will?!"

Adam shrugged. "Unless your invitation was just to be polite and you'd much rather that I had declined. Want to ask again and I'll try another answer?"

June flushed. "No, *no,* that's not at all what I meant. I'm delighted you'd like to go. You just, well, you never ..." The sentence hung unfinished while June struggled to get herself out of the awkward corner she'd painted herself into.

"Socialize?" Adam volunteered helpfully.

June nodded. "Yes, that's it. The couple of times that I've had dinner with Miles -,"

"You've had dinner with my butler?" Adam didn't care if it was rude to interrupt.

June flushed again but this time it had nothing to do with Adam or his feelings. "Well, yes, we have. I asked him out to dinner the first time in the hopes of stealing him away from you."

Nodding, Adam said with absolute sincerity, "I tried to get him to go."

She smiled. "Yes, I know. He told me you did. But he's tremendously loyal and wouldn't hear of it. Anyway, that first evening, I

ended up enjoying myself tremendously. He's quite witty, you know."
Again the flush.

"Try living with him day in and day out. Always mumbling those
annoying quotations." *So conniving. So shifty. So...*

June interrupted Adam's thoughts and said with real admiration,
"Don't you think it's impressive though? He's got magnificent retention.
That's why he's such a good ... I prefer 'personal assistant' to butler."

"I prefer butler. Keeps him in his place."

June looked at him with a slight frown. Adam suspected she was
trying to figure out if he was serious or not. He gave her his 'yes, I really
mean it' face. "Hmm, I see," she murmured, but there was absolutely no
way she could. "Well, whatever his professional title, on a personal level he
is quite, um, *nice.*" She cleared her throat and went back to clearing up her
desk and loading her briefcase, suddenly looking for all the world like a
flustered schoolgirl.

Well, now isn't this interesting. "So, there's been more than just the
initial 'professional' dinner I take it?"

Feigning nonchalance, June smiled, "Hmm? What? Oh, yes, well,
just twice we've gone out. We're both very busy people. I'm sure you
know how it is."

No, actually he didn't. How about that. His *butler* was getting
more action than he was. How pitiful was *that?* Curiosity was burning a
whole in his brain. "Planning on seeing him again any time soon?"

She appeared to debate whether she was going to answer him or
not. "Actually, I see him every Sunday at church. Lately, we've been sitting
together, and sometimes we go out for coffee or lunch or something."

"*Miles goes to church?*" There was no way he could mask his surprise.

June Willoughby stood there staring at Adam's shocked face.
Finally she said, "Can I ask you a personal question, Adam?"

No. "Sure."

"How can you spend so much time with a person and not know
him *at all?* How do you maintain such emotional distance?"

Now it was his turn to gather up his papers and appear busy as he
filled his briefcase, regretting every moment in which he'd left the

professional realm and ventured out into this "fun and friendly, I'm Mr. Personal realm." Finally, Adam looked at the Mayor and decided she'd better know what she was in for this evening, having invited him along for her after hours personal bonding time. "It's an amazing gift I have, along with my computer brilliance and business acumen. I call it strategic alienation." Adam arched a casual eyebrow and gave her his "dead, emotionless" face.

He saw Kathryn sitting with a small group of men and women in a far corner of O'Reilly's almost as soon as he walked in the door. If he hadn't already been in deep regret for saying he'd go along, that would have cinched it. In high gear, tense and uncertain because of the circumstances, he was a bundle of sarcasm and wit just waiting to explode and destroy everything in his path. He concentrated on keeping his mouth shut, smiling his sincere "I'm really interested in everything you're telling me smile," and nodding appropriately when it was required. *Initiating* small talk was just about impossible for him, but he was determined to *sustain* any that came his way. In the brief few moments it took for everyone to park their cars, meet, walk into the restaurant/bar, and wait for a table he was ready to run screaming into the night. It seemed perfect that beautiful, sophisticated, laughing-casually-and-easily-with-her-group-of-friends-and-colleagues-Kathryn should be on hand to witness his imminent failure. What would she call it? Oh yeah, *strike three.*

He ordered a beer although alcohol was rarely a drink he chose. He liked to remain sharp and aware, something that never happened when he drank. Besides Adam and June sitting at the round, cloth-covered table, were June's personal assistant, Rebecca, a short, glum young woman and Jonesy, as everyone called him, a quiet, thoughtful man who had skin as dark as ink and was one of the township lawyers. While Jonesy ordered a collection of appetizers, Adam wondered if Rebecca was aware that June had been shopping around for her replacement in the form of his butler. Probably not, and probably not a good subject to bring up in casual conversation either. *Make note of that.*

The music was thankfully loud, making conversation sporadic at best. Adam forced himself to sip his beer, try to enjoy the music, and act like he was relaxed and enjoying himself. He knew he failed miserably, but everyone was far too polite to make note. Each person went out of their way to make polite conversation on at least two occasions, which he suspected was the requisite number necessary. After spending a little more than an hour (which *he* hoped was the requisite length of time to be polite) he began to make excuses to leave.

June gave him a sympathetic smile, confirming his lack of casualness and false enjoyment of the evening when he shouted across the table he had to be going. As he pushed back his chair to stand, Rebecca said, "Look out!" a split second too late. With all the grace of a Mack truck he bumped into a waitress passing between chairs behind him sending her and her tray of drinks and food flying.

Right on to Kathryn McFadden.

Conversation stopped. Even the band chose to go on break and the piped in replacement music dropped the sound level by a number of decibels. All attention swung to the clumsy idiot and the woman covered in table twelve's drinks and appetizers. "What are you doing standing there?" Adam said to Kathryn. "You were sitting all the way on the other side of the room!"

Wrong. Wrong thing to say. He knew it. The waitress who was hauling herself up off the floor knew it. Both tables close enough to hear knew it. And boy-oh-boy, did Kathryn McFadden know it. If looks could kill. Adam had heard that expression but had never truly appreciated its full meaning. He did now. Right down to the various painful methods with which she wished to bring about his death.

"I'm so sorry, Ma'am!" the waitress sputtered as she whipped a cloth out of her apron pocket and made useless attempts to help repair the irreparable.

Right thing to say. What *he* should have said. Kathryn took the cloth from the waitress and wiped her hands. She stilled as she looked at the front of her suit and came to the obvious conclusion that there was absolutely no hope. "It's okay. It was an accident. I was about ready to go home anyway and this just makes the decision final." She tried to smile reassuringly contorting her lovely face into a grimace.

"Kat! What happened!" Maria Gonzalez suddenly appeared looking at the disaster.

"Minor mishap," Kathryn said. She glanced over at their table and waved to the collection of people staring at her. As she smiled at the two men and one woman looking curiously at her, she said out of the side of her mouth to Maria, "You go back and close the deal. I know you can do it, Maria. Remember: you have what they want and *only you* can provide it in the way they need. Be polite, but don't be a wimp. They won't respect that."

"What if I blow it?" Maria said in an agonized whisper, indecision pouring off her in palpable waves.

"You didn't blow it with me," Adam said honestly. "You quite impressed me. And I had come only to be polite and let you down gently. Your sincerity and honesty couldn't be ignored."

Maria looked over at Adam and smiled, noticing him for the first time. "Hi, Mr. LeGrande."

"Adam," he corrected her.

She nodded. "Adam. Thanks for saying that." She looked at Kathryn who was standing silently, dripping on the floor. Adam watched a dark reddish ooze slowly make its way out of the open toe of her shoe. "I can do this?"

"You can do this." Kathryn looked down at herself and then back up at Maria. "I'd hug you but I don't think it's a good idea." She looked over at their table again. "Go. Don't keep them waiting. And," she looked at Adam, "remember what Mr. LeGrande said. He was definitely a harder sell than these guys are."

"Is it too late to say I'm sorry?" Adam said as Kathryn made attempts to wipe off her purse.

She sighed and looked at him pointedly. "I don't think it's ever too late to say you're sorry."

Something told Adam they were suddenly talking about a lot more than spilled food and drinks. "Do you have your car? Can I offer you a ride home?" He made a stab at humor. "I know where you live."

"No, I've got my car. Thanks. Don't let me spoil your evening." She gave him what passed for a vaguely polite smile, peeled her feet off of the floor, and squished out the door. *Couldn't get away from him fast enough.*

At least she didn't say, "Strike three." That was somewhat positive, wasn't it?

"Where's Kat? Did she leave already?" Maria was standing next to Adam again, looking around the restaurant as the bus boy came with a bucket and mop.

Adam looked at Maria. "Yeah, she just squished out of here."

"Darn. She left her briefcase and computer. Even her cell phone. She must have really been addled." Funny, she just looked annoyed as hell as far as Adam was concerned.

Adam extended his hand. "I was just leaving. Give it to me. I'll take it to her."

Maria looked at him and said in all seriousness. "I don't know. You two don't do too well together." So now the woman was gifted at making understatements of the year. Wonderful.

"I promise to be nice." He smiled his "Honest, I'm being completely sincere" smile. "Besides, maybe I can catch her in the parking lot."

Maria glanced over her shoulder at the table of business executives and back at Adam, clearly torn. "Okay." She handed over the briefcase with the cell phone holder strapped to it. "I appreciate it and I'm fairly certain Kathryn will, too." The element of doubt, though, was clearly in her voice.

Taking the positive outlook, Adam smiled. "Thanks for the vote of confidence."

Kathryn wasn't in the parking lot, so, Adam drove with growing trepidation to her home. She didn't answer the doorbell either, but Adam could see lights on all over the house and supposed she was in the shower hosing herself down. He sat on the front porch to wait.

He'd returned to the scene of the crime, like all criminals destined for eventual apprehension and incarceration for crimes against humanity. Exactly a week ago, he'd lost his cool and said some pretty cruel things to

Kathryn on this very porch. Of course, in retrospect, he'd shafted himself as well. *You may be good at what you do but you're not any more likeable than I am!* Wasn't that pitiful? He couldn't even do a decent insult without lumping himself into the mess.

He struggled to change the focus of his thoughts and succeeded in picturing Miles and Mayor Willoughby holding hands and giving each other tender looks. That practically made his brain spasm, so he flipped his thoughts to Miles sitting in church and a priest sprinkling holy water and incense all over him. That made him laugh and shake his head in disbelief. Maybe he should try some number sequencing calculations ...

"Remembering all the fond memories of your last time on this porch, Mr. LeGrande? I thought I heard the doorbell when I was in the shower."

He practically jumped out of his skin. He stood, picking up her briefcase. Through the screen door she looked down to see what he was holding, and her face registered shocked surprise and then intense relief. "Oh, whoa, I was so flustered I forgot my stuff. Wow. Thanks for bringing it over. I go into withdrawal when I'm away from my computer for more than thirty minutes."

She was wrapped in a big, faded light green terry robe and her hair was twisted up in a dark blue towel on top of her head. He could smell her shampoo and soap. Warm. Fragrant. Enticing. He stood there like an idiot just staring at her. Cocking her head, a bemused expression on her face, she finally asked him, "Are you going to say anything?"

He knew for a fact that if he opened his mouth he'd only annoy her. Again. Make a comment about the tacky robe ... Ask to get close to have a better whiff of her skin lotion ... Oh yeah, that would go over big. Another disaster was an absolute certainty. *Keep your mouth shut.* He shook his head no.

That made her laugh. "*Really.*" She crossed her arms, leaned against the doorframe, and studied him for a moment, the picture of casual indifference. Her robe gaped slightly and he swallowed and looked pointedly *up*. "That might be safe for a bit, actually. How about you come in for a cup of coffee and I'll talk a little while you stay silent. Then, once the coffee is made, I'll gag myself and you can have a turn."

Of course, he realized, he'd managed to infuriate her at the restaurant without saying a word. He'd managed strike three without uttering a single syllable. Staying silent guaranteed absolutely nothing.

Kathryn seemed to read his mind and grinned. She had a smile that could light a dark room. He certainly hadn't had the fortune experiencing *that* until now. "There is a much lower probability that you'll bump into a waitress carrying a tray of food and drinks here. I'll even let you pour your own coffee." Adam sighed. Maybe it would work ...

At last he nodded and she opened the screen door.

The coffee was already on, he could smell it as soon as he walked into the front hallway. "I'm going to go upstairs and get dressed. Make yourself comfortable."

Adam walked into the living room that he'd only briefly walked through on the day he'd met with Maria. He was drawn to the huge bookcase dominating the far wall and he was surprised at the titles. *The Interlinear KJV-NIV Parallel New Testament in Greek and English* and *The Englishman's Greek Concordance of the New Testament.* Whoa. She spoke Greek? He'd taught himself French, German and Latin, but even he'd not attempted Greek. *Ancient Israel, Its Life and Institutions* and *Peoples of the Old Testament World.* Israel? Was she Jewish? He thought she was one of those born-again Christians. But sure enough, there was *1,301 Questions and Answers about Judaism* along side *Webster's New World Hebrew Dictionary.* She spoke Hebrew, too? There were at least two full shelves of books concerning people of the Bible, in particular women's roles in the church: *All the Men of the Bible, All the Women of the Bible,* and *Women, Authority, and the Church.* The last one made him roll his eyes. It sure sounded a bit confrontational.

He wandered over to the large, old fireplace dominating the room with a huge, dark wood mantle. It was cluttered with photographs and knickknacks and he took his time looking at each one. He found a photo of Kathryn with an older woman, a formal portrait of the same older woman, and photos of Kathryn with various women laughing and smiling into the camera. Interspersed amongst the pictures were a preponderance of figurines, most of them angels. There was a plaque with a saying, *For God has not given us a spirit of fear and timidity, but of power, love, and self-discipline.*[20] It sounded like it could be the theme of that She-Woman-Man-Haters Club.

A wave of panic hit him as he realized the reality of his situation. What was he doing here? Was he out of his mind? Mr. Strategic Alienation himself. The history between the two of them was bad enough that he probably could make her angry enough to resort to physical violence this time. He had to get out of here.

As he walked purposefully out of the living room, she was coming down the stairs. Her hair was still wet but combed out now, and already starting to dry and curl around her head. It looked a darker brown when it was damp like this, and it was the first time he'd seen her hair down and casual. She was wearing a worn pair of jeans and a tee shirt that said in big huge letters 'Whatever.' There was more writing in smaller print but Adam didn't want Kathryn to think he was staring at her chest. Which was a very *nice* chest, of course, but not his business to be looking at. Oh man, this was a huge mistake …

Get out. Like a fire drill in a school that makes children and adults alike instinctively evacuate the building - no questions asked - the urge to leave Kathryn McFadden's house was as overpowering. He glanced at the door.

"Cutting out?" Kathryn was standing three steps up watching him. Her words were carefully spoken, an observation not a condemnation.

Keep your mouth shut.

Get out.

He nodded.

She came down one step and again cocked her head to one side. Her wet, dark hair swung out from behind her like a fragrant curtain. "Are you *always* this awkward with people or is it just me in particular?"

He sighed and closed his eyes, beginning to feel actual, physical pain. When he was in an uncomfortable position (which had been most of

---

[20] 2 Timothy 1:7, New Living Translation

his life) he always relied on his quick wit and/or sarcastic mouth. Dazzle or offend was his *modus operandi* since he had understood he needed one, since he realized pushing people away was significantly easier than dealing with the hurt and abuse of letting them come too close. If he had to be silent, he couldn't be flip and acerbic. If he couldn't be flip and acerbic, he was lost. If he was lost, he was vulnerable. Vulnerability meant discomfort, pain, misery ...

"I promise not to be abrasive, unyielding or," she hesitated, "... holier-than-thou for the entire time we drink our coffee."

Ah, crap. Now they were *reliving* the crime. He opened his eyes expecting to see her fury and saw, instead, tremendous hurt. Huh? Hurt? Her eyes glistened with what could possibly be tears. Where had that come from? She gave him a small smile, walked down the remaining stairs, and headed down the hall to the kitchen without another word.

Common sense deserted him. Self-preservation abandoned him. Curiosity taunted him. He couldn't help himself. He followed.

Sitting at the large, round, oak kitchen table, Adam watched her pour the coffee into a thermal carafe and set it in front of him. That was followed by two mugs, spoons, a sugar bowl, and a quart of milk. Only the plastic container she set down required explanation. "The most delicious cookies on the face of the earth," she told him with a pointed look. "Be *very impressed* that I'm sharing them with you. Maria's a fantastic baker and when she can't sleep she bakes. Lousy for her, but great for me." She peeled open the container and helped herself to a cookie.

"So you really aren't going to talk, huh?" She shrugged as she poured herself a cup of coffee, adding sugar, and milk. "Okay. I'll start. I'll start by saying, 'Thanks.' It was very kind of LeGrande Incorporated to recommend Computer Dynamics before Maria's even had a chance to prove herself."

Huh? What was she talking about? He bit his tongue. Literally.

"I mean, after all," Kathryn continued, completely oblivious to his confusion, "Maria was grateful enough when you were willing to go along with the mentoring. Especially after she'd heard our last, um, *encounter*. But then when Body Gloss called us and said that they'd been referred to us by you," she hesitated and then smiled, "well, just *thanks*. The vote of confidence meant a lot to Maria."

With a puzzled frown, she said, "What I don't understand is why LeGrande Incorporated turned down the job? I mean Body Gloss said that you had implied that they were just too small to bother, but they're a chain. I would have thought you would have jumped to get your foot in the door with that corporation even if it was only one small shop being set up here."

He would have, too, if *he'd even known about the opportunity*. Confusion was joined with irritation about such a significant slip up.

Kathryn smiled and helped herself to another cookie. "Business must be very good indeed when you can reach the point where you pick and choose jobs like that."

Business was good, but it wasn't good enough to start behaving like cavalier imbeciles. He took a sip of his coffee and then helped himself to a cookie. Anything to keep him from speaking.

"Aren't they good? Before I found out how brilliant Maria was with computers I tried to get her to open a cookie shop." She laughed. It was a magical, light-hearted sound that he felt all the way down to his toes. "Then she revamped my entire house so that I had a personal wireless interface network and I forgot very quickly about the cookies. You know, her casual reading material is tech manuals and computer tech sites? She actually went on vacation and brought the schematic drawings for her computer so she'd 'understand it inside and out'." Kathryn shook her head in disbelief.

She rested her chin in her hand and looked at Adam. She had short, carefully manicured nails painted with light pink nail polish. He glanced down at her bare feet. Yup, toes were pink, too. *Nice*. While he was still admiring her toes she said, "Okay, I've run out of polite conversation. You're turn." She looked at him as she took another sip of her coffee. "But you should know I lied. I don't plan to gag myself and consequently will probably be incapable of staying quiet."

He was safe if he kept it business. Taking a sip of his coffee he asked, "Who'd Body Gloss say they talked to at LeGrande?"

Kathryn frowned in concentration. "Gee, I assumed it would have been you?" Adam shook his head. "Don't know then. Who's in charge of business development?"

"Me. I do that. Scout it out. Most people want to talk with me directly first anyway. Then, once they're hooked I can usually turn them over to others."

"Who's your business assistant?"

Adam sighed. Suddenly the confusing pieces morphed into a clear image. "Miles."

"Your butler?!"

Miles. It had to be Miles. "Yeah, my butler. He's only my butler to annoy me. He's also my personal assistant, chef, and chauffer. He's managed to completely alienate every household employee causing them to quit and now he's in control of all aspects of my home office. I can't get away from him."

She looked suspiciously pleased that he seemed unhappy with Miles. "You're kidding me."

Adam gave Kathryn a disgusted look. "Have I given you the impression that at any time I would actually have a sense of humor?"

Kathryn shrugged. "Sure. You just don't have an *appropriate* sense of humor. It's vaguely possible that *someone*, not of the female persuasion of course, would have found your comments on our first meeting vaguely funny."

Uh-oh. Approaching dangerous territory. Danger! Danger!

The agony of personal small talk without the ability to be sarcastic and cutting. *Ask a question*, his panicked mind urged. *Get her to keep talking so that you can shut up.* "Why did you look so hurt - as opposed to angry - when you made reference to the things I said to you the other day on your porch?" *Not necessarily safe territory, but a change of subject anyway.*

Kathryn struggled to keep up with Adam's train of thought. "They were hurtful things you said to me. Didn't you realize that?"

Adam made a dismissive gesture with his hand. "You weren't hurt when I said them. You were *angry*."

Kathryn searched his eyes for a moment or two. She had the largest brown eyes he'd ever seen, surrounded by long, dark lashes. "You're serious, aren't you? You're really asking me to explain my reaction then and now to your telling me I was 'abrasive, unyielding, and holier-than-thou'?" He broke eye contact with her, hearing the *Get Out* fire alarm in his head again. He suspected he wasn't supposed to say 'yes,' but he'd already asked the question, hadn't he?

Kathryn sighed. "Okay, since you asked, I'll tell you. *Yes, I was* mad at first. I thought you had a … heck … of a nerve saying those things to me. In the business world, men are always so quick to call strong, independent women bitches." She shrugged. "I can handle that. I think it says more about the man saying the word than the women the word is directed to. But, my reputation *as a Christian* is more important. I was angry at your accusation that I was holier-than-thou. Holier-than-thou implies that I feel I'm superior to everyone, above reproach, unable to make mistakes. *That's* when I was angry. But after you left and I thought long and hard about it I realized, perhaps, you may have had a point. My behavior, in a number of instances, could have been perceived exactly in that manner. So my anger shifted to sadness. I was unhappy with myself that that was the image I had projected to you."

Adam gestured with his chin towards her shirt as he helped himself to another cookie. They *were* exceptional. "Why does your shirt say, "Whatever"? I'm afraid to read all the fine print because I don't want you to think I'm staring at your breasts. Not that it's not a very nice set of breasts, but, well, you know."

Kathryn sat there with her mouth hanging open. Leaning forward to make more of a point she said, "I just worked *really hard* trying to answer your question. I just told you some really intense and personal information and all this time *you've been thinking about my chest?!*"

Adam shook his head feeling the need to clarify. "No, actually I was thinking about your chest since you first came down the stairs."

She started to laugh, a high hysterical sound, leaning back in her chair and staring at the kitchen ceiling. He grabbed the opportunity. Her shirt said, "WHATEVER: whatever is true, whatever is honorable, whatever is right, whatever is pure, whatever is lovely, whatever is of good repute, let your mind dwell on those things. Phil. 4:8" He frowned. Phil?

Adam waited patiently for her to settle down. She finally got up, went over to the sink, and poured herself a drink of water, seemingly deep in thought. After taking a long drink, she turned, leaned against the sink, and studied him. He had been right to avoid the whole breast conversation in the first place. He looked at her, trying his best to read her mind. Kathryn didn't *look* annoyed; God knew he was familiar with *that* emotion. She looked ... vaguely curious. "Perhaps I should go," he finally said in the face of her silent observation.

"Did you even hear what I told you?"

He was completely insulted. "About being angry versus being hurt? Sure I did. I *was* listening. *I can multitask.* My problem is that things that puzzle me keep buzzing around in my head until I solve them."

"So what my shirt said was bothering you." Again, no anger. She seemed to be studying him like he was some kind of science experiment gone wrong.

He certainly wasn't that complicated. Just because he was a computer genius and financial whiz didn't mean he was exceptionally complicated. Adam spelled it out for her. "Yeah, not knowing stuff bothers me. It used to be a problem when I was in school, too. In kindergarten, all the kids wanted to get to lunch and I really needed to read all the information on the bulletin boards. Once I got everything read I could relax for a bit, until the teachers changed the boards the next month and it started all over again. But until I could read all that information ..." he shook his head, "man it would bug the heck out of me."

Kathryn put her glass down and held the bottom of her tee shirt out so he could see. She looked up at him questioningly. "Read away."

"I did already. When you were laughing so hysterically."

She had the audacity to roll her eyes. "So, everything's solved now?"

"Well ..."

"What?"

"Who's Phil?"

She let go of her tee shirt and came over and sat down at the table again. "Tell me you've never read the Bible."

Adam shook his head and said sincerely, "I don't think I've ever read any fiction. There was never any time."

If she'd been a cat her back would have arched, her tail would have gotten fat, and she would have spit at him. He watched her fight down the anger, take a deep breath, and walk over to the edge of the kitchen counter. Picking up a large book she came over and sat down. "This is my Bible, Adam. I don't consider it fiction, okay? To say that, even if you were only trying to be honest, is insulting. 'Phil' is short for Philippians. The Bible is so large its broken up into sixty-six books. Each book is broken down further into chapters, and each chapter is broken down into verses. My shirt has a Bible verse on it." She flipped through her Bible, found what she was looking for, and turned it around so Adam could look down at it. Pointing to the top corner she said, "Philippians," pointing on the page she pointed, "chapter four," then sliding her finger down the page she stopped, "verse eight. Go ahead, read it."

And now, dear brothers and sisters, let me say one more thing as I close this letter. Fix your thoughts on what is true and honorable and right. Think about things that are pure and lovely and admirable. Think about things that are excellent and worthy of praise.[21]

"It's a letter," he said.

Kathryn nodded. "A letter that a man named Paul wrote to a church he had started in Philippi. That's why the book is called 'Philippians'."

"Sounds different than the way it is on your shirt."

"Yup. There are all kinds of translations of the Bible from the original Greek and Hebrew." She tapped her Bible. "My version is called the New Living Translation."

"Why don't you read it in the original Greek or Hebrew?"

Kathryn laughed. "It would be pretty hard, especially since I don't read Greek or Hebrew."

---

[21] Philippians 4:8, New Living Translation

"I saw all kinds of books on your book shelf about Greek and Hebrew."

"Yeah, well," she rolled her eyes, "Maria reads tech manuals. I read Biblical reference books in my down time."

"Really?"

She shrugged. "Well, you know how you have to have the answer or it 'buzzes around in your head'?" When he nodded she said sincerely, "I'm one who likes to know as much as I can about what I believe in."

It was Adam's turn to roll his eyes. "Aren't you going about it backwards? Researching information about something you claim to *already* believe in? Shouldn't you know all the facts before you buy into something?"

Adam's answer didn't faze her in the least. Shaking her head, she said simply, "Nope." Pulling her Bible back towards her, she flipped through the pages. The book was worn. The gold edging was worn off and the leather cover was pretty scuffed. "Here," she said, turning the Bible back to him. "Read this."

What is faith? It is the confident assurance that what we hope for is going to happen. It is the evidence of things we cannot yet see.[22]

When Adam looked up at her she smiled one of her breathtakingly beautiful smiles. "My belief in God is rooted in *faith*. My desire to learn more about God is rooted in *love*."

Surprisingly, Adam did not feel compelled to make even one snide comment.

---

[22] Hebrews 11:1, New Living Translation

Why be a man when you can be a success?[23]

Chapter Seven

"How dare you!"

(Said in a very bored voice.) "What? Unhappy with my suggestion of how we can finish off the evening?"

"Your money and power cover up all that you lack in finesse. Is that the way you see it, Adam?"

"Get off you're high horse, darlin'. Don't stress yourself. If it doesn't suit you to go along with my proposition, then I'll just drive you back to the party and ask someone else to come home with me. The night's still young."

"You thought, because I accepted your invitation to come over for a drink that I would ..."

(Now working up a bit of righteous anger.) "And YOU thought that I was inviting you home for drinks and ... what? ... a few rounds of Scrabble? (Shakes head in complete disbelief.) "Hurry up and decide. I'm a busy man. My time is worth millions."

---

[23] Bertolt Brecht, 1898-1956

"Miles!!! Hey! Where are you? I think I should have a bell pull installed by my desk! MILES!"

"Good morning, Sir. It is unnecessary to shout unless the house is on fire."

"Did you talk with someone from Body Gloss last week?"

"I did, Sir."

"Did you tell the representative we didn't want to do business and pass the chance off to Computer Dynamics?"

"No, Sir. I simply explained to the him that his job was of a size that we no longer tended to gravitate towards but offered him the name and contact information of Computer Dynamics. I explained that they were a new, start up company but were currently in charge of putting in the township's new computer system under your direct supervision. I implied that pricing might be much more to their liking as well."

Leaning back in his desk chair and crossing his arms, Adam said, "You're up to something again. I can see it in your shifty eyes. Who gave you the authority to turn away business?"

Miles blinked his devious eyes. "I beg your pardon, Sir, if you feel I have overstepped my bounds. In the future, I will simply take messages and leave them on your desk for you to sort through. On average we get approximately ten to fifteen business queries a day. This past year that I have been serving as your assistant, I was of the impression that my handling of these types of business matters had been to your satisfaction." Miles turned to leave.

"You doing the Mayor, Miles?" Miles stopped and slowly turned around. But as Adam expected, Miles refused to respond to his purposely crude remark. "I went out with her and a group of people from the township last night and had a beer with them." *And made a fool of myself again.* "June seems to be a bit *smitten* with you. Tell me, do you guys hold hands in church?" Still, Miles stood silently watching, waiting, and emanating superiority. "So that's where you disappear every Sunday morning. And I thought you were just taking the opportunity to sleep in late and scratch yourself." Once again they were in the waiting game in which Miles always won. The two men stared at each other. *Let's give just one more push. How far can I go before he'll be unable to remain silent?* "The Mayor is cute when she blushes."

Bingo. Miles took a few steps towards Adam. "It is my earnest hope that you said nothing inappropriate to her." Pause. "Sir."

"Nah, I was my usual charming self," Adam smiled his "oily and hardly sincere" smile.

"Perhaps that is as I feared."

Shrugging, Adam said, "She asked me how I maintained such an emotional distance from people I spend so much time with. Perhaps I should have told her I learned from a master."

Miles shook his head. "No, Sir. In that respect, you have set the bar yourself. I do not believe that anyone could top you in that area."

Adam spread out his arms, suddenly furious with everyone and everything. "This is me. 'Take it or leave it.' 'What you see is what you get.' Isn't that what they say? But I'll help you pack your bags if you're inclined to go work for the Mayor. She used words like 'tremendously loyal' in regard to you." Adam shook his head and frowned, the picture of complete confusion. "I was so very puzzled."

Miles sighed and shook his head. "No, Sir. I don't need you to help me pack my bags. You know I'm going to continue working for you unless you dismiss me. But I must disagree with you. I do not believe 'what you see is what you get.' Nor do I like the phrase 'take it or leave it.' Each of us is ultimately responsible for the person we become. At some point, the right to point a finger and to cast blame at others no longer works. It's called *becoming an adult*. It's about assuming responsibilities for who you are, what you are, where you are planning to go, and how you are planning to get there. History is full of the successes and failures of people who had far worse beginnings than you did."

"Go on, Miles," Adam said with biting sarcasm and anger as he leaned forward, "lay a quote on me. Drive home your point. Let's hear it. I'm holding my breath with anticipation."

That kept Miles silent, but only for a minute. *"Change your thoughts and you change your world.[24] "* As he turned and made his way out of the study, he said to Adam, "You have a meeting with Matthew Liccardi at ten a.m. I remember he quite enjoyed my puff pastries and Earl Grey tea. I'll bring in both at about ten-thirty, Sir."

Thursday evening, sitting in Gwen's cozy living room, Kathryn attempted, once again, to impress upon the ladies why she and dating did not mix. "It was a classic example of you can't judge a book by its cover. On the outside, he looked polite, successful, and sincere. I'd seen him at church a few times over the last year so that was a huge plus. It was pretty amazing that just last Thursday you all were pushing that I go out on a date and that Sunday he made a point to speak with me after church and ask for my phone number." Kathryn shrugged. "I thought you would all be *so proud of me.* It seemed like a safe enough request so I gave it to him."

"I take it he called," Gwen said, with trepidation in her voice.

"Oh, he called alright," Kathryn said giving them all a piercing glare. "We had a lovely, long chat on the phone, too. Think we talked for close to an hour Tuesday night. Told me all about how his home base was Cincinnati, but that he did significant business out here, sometimes two or three weeks of the month. He told me about his work, I told him about mine. He was very easy to talk to, I have to admit. We talked about how lonely the traveling life was and how difficult it was to meet *nice* people." Kathryn glared at her friends as she ground out, *"We talked about what a strain all his traveling was on his marriage and how bitter his wife was with him away all the time."* Kathryn paused, letting the information sink in as she extended her hands out in supplication to the group. "Tell me. W*hat* does it say about me and the image I project that he felt comfortable enough to *tell* me about his wife and still think I would be interested in going out to dinner with him Wednesday night and back to his hotel room for nightcaps?!" She

---

[24] Norman Vincent Peale, 1898-1993

turned to her friends, taking in their various expressions of shock, outrage, and not a small amount of stifled laughter. "This is *all your fault*. I *told* you I was a loser magnet."

"But you made the right choice," Gwen said encouragingly.

Audrey nodded, smiling and giving her a wink. "On the plus side, he was *so bad* that *even you* weren't willing to make the effort to transform him into something bearable."

"Give me a break, Audrey, I'm not that bad," Kathryn said with annoyance.

Meredith looked up from the pile of new make-up booklets she was collating and getting ready to hand out. "Oh, I don't know," she said, "I still can't believe you stuck with that guy and all of his addictions for two years *and got within six weeks of marrying him*. You can be pretty determined when you find a really desperate man who needs to be saved." As she began to pass out the catalogs she said, "Page twenty-two in this one's got a great sale on sunscreen: two for the price of one."

"And married men haven't necessarily discouraged you before," April said. At Kathryn's sharp look, April said meekly, "Well *you* were the one who told me about that." Taking the catalog from Meredith she studied the front cover's showcased pair of rhinestone sunglasses. In an effort to placate Kathryn, April offered, "My stepbrother has his own business."

"How about his own teeth and his own hair?" Meredith asked with a completely straight face. "Anyone still need another copy of the latest cooking catalog I gave out last week? I've got a few extras." She pulled a pile out of her bag and waved them for all to see.

"Of course he's got all his own teeth!" April said in absolute seriousness, "He's only in his mid thirties!" Meredith handed April a kitchen catalog.

"I got fixed up on a blind date one time," Meredith said, suddenly lost in memory, as Audrey rolled her eyes and Lydia stifled a giggle behind her hand, "and I'd been told that the guy owned his own business and had 'really nice brown eyes'."

"And?" Pattilou said, making an effort to contain her laughter.

Meredith grinned. "Turned out he *did* have his own business chemically spraying trees and grass for bugs and stuff. The guy had *five teeth* in his entire head."

"But did he have nice brown eyes though?" Pattilou said. How she continued to keep a straight face was a lesson to all of them in self control.

Meredith just laughed and shook her head. "I honestly can't say. I never could get past the teeth."

"Hey, let's get back to me!" Kathryn laughed. "Am I released from my quest to find a personal life? Have I proved my point regarding me and men?"

"NO," they all chimed together.

"Absolutely not," Gwen said sounding more determined than ever. "Perhaps, God is going to work you into this whole back-to-dating-and-having-a-personal-life thing gradually. He's going to start out easily. Hooking you up with obvious, even-Kathryn-has-no-trouble-identifying-them, losers -,"

"Hey!" Kathryn shouted, laughing.

"- and then," Gwen continued giving Kathryn a grin, "He's going to gradually work you down through less and less obvious losers until, Eureka!, your prince is standing before you."

"I like that. *A prince,*" April said with a sigh and a wishful stare. She'd already folded over numerous corners in both catalogs.

"Or we'll all take up a collection to ship you off to Mount Holy Shrine of the Perpetually Single Sisters," Audrey said. She glanced at April. *"Kidding."*

"I hear from Maria that you actually had a conversation with Adam LeGrande in which the two of you didn't even consider coming to blows," Lydia said with a twinkle in her eye. "It's a good thing she keeps me updated with *the facts* or we'd never hear all the good stuff that's going on in your life."

"You know, I think you two need to stop talking," Kathryn groaned.

"No way. If that happened we'd never get to hear anything," Meredith leaned forward. "Spill it."

"Well, we *did* have a relatively hostility free conversation, but that was *after* he knocked an entire tray of drinks and appetizers down my new gray suit," Kathryn murmured.

"Yeah, I heard that, too," Lydia laughed, nodding and rolling her eyes.

"Oh, now even I want to hear the whole thing. We need *all* the details before we move on to praises and prayer requests," Meredith commanded.

"Well," Kathryn said, "can you believe that this guy, Mr. Brilliant, graduated from MIT with a *doctorate* at age sixteen and had never even *once* read a Bible?"

"Miles!"

"Yes, Sir."

"Do we have a Bible anywhere?"

"A Bible, Sir?"

"Don't look so stunned. I was just curious. Do we?"

"Well, I suspect there might be something in the library. And of course I have one."

"You do?"

"Yes, Sir, I hold the Bible with one hand while I hold Mayor June Willoughby's hand with the other," Miles said deadpan.

Adam sighed, "What a cute picture. What translation is your Bible?"

Miles looked absolutely bemused. "The New International Version, Sir."

"Kathryn McFadden has the New Living Translation. What's the difference? Do you know?"

"Not specifically, Sir. I'm sure that you could do some comparative research on the web. There are a number of free Internet sites that let you read the Bible online and there are numerous versions available."

"Really."

"Yes, Sir."

"Can I see your Bible, Miles?"

Miles hesitated. "Sir, with your penchant for insult and irreverence, I am unwilling to suffer through a debate with you on this subject."

Adam studied Miles. "Hmm, Kathryn McFadden said something along those same lines - although not in such stiff, snooty language - when I called the Bible fiction."

"You called the Bible fiction?"

Adam shrugged. "Yeah, she got all pissy for a few minutes but did a good job keeping her cool in the end."

"Sir, you are a multimillionaire with a 25,000 volume library just across the hall. Might I suggest you go online, do a bit of personal inquiry and exploration, and then purchase a copy of the Bible for your own? That way you can pick it apart, laugh, ridicule, or - hopefully - find some enlightenment at your leisure. I *will* tell you that the New International Version is currently one of the most popular versions. Perhaps you should ask Ms. McFadden why *she* chose the New Living Translation. And here's an important tip I certainly hope you will take to heart: avoid reminding her that you referred to the Holy Bible as *fiction."*

Kathryn sighed as the phone's jarring ring interrupted her thought process again. If the phone didn't stop ringing and she didn't get this proposal finished she was going to be in big trouble. Bishop Pharmaceuticals had expressed an interest in Advancement Corporation. *Bishop Pharmaceuticals.* The chairman of the board of *the* premier pharmaceutical company *in the world* had read an article in the know-nothing weekly town paper about Kathryn and her company and had contacted her. He had invited her to convince him why her company might be worth his company's consideration for investment purposes. No one had to tell her that this was the chance of a lifetime, a one shot deal. She had been working for days trying to put together a proposal that would show her, and consequently her company's, passion, mission, and goals. *If* she could make herself convincing enough on paper, *then* she might have the opportunity to dazzle in person. But the day had been riddled with interruptions. "Kathryn McFadden."

"It makes no sense why you chose the New Living Translation. According to their website the New International Version took over ten years to be completed and was faithfully translated from the original Greek, Hebrew, and Aramaic."

Absolute silence greeted Adam on the other end of the phone. He waited. He might not be able to out wait Miles, but something told him Kathryn McFadden would be a piece of cake. He was right. But still she surprised him. In a deep voice, imitating a man, she said, "Hello Kathryn. This is Adam LeGrande. Am I disturbing you? I've got a few questions to ask you."

Now it was his turn to be silent as he thought through his options: comfortable sarcasm or awkward politeness. "Will I have to repeat the question again?"

"Probably, because your rudeness was so distracting, I'm not sure I processed anything correctly."

He sighed. "Hey Kathryn. Adam LeGrande here. How the hell are you?" Adam heard her amused chuckle in his ear and grinned. Maybe this idle chitchat wasn't so hard after all.

"Adam!" she said with false enthusiasm, "what a pleasure to hear your voice. I've been sitting here all afternoon thinking about you and hoping you'd call."

That was stunning. "Really?"

Now she burst out laughing. "*No.* I'm up to my eyeballs in tables trying to get a proposal done by five o'clock."

"So you don't have time to discuss the ins and outs of Bible translations, huh?"

"Not even a minute."

"Oh. Okay. Well, goodbye."

"Adam!"

"Yeah?"

He could hear the frustration in her voice and it made him grin again. "*Now* you're supposed to say something like, 'Gee, when will you have some free time? We could catch a meal and discuss things over some moo-goo-gai-pan."

"You like that stuff? It's loaded with additives and fillers."

Kathryn chuckled. "You know, I don't think you are as inept as you let people think you are. I think you really just don't care."

"It's probably a lot of both." Adam leaned back in his chair, put his feet up on the desk, and smiled smugly. This had to be a personal record for him. Having a sustained conversation over the phone for several minutes and *all of it casual, chitchat.* He could do this. He really could do this.

"Oh. Well then. Good-bye."

Before he could get a word in, she disconnected the call. He sat for a long time looking at the receiver, absolutely stunned. Had he annoyed her again? Or was she just giving him a dose of his own, barbaric medicine? He had no way of knowing, short of calling her back, which given that she was so pressed by work, might only annoy her even more. And why was it that with every encounter he had with Kathryn McFadden, his desire to see her again increased? Very curious. *Very curious.*

One minute after five, Kathryn's phone rang. "Kathryn McFadden."

"Hey Katty-Girl. Adam LeGrande here. Want to step out on the town, hit the light fantastic, and discuss Bible translations?"

She managed a tired sigh. "You are the strangest man I have ever encountered. I *told you* I'm under pressure to get a proposal finished."

"Yeah, I heard you. You said it had to be done by five. It's five-oh-one. Deadline's over. So, are you free?"

"*No.*"

"When do you think you'll be done?"

She sighed, clearly exhausted and frustrated. "At the rate this thing is coming together, probably midnight."

"Okay," he said and the line went dead.

Kathryn rolled her eyes, shook her head, and went back to work. Hours later when she stopped to grab a cup of coffee and eat a quick peanut butter sandwich, she recalled their conversation. Adam wouldn't call her again at midnight, would he? Or worse, *show up* at midnight ... Oh, no ...

Actually, the proposal was finished by eleven o'clock. But as exhausted as she was, she was far too wound up to fall right into bed. Kathryn showered and changed into her pajamas, fixed herself a cup of herbal tea, and curled up into one of the big, white wicker rockers at the far end of the front porch.

She could not believe her eyes when, like clockwork, Adam pulled up to the front of her house at midnight.

She observed him as he walked briskly up the front walk, cool and confident. Did he see nothing odd about showing up uninvited at someone's home at midnight? There was no hesitancy, no uncertainty in his posture. He was dressed casually and Kathryn noted wryly that he did that as well as he did his custom made suits. Between the bright moonlight and the light spilling out of the front room's windows she could see he was relaxed enough that he had a dark dusting of a beard beginning. Taking in the whole package, sneakers, worn jeans, and an old MIT sweatshirt never looked so good. He repositioned a paper bag he had under his arm, leaned over, and peered through the small curtained window on the side of the front door, then straightened up and rang the doorbell. Just like that. No hesitation. No big deal.

What would he do if she didn't answer? She made every effort to remain silent, having fun watching.

He didn't stand still. Kathryn suspected he rarely did. Adam turned, walked to the edge of the porch, and looked out onto the moonlit front yard. It was bright enough that the trees actually cast shadows on the ground. He sighed. He fidgeted. He walked over to the door and looked in the window again.

Kathryn couldn't help it. "So, what would be the polite thing to do if I never answered the door?"

He was fairly good at masking his surprise. Walking toward her he collapsed into one of the other wicker chairs. "Jeeze, Kathryn. It's a good thing I didn't scratch myself or something while I was standing there."

"That would have made me laugh out loud," she smiled, imagining his shock and embarrassment.

"I bet it would." He placed the bag down on the floor, reached in, and pulled out a Chinese food container. Extending it to her, Adam said, "Here, I hope it's not cold."

"You got me moo-goo-gai-pan?!" She smiled with delight and began ripping open the container with undisguised enthusiasm.

Adam looked at her like she was insane. "*Of course not.* I told you that it's loaded with fillers. I got you vegetable tofu teriyaki. No MSG. No fillers. One hundred percent healthy."

Staring down into the dark contents of the container, she looked back up at him, disappointment clearly evident in her voice, "Really?"

He hesitated. *Perhaps* suddenly realizing that *maybe* he had erred in his decision. "Well, vegetable tofu teriyaki *is* healthier, you know."

Kathryn sighed. "Thanks." Her enthusiasm had dimmed substantially.

Reaching inside the bag, Adam pulled out another container and two sets of chopsticks. Handing her a set, he opened his container and expertly began shoveling food into his mouth.

"What did you buy for yourself? The same thing?" Kathryn asked as she took a hesitant bite of her vegetable tofu. It wasn't too awful.

"Uh-Uh," he mumbled with his mouth full, glancing over at her, "I got myself moo-goo-gai-pan."

At her stunned expression he threw his head back and roared with laughter. His green eyes crinkled with delight and two dimples appeared. She still hadn't managed to say a word when he switched containers. Sure enough, she was looking down and smelling the delicious aroma of her favorite Chinese dish. For long moments, they ate in companionable silence. Finally, he put his container down, wiped his mouth with a paper napkin, and said, "You don't expect much from me, do you?"

Sounding a bit defensive Kathryn said, "What's that supposed to mean?"

"Well, you thought I'd bought you the tofu dish rather than what you had told me you wanted. Show's you have a rather low opinion of me."

Kathryn leaned forward. "First of all, I *never* told you to bring me moo-goo-gai-pan at midnight. Second, you've *created* the opinion I have of you, Adam! You were a blank slate when I pulled up in front of your house three weeks ago. You've worked diligently to create a rather ... *negative* ... image of yourself." She took another bite of her food, chewed and gave him a sideways glance. "And 'negative' is a politically correct term." When he didn't respond, Kathryn felt a wave of compassion. Holding up the food she said, "This was very sweet, you know. This is a good thing on your slate. It proves to me that there *may be* a nice guy somewhere in there."

"Why do you have the New Living Translation?"

Kathryn sighed in exasperation. "So, what, this has been one of those 'unanswered pieces' you talked about last time that buzzes around in your head until you solve it? It bothers you so much that you spring for food you disapprove of and show up here at my house in the middle of the night?"

Something told him he wasn't *supposed* to say 'yes'. That 'yes' was a *very* wrong answer. She was looking at him so intently, like she was trying to see inside his skull. Adam swallowed and mentally shrugged. "Yes."

Kathryn put her food container carefully in the bag, along with her chopsticks, and her used napkin. "Okay. I don't want you to lose sleep or stress over this anymore. I chose the New Living Translation because it has more inclusive language than some of the other popular translations." When Adam started to open his mouth to ask more questions, she glared at him to be silent and continued. "That means that the translators took special care to correctly translate specific gender related terms more accurately than previously done - like 'man' is translated to 'mankind'."

Oh, now he got it. The She-Woman-Man-Haters-Club again. He nodded in satisfaction as all the pieces fell into place. "Oh, now I get it.

The feminist agenda. Are you one of those people that claim that God is a woman and the whole Mother God thing?" Adam looked at her. "Did you know that Bon Jovi's got a song about that? Have you heard it? The chorus is something like, *If God was a woman with long blond hair, would you kneel at her altar and offer her a prayer, could she be your addiction, could she make you sin*[25] ..." He grinned at her. "Sorry, I don't have the best voice."

Kathryn stood. "Good-night," she said through tight lips and walked toward the front door.

Adam scrambled up after her. "Hey! Kathryn! Wait! What did I do now?" As she turned to look at him he gave her his "I'm really trying to be sincere" face. Trouble was, he really meant it this time.

Hands on her hips, she drew a deep breath, looked down at her feet, and shook her head. Adam waited. She had the just scrubbed from the shower, fresh and clean look going on again. He took a deep breath. Man, she always smelled *good.* Finally, she looked up at him. With an effort, he concentrated on her serious expression. She was angry again, but working hard to tamp it down so she could speak without gritting her teeth, he supposed. With forced patience she said, "Perhaps you have nothing in your life that is ... precious. Cherished. Prized. So you may not understand. But my faith is not a laughing matter to me. Or a mocking one. Or one you are allowed to ridicule. *I can't have it.* I enjoy discussing my faith, researching my faith, puzzling over certain aspects of my faith with others of like mind. *But I will not defend it.* I don't have to defend the fact that I'm a woman, that I'm single and independently wealthy, or that I'm a brunette, for goodness sake! So, I *will not* enter into disrespectful conversations with you about my faith."

Kathryn rubbed her eyes and then looked up at him. He suddenly realized that she was exhausted. "I don't condemn you or ridicule you because you *don't* believe in God, Adam," she said earnestly, "I'd just like the same courtesy." She didn't wait for his response, but simply turned and walked into the house. Through the screen door, she said, "Good-night, again. Thanks for the food."

---

[25] "If God Was a Woman", Artist(Band):Bon Jovi, R. Sambora, R. Supa & D. Bryan

Adam stepped up to the screen door. It was suddenly supremely important that this evening not end poorly. He didn't want any more times like that with this … intriguing … woman. His inability to adequately and accurately express himself rose up in his mind like a big, laughing demon. *He could do this.* He said intensely, "Do you remember that night at the country club and what you told me you did for a living?"

Kathryn looked at him, hesitated, and then nodded.

"What did you say you did? Tell me again."

She was afraid he was going to make a sarcastic remark. He could see it in the wariness of her expression. Adam felt a wave of anger at himself for the person he had created in her eyes. Kathryn took a deep breath, lifted her chin a bit, and looked him defiantly in the eye. "I said that I help make dreams come true."

Okay. Here it goes. "I have never, ever fit in anywhere in my life, Kathryn. I have never felt a sense of belonging, a sense of comfort in any aspect of my life. My life revolves around my business that is built on *me*. I have no family, no friends, not even any close acquaintances. You're right. I have nothing precious or prized in my life. Everything I've got I've achieved through some flash and dazzle intellectual skills that I don't even have to think twice about. What I am is the result of my crazy mother and an unknown sperm donor's scrambled DNA. The only things that spark my interest are bits of information I hear during the course of a day. They spark my interest because I don't understand all there is to know about them. This unknown sparks my interest - gives me some crazy kind of enjoyment. Otherwise, all I have is one annoying as hell butler and a bunch of business people who are consistently trying to get a piece of my pie." He thrust his hands in his pockets and hunched his shoulders. "I can't even make polite, casual conversation with someone because *I never needed to learn how*. It was an unnecessary waste of my valuable learning time."

Moments of silence passed between them with nothing but the sounds of the night breeze stirring the trees. Adam put both hands on either side of the screen door and leaned in as close as he could without getting screen marks indented on his forehead. "You want to make a dream come true, Kathryn? A really big one? Give me a real reason to get up in the morning. Teach me some things I don't know. *Make me into a human being* instead of some gifted, trained dog who does tricks for his daily performances. *Now that would be one hell of a miracle."*

Adam and Kathryn stared at each other through the screen door. He put on no face at all this time. He just let her see what a complete and utter void he really was. She looked back at him and slowly, two tears made parallel tracks down her cheeks. Great, now he'd gone and made her cry.

"*Why me?"* she finally asked in a soft, anguished voice.

He answered without hesitation. "Because you are the first person I've ever met who seems to see the person I truly am: a lonely, miserably, rude *nobody."* He shrugged and said with absolute sincerity, "If you can see the *reality*, maybe you could help me figure out what's missing."

He was in his car, driving away, and Kathryn still couldn't think of how to respond.

*Learning is not attained by chance, it must be sought for with ardor
and attended to with diligence.*[26]

Chapter Eight

*"I have a really lousy history with men, guys. I mean Really Lousy. I seem to
lose all of my goodness when I get involved with someone; I forget what's important, I lose
proper direction, I compromise my standards. It's kind of like I become possessed."*

*(Incredulous expression.) "So, are you telling us you're going to swear off men,
Kat?"*

*(Slight laughter.) "Actually, I'm telling you that I've already sworn off men!
(Said intensely.) This last relationship was … worse than the others because I almost
married the guy. I need to get my priorities straight. I need to get strong and confident
and be the woman God wants me to be."*

(Said with deep concern.) "Don't you want to get married? Have kids?"

*"Yes. Quite passionately, actually. It's been a dream of mine since …
(sounds wistful) … forever. But I'm even more determined to find The Right Man for
me and never end up in divorce court. At the rate I'm going, divorce court is a much
greater certainty right now."*

---

[26] Abigail Adams, 1744-1818

"You're a beautiful, vibrant, intelligent woman, Kathryn ..."

"Yup. That's why I'm making this choice. And I would like you all just to support me with your prayers."

"Sir, this package arrived this morning. As it is marked "Personal" I felt you should open it." Miles extended a medium sized package across Adam's desk.

Making no effort to take the package, Adam leaned back in his chair. "How was church Sunday, Miles? Sit with the Mayor?"

"Church was exceptional. A fine sermon. And, yes, Sir, I did sit with Mayor Willoughby."

"You call her 'Mayor Willoughby' and she still blushes when she talks about you? You must really have some moves." At Miles' stoic expression, Adam asked, "Have a cup of coffee afterwards?"

Tired of waiting for Adam to take the package, Miles set it down on the desk. "Actually, we decided to go to a nice little Italian bistro a few towns over and have lunch."

"Catch any action?"

Miles nodded, refusing to rise to the bait. "We did. Saw a movie after we finished our lunch."

"You wear your butler suit and gloves when you go out with her?"

"No, Sir, I wear them only for you. As you required when you hired me over a year ago."

Adam shook his head as he reached for the package and began to unwrap it. "Oh no you don't. I take no responsibility for this ridiculous masquerade party you insist on perpetually attending. I never told you you had to wear those butler duds. You came up with that all by yourself."

Miles leaned forward onto Adams desk, his immaculate white gloves making a stark contrast against the deep mahogany wood. "I remember your exact words as if they were spoken only yesterday, Sir. Need I remind you of them? You said, and I quote, 'The only opening I have in my life right now - personally or professionally - is for a butler.

Take it or leave it.'" Miles waited a beat and then said, "I chose to take it. *Sir.*"

Adam met Miles' gaze uncomfortably. Finally he ground out, "Aren't I the lucky one?"

Standing, Miles shot back, "Not as fortunate as I am, Sir." He then took the time to adjust his cuffs and straighten his jacket. It was completely unnecessary as he always presented a perfect appearance. Adam knew it for what it was; simply another subtle ploy meant to annoy.

Their verbal sparing came to an abrupt stop when both men realized what Adam had unwrapped. It was a brand new, New Living Translation Bible. Adam opened the attached note, although he knew who had sent the package.

Adam,

Many people feel as if something is missing from their lives. I was one of them. The trick is finding the right thing to fill the void. I can't do that for you. But I can share with you what made me feel content with the person I am.

Kathryn

Adam looked up at Miles' curious expression. "Well, well, well. What do you think, Miles? Kathryn McFadden is sending me gifts now. I think the woman has the hots for me. What do you think?"

Turning to leave, Miles said, "How could she not, Sir? You are such a likeable fellow."

"Kathryn McFadden."

"You know, if you had caller ID I wouldn't have to go through all of the useless small talk that is involved with trivial phone greetings."

"'Hi, it's Adam' is significantly shorter than what you've just said already," Kathryn replied. Her voice didn't have an annoyed edge to it. Yet.

"Okay. You've made your point. I -," Adam caught himself before he launched into a question. "Do you have a moment to answer a few questions?"

Kathryn chuckled in his ear. "Oh, good job, Adam. You're proving that you are capable of learning and improving." She sighed. "Sure. I've got a few minutes. I just made myself a cup of tea and was going to take a break. Go ahead. Shoot."

"Okay, so I read it. And I just can't get how you can believe all the wild and crazy stuff that's in there. I mean -,"

"Wait. Are you telling me," Kathryn interrupted him, "that you've read the entire Bible in two days?"

Uh-oh. Another one of those questions where Adam was absolutely certain that 'yes' was not the correct answer. Swallowing, he said hesitantly, "Yes."

Kathryn burst out with an incredulous laugh.

"I read fast," he said defensively.

"Okay. Sure. Fine. Go ahead. Ask your questions. Then I've got a couple."

"Well, like I said, I don't see how an intelligent person like yourself could swallow all of that stuff."

Adam could almost hear her wheels turning as she prepared her answer. Finally, with a tone of voice that didn't seem to be annoyed - yet, he thought, Kathryn said, "You know, Maria's got tons of these high tech, computer books lying all over the house. I've looked at them a few times and there's no possible way that what's written in there could really mean anything of quality."

He knew where she was heading. "Kathryn, you cannot compare Maria's tech manuals to the Bible."

"Why not?"

Adam shrugged even though he was all by himself in his office. "Because. She's had extensive training, years of school, and vital hands-on experience in order to be able to make sense of all that information."

"So, you're telling me that prior to her extensive training, years of school, and vital hands-on training Maria would not have understood those tech manuals?"

"Of course not."

"She might even have called it, hmmm, now what would be a good phrase? How about 'wild and crazy?'"

"So, you're saying I've got to get training, schooling, and experience before I can understand the Bible? Great," he said with real sarcasm. "No wonder so many people can't figure God out. This book is only designed for the educational elite."

In patient tones, Kathryn said, "Schooling and training and experience are good in anything you want to learn and understand in depth. But you know what? Before Maria did all that stuff she had an active interest, a real passion for computers. Even before she understood it all she was tinkering with it, asking questions, reading stuff she could understand, and saving up her money to go to school. She'd made a decision, a life choice, before any of the big intellectual and experiential acquisitions happened.

"I'm guessing you picked up that Bible, Adam, and with pride in your impressive ability to speed read, you whipped through that book without even once considering why you were reading it and what you were hoping to get out of it." Kathryn made him sound like a pompous idiot.

"I just wanted information. Understanding what all the buzz is about."

"Okay," she responded briskly. "Good job. You're done then."

"You going to hang up on me?"

She laughed. "No, not yet. How about this? My turn to ask you questions, okay? I'll ask you some basic comprehension questions to see how much you retained and got out of your World Record Speed Read of the Bible. Okay?"

"Sure," he said. Feeling compelled to prepare her, he said, "I have miraculous retention. I bet you're going to be surprised with what I remember." He frowned. Jeeze, he sounded smug even to himself.

He could hear the smirk in her voice when she said, "Great, let's just see how terrific you really are. I'll keep asking you questions until you get one wrong. But when you mess up, then this conversation is over."

Okay, the gauntlet was thrown. Kathryn had no idea what she was getting herself into. "We could be here all day, you know."

"Yeah." Why did Adam get the feeling she was rolling her eyes? "We'll see. Let's start off with an easy one: what did God call the first two human beings that He created?"

Adam groaned. "Kathryn, you can ask something a little harder than that. I could have answered this one without even reading the Bible."

"You're so sure, huh? If I can't be sure that you've got the basics down, then how can we discuss the heavy-duty stuff? Come on, let's hear your answer."

Adam sighed. "Okay. God called the first two human beings he created Adam and Eve. There. Satisfied?"

"Wrong answer," she said, and Adam could hear laughter in her voice. And then she hung up on him.

"Miles!! MIIIIIILLEEES!!"

"Sir, I'm making a soufflé for dinner and I cannot leave it unattended." Miles stood in the doorway of Adam's study, wearing his standard butler suit, sans jacket and white gloves, with his shirtsleeves rolled up and a white apron on. Not waiting for Adam's response he turned and walked briskly away.

Adam found Miles in the kitchen, working with all the intensity with which he did everything. Pulling up a stool, Adam took an apple from the fruit bowl and took a bite. "You know, I could hire a cook. Again. If you promise you won't drive them screaming away down the driveway. Again."

Miles gave him a pointed look. "You're so certain it is *my* difficult personality that drove all your help away?"

Adam shrugged and took another bite of apple. "Hey, I pay a good wage and offer excellent benefits. Works for the rest of my hundreds of employees."

"The ones that are fortunate enough to work in offices *other than* your home office, you mean."

Grinning a wily grin, Adam said, "Unhappy Miles? Want to quit? I'd give you two weeks' severance and references."

Miles did what he did best, ignored him. "After the last chef left - tearing her hair out as she ran screaming into the dark night - I've enjoyed dabbling in the kitchen. We've discussed this before. I take pleasure in cooking. As long as you are prepared to consume my culinary creations willingly, I see no need to make any changes. Besides," Miles glanced up at Adam with a knowing look, "we both know, Sir, that I seem to be the only help here at the home office that you've been able to keep for any length of time. History seems to imply that you are rather difficult to work for."

Adam refused to rise to the bait. "Have you cooked all your life?"

Miles looked up at him, as if gauging the sincerity of his questions. Adam gave him his 'I'm really interested' look. Miles rolled his shifty blue eyes. "No, Sir. I have not cooked all my life. In earlier stages, I was a chauvinist imbecile who believed cooking, cleaning, and general household responsibilities were beneath me and only worthy of the 'little woman'."

"You've come a long way, baby," Adam said.

"Exponentially, Sir."

"What did God name the first two humans he created, Miles?"

After carefully transferring a dish into the oven, Miles wiped his hands on a towel. "Is this a trick question, Sir?"

"Well, everyone knows that the first couple was called Adam and Eve. But Kathryn just told me that that was the wrong answer."

Adam detected just a hint of a smug expression on his butler's face. "The first couple of the Bible was called Adam and Eve. But Ms. McFadden is correct in that it was not what God named them." As Miles began wiping down the counter, he said almost to himself, "I'm almost certain that Adam gave the woman the name of 'Eve'."

"Well, do you know what God called them?"

Pause. "Yes, I do, Sir."

Adam sighed. "But you're not going to tell me, are you?"

Miles looked at him. *"Get your facts first, and then you can distort them as much as you please."* [27]

Adam rolled his eyes and pushed off from the kitchen stool. "Shut up, Miles."

As he stormed out of the kitchen, Adam heard Miles call after him, "Genesis 5:2!"

Moments later Adam frowned at his Bible. *He created them male and female, and He blessed them and called them "human."* [28] Human? God called them human? Hadn't Miles said there were different Bible translations on the web? Googling 'Bible translations' got him onto www.biblegateway.com. He was amazed at what he found.

He created them male and female and blessed them. And when they were created, He called them "man." [29] The New International Version had God calling them both man? Huh?

The New American Standard Version, whatever that was, said, *He created them male and female, and He blessed them and named them Man in the day when they were created.* [30]

But the most stunning of all was the King James Version, because it said, *Male and female created He them; and blessed them, and called their name Adam, in the day when they were created.* [31] God called both of the first two humans He created Adam!

Wandering back into the kitchen he found Miles, cleaned, polished, suit-jacketed, and gloved, sipping tea at the breakfast table. "God called them both 'man' or 'human' or – here's a really wild one – 'Adam.' She was right."

Miles just sipped his tea and arched his eyebrow.

Crossing his arms and leaning against the doorway, Adam said, "I'm not going to acknowledge anything about whether you were right or wrong. You wouldn't give me an answer."

---

[27] Mark Twain, 1835-1910
[28] Genesis 5:2, New Living Translation
[29] Genesis 5:2, New International Version
[30] Genesis 5:2, American Standard Version
[31] Genesis 5:2, King James Version

Another dignified sip. "But, Sir, I did tell you exactly where to look."

"How come everyone goes around saying that God called the first couple Adam and Eve? Why do they go around telling inaccuracies like that?" Adam dealt with facts. Facts were easy to prove and always solid.

Miles set his teacup down and folded his hands carefully. Adam puzzled briefly about how Miles managed to keep his gloves so white. Did he have a couple gross of them stuffed under his bed or something? "The Bible is a complicated book, Sir. You can study it all your life and about the only thing you will become certain of is the more you know the more you need to study. But in answer to your question, I think there are two schools of thought regarding that. The first school is full of people who are brilliant, educated, confident men and women who have neither the time nor the desire to really sit down and study God's word. They just operate on hearsay and what they might have heard casually in their brief brushes with religion as a child. They are in the dangerous position of thinking that they know all they need to know. They've made an uninformed decision based on insufficient evidence.

"The second school is full of people who have a sincere desire to get to know God more with each passing day while at the same time help others to get to know Him, too. That school really doesn't have time to deal with the inconsequential things such as whether God called the first woman Eve, Adam, or man or whether or not the Wise Men were present on the night of Jesus' birth. They want to make sure that when they get that opportunity to 'talk God talk' that they share the Most Important Information. The Nitty-Gritty, as they say, Sir. So all these "inaccuracies" as you so accurately put it, rarely get addressed. You usually have to hang around, do your own research, and talk with other like minded folk before that kind of information comes to the surface."

"Which school are you in, Miles?" Adam couldn't help but goad, waiting for the expected pompous answer.

Miles stood and put his cup in the dishwasher and walked over to check his soufflé that was still in the oven. He looked directly at Adam.

"Wrong question, Sir. The question that should be foremost in your mind is *which school are you in?*"

"You hung up on him?" Meredith asked incredulously. To emphasize her shocked horror, she let her mouth hang open dramatically.

Kathryn looked a little sheepish, "He brings out the worst in me! I can't help it. He's so boorish in his behavior. I can't believe I'm even using that word! And so full of himself! He's rude, arrogant, and the most self-confident individual I've ever met."

"Is he still handsome, intriguing, and loaded with potential?" Pattilou asked, quietly watching Kathryn closely.

Kathryn looked directly at Pattilou but said nothing. What could she say?

"Doesn't sound that full of himself to me," Audrey pointed out, classically diving right into the center of the storm. "What words did you say he used to describe himself? A 'lonely, miserable, rude, nobody'…? Sounds to me like he knows exactly what kind of image he projects and he hates it."

"What are you going to do?" asked April quietly. One of her two dogs, Snoopy, was curled up at her feet. She'd brought him along to Bible study because, according to April, he was suffering from severe 'separation anxiety'. Translation, he was tearing apart the house April was 'sitting' every time he was left alone. April had been surprisingly silent all evening, listening to Kathryn's account of Adam's surprise visit and everyone's reaction to it.

Kathryn shrugged. "I sent him a copy of the New Living Translation Bible and a note that said I wasn't the one who could make the change he was looking for, he had to do it."

"Are you feeling well?" Audrey said with real amazement in her voice. "This is the woman who claims to see potential in every man she meets? A woman who has such difficulty discerning the good ones from the bad ones that she's avoided the entire race of men for over six years?!

A handsome, single, gainfully employed man asks you for help and who you admittedly find 'intriguing', and you shied away from him? Are you listening to yourself?!" She glanced at the other women nodding, "Woo-whoo! I think our Kathryn is growing up!"

Yeah, I was going to write a book about guys that have potential ... Kathryn stuck her tongue out at Audrey and again chose to not respond.

"Audrey does have a point, Kat. That's amazing progress for you." Gwen grinned. "After all, by your own account the guy is handsome and rich. That's enough potential for most women to consider marriage, let alone a relationship."

Kathryn shook her head saying with absolute certainty, "He's not interested in me romantically. That's not an element of our ... interaction. I don't even feel comfortable calling it a relationship. We can't be together for more than about ten minutes without annoying each other profoundly." At Lydia's knowing grin, Kathryn acknowledged with a sigh, "Yes, he's handsome. But his good looks are completely overshadowed by his monstrous ego and his inability even to pretend to make polite conversation."

"You've just described two of my three husbands," Audrey pointed out. "And the only reason all three of them didn't qualify for that description is that Bill could never be described as handsome."

Gwen laughed silently and shook her head.

Kathryn continued trying to drive home her point. "I even suggested one time that he ask me out for a cup of coffee to talk about things, and he just blew me off."

"The picture doesn't fit," Pattilou said, her forehead wrinkled in concentration. "This guy wouldn't keep showing up if he wasn't interested."

Kathryn groaned in frustration. "He doesn't keep 'showing up'! A number of times that we've encountered each other were either by accident or because of business, not because either of us was seeking the other out."

"That's not what happened Friday night," Lydia pointed out. "The guy brought you moo-goo-gai-pan *at midnight* and then literally poured out his heart and soul on your front porch."

"Oh puhleeze," Kathryn rolled her eyes.

"And you did think enough of him to send him a Bible," April The Silent pointed out.

Everyone turned to look at April and then back to Kathryn. "She's got a valid point," Audrey said in a voice filled with amazement and wonder.

"It's called *witnessing*, people," Kathryn said. "I would have done it for *anyone* who gave me the same opening."

"We'll see," Gwen murmured. "This is going to be very interesting ..."

"Maybe it's time we let April fix you up with her stepbrother," Meredith said with a twinkle in her eye and a wink at April.

April just smiled and shrugged.

"Well, before we get started, I've got someone I want to talk to Kathryn about," Pattilou said.

"Oh, no," Kathryn said, "not another one!"

"But he's *nice*. I've met him ..." Pattilou said in a pleading voice.

Kathryn sighed with defeat. "Let's hear ..."

Chapter Nine

(Impressed male laughter.) *"You're my idol, LeGrande."*

"Why's that?"

"Oh, come on. You have to know that every guy in here would give anything to trade places with you. Every time I see you, the women are practically throwing themselves at you, like that one over there who just sent you the drink. You make no effort to be polite or even subtle about what you want from them, and still they come! We poor average Joes have to do the whole wine and dine routine, being polite, acting sincere, listening to inane conversation ..."

"Yeah, my life's a blast."

(Gesturing to the beautiful blonde woman standing at the bar.) *"You going to go for it?"*

"And risk disappointing my fans? Of course ..."

"Kathryn McFadden."

"Hey Kathryn, it's Adam. I was wondering if you'd have dinner with me tonight?"

"Why?"

Adam chuckled. In a high, falsetto voice he said, "Why Adam! What a nice invitation. I'd love to." Dropping back down into his normal voice he teased, "Why does it feel, all of a sudden, as if our roles are reversed?"

"I can't. I've got a date."

"*You date?*"

"Why does that seem so incredible to you?" She sounded furious. Looking at his watch he noted that it was exactly twelve seconds since she'd picked up the phone. Adam wasn't sure, but he thought it might be a personal record for him.

"You just seem like the 'all business, no pleasure' type."

In a snippy voice Kathryn responded, "Along with being in the … hmmm, let me see if I can remember how you put it, oh yes, 'dog with a capital 'D' category of woman. So ugly even her own mother doesn't acknowledge her'."

Adam rested his face in his hand and inwardly groaned. Not only did he constantly have to contend with his inability to engage in casual conversation, he had to deal with his past disasters as well. "Didn't I apologize for that?"

Kathryn was silent for a moment and then sighed. "Yes. Yes, you did."

"Would it help if I admitted what category you fall into?"

"*No.*"

"Because it isn't the dog category."

"I wasn't fishing for compliments, Adam," Kathryn said quickly.

"You could easily fall into the fantasy dream scenario, if you spiced up your wardrobe a bit. With your -,"

Sounding a little bit desperate, Kathryn interrupted him, "I *said* I didn't want to know this -,"

But Adam kept talking right over her, getting just a bit louder, "- beautiful dark hair and those fantastic brown eyes. Did I ever tell you how

I figured out that you and Maria shared the same house? I was leaving the meeting with Maria and passed this really hot chick – dressed much more closely to my dream scenario I might add – jogging along the side of the road. Nice butt, really sweet legs, and when I drove past I of course wanted to check out her -,"

"ADAM."

"What?"

"Thanks for the invitation to dinner, but, as I said, I'm busy."

"Whom are you going out with?"

She groaned. "My *friends*," she forced the word out almost as if she doubted its validity, "are determined to get me back into the," she paused, "*social scene* shall we say. One of my friends, Pattilou," she sighed, "the one I trust the most actually, well her husband works with some guy." Kathryn blew out a frustrated burst of air. "She promised me that she's met him, he's nice, although we haven't done a background check he's supposedly not an ax murderer or anything. Last night I agreed to talk with him if he called and, well, he called this morning."

"And just like that, you're going to go out with him?"

Now she sounded defensive. "He was nice enough on the phone. *Polite. Didn't annoy me so that I felt compelled to hang up on him or instruct him in civil conversation.* A mutual acquaintance introduced us so there is *some* level of familiarity."

"But he's still a stranger, right? You've never met him."

"Yes …"

"How are you going to recognize him? You going to wear a red carnation in your teeth or something?" Adam had the gall to laugh.

"How do you meet women, Adam?"

That stopped him mid-laugh. "I don't. They find me."

"What is *that* supposed to mean?"

"Just like it sounds. When my solitary existence starts to get to me, I go to some business function. Nine times out of ten I get hit on and I just pick one."

"*You pick one?*" Kathryn's tone made it sound like he was the absolute scum of the earth.

Another example of when not to say yes. "Yes." Now it was Adam's turn to be annoyed. "In case you haven't noticed I'm not too bad looking, I'm wealthy, I have a chauffer ... Women like that kind of stuff."

"Enough for a one night stand anyway," she ground out.

He was silent for quite a while. "Sometimes they hang around for more than one date. But they don't usually last long." Adam got defensive. "Women don't have staying power. It's a known fact."

She let out a burst of disgusted laughter. "You are such a pig. The truth is, after a few encounters with you, even your oodles of cash can't overshadow what a horrible, egotistical, abrasive man you are."

Ah, well. At least he didn't have to pretend with her. That was good, wasn't it? "Yup. That about sums it up. What's your excuse?"

Her hesitation was telling. "What do you mean what's my excuse?"

Adam spoke slowly and clearly like she had learning issues. "How come someone like you who is attractive, wealthy, *has all her own limbs and doesn't drool*, is alone and single at – what are you? Thirty?"

"Thirty-one."

"Wow. *Thirty-one*." Adam purposely made it sound like it was a horrible indictment on her character. "So? What gives?"

"I've got a lot of work to do before my *date*. I should go."

Adam could almost hear her grinding her teeth. He smiled to himself. Casual conversation could be quite fun actually. He'd had no idea. "Hmmm. Sounds like you're avoiding the issue."

"No, I'm avoiding your intrusive question."

"Chicken."

Kathryn sighed loudly over the phone. "I've not had a good history of choosing ... *nice* ... men. Okay? It's just easier to avoid the whole dating scene entirely."

"Ahh, the necessity that Mr. Good Guy Tonight not be an ax murderer now makes more sense to me."

"My friends seem to think that it's time I stepped out and tried the social scene again."

"You sound thrilled."

"Oh, *I am*." Frustration and sarcasm were both evident in her words. "The last man that I considered dating - whom I met *at church* mind you - wanted me to listen to his woes about excessive business travel and a wife who didn't understand, while he expected me to accompany him to his hotel room."

Trying to be funny he said, "Did you go?" At her hissed breath, he quickly shouted in the phone, "Don't hang up! I was kidding!" Kathryn didn't hang up, but she didn't say anything either. "So, what are tonight's plans?" he prompted.

She sighed. "Why do you care, Adam. What's your interest? Am I intriguing to you because you can successfully annoy me inside of a minute?"

"Actually, it only took me about fifteen seconds this call. I think that's a personal record for me." They were both silent on the phone for long moments. Something told him that he was *not* going to win this waiting game. He sighed. "Okay. I'll be straight with you. You *do* intrigue me. I like you. I like your quick wit and your quick mouth. I like that you stand up for what you believe in and aren't afraid to call someone out when they deviate from what is true and fair. I like that you don't put up with my crap and can give as good as you get. I think I could learn a few things from you," Adam hesitated. "Don't get annoyed at my repeating myself, but I think you're beautiful, too. Dream category, minus the wardrobe, remember?"

She was absolutely silent.

"Are you still there, Kathryn?"

Deep sigh. "Yes."

"I guess this is a long winded way of saying that *I'm* interested in dating you. I know I'm very rough around the edges, but I can guarantee you that I have no criminal tendencies or a past record. I know that I annoy you to no end and can be completely clueless and rude. I've told you that I have absolutely zero experience with healthy, committed, communication-based relationships. But I'm nice looking, have all my own teeth, am gainfully employed, and am willing to listen to positive suggestions and helpful hints." Adam chuckled warming to his topic, "You've got to admit, I've got potential, don't I?"

"OH. MY. GOD!" she said with a strangled, horrified gasp. And hung up on him. Again. As usual. Adam looked at his watch. It had taken her twenty minutes before she'd hung up this time. He actually had managed to have a casual, non-business conversation with someone for *twenty whole minutes!* He wasn't sure but he thought that was another personal record. Things were *definitely* looking up for him.

Anthony Lombardo had sounded nice. *Really nice* in fact. Sitting across from him at the Italian restaurant, Kathryn let herself relax and started to enjoy herself. So far, so good. He was nice looking, too, - although that could be a detriment when it came to accurate first impressions. Just shy of six feet with a muscular build, dark hair, and dark eyes, he had a quick wit and an easy laugh. And so far had no glaring issues.

"Does being a divorce lawyer depress you?" Kathryn asked. They had enjoyed a delicious meal and were sharing a slice of cheesecake.

"Yeah, it can," he gave her a smile and a wink, "but doing real estate balances things out. The market's on a huge upswing." Anthony suddenly got serious. "I know a really good marriage counselor and I do encourage them to seek counseling if they haven't already."

"Did you always want to be a lawyer?"

Anthony shrugged. "My dad was one and so was my grandfather. I rebelled for a while when I was a teenager." He blushed and said with an eye roll, "I was going to be a rock star for a couple of years," he shook his head and laughed. "I can never take you home to meet my mother because she actually has *videos.* But then I wised up. Truth is I'm good at being a lawyer and I enjoy it. Passed the bar on the first try." He grinned again. "I'm happy."

"How do you know Pattilou and George?"

"I found him space when he expanded his office." Anthony rolled his eyes. "I had no idea how particular architects were about office space, but in retrospect it made sense. Pattilou told me she owed me big time for finding someplace he was happy with. Apparently George had gone through three agencies without success until I was able to find him something. I told her -," He stopped and blushed.

Kathryn grinned. "What?"

"Ah, I should have quit while I was ahead." At her arched eyebrow, Anthony continued. "I told her if she knew any attractive single women she could fix me up with we'd call things even."

"Me?"

He shrugged. "She said she knew someone *very nice* and *very attractive* but she wasn't sure she was available." He blushed again. "Her description certainly was accurate."

Kathryn looked down at her coffee cup. "Thanks."

"And I'm beginning to think it was worth the ten month wait."

That got her to look up at him. *"What?"*

"Apparently you weren't available originally. Pattilou called me last week to find out if I was still interested."

Kathryn covered her face with her hands. *"How embarrassing."*

Anthony looked absolutely puzzled. "Why?"

She groaned. "Suddenly it seems as if everyone's scrambling to try to fix me up."

He looked bemused. "Gee, what is there a line or something?"

She laughed. "I certainly hope not, but you never know with my friends."

Anthony gave her a sweet smile. "I guess I'd better keep you too busy to find out then, huh?"

They had planned to go to a movie after dinner, but opted instead to go to a local coffee house/Internet bar that Anthony said he enjoyed. It was furnished with an eclectic mix of old cast off sofas, coffee tables, and lamps that cast a muted, soft glow. Staring at the menu, Kathryn chose an interesting sounding mint green tea while Anthony ordered a double espresso.

"So, got any good stock tips for me?" Anthony said casually as they carefully carried their hot drinks and settled themselves comfortably on a huge green velvet couch with lion claw feet peeking out from under its gold fringe.

"Excuse me?"

"Pattilou and George talked about your newest venture, Advancement Corporation, but I did some reading up on you and you were a whiz on Wall Street. I can't believe you still don't have connections and dabble now and then. I'll tell you, I'm still struggling with law school loans. I'm going to be doing that *for years* and I could use all the help I can get. Help me out here, Kathryn. You've got to have a few suggestions for a guy who's bought you such a nice dinner."

Why did she suddenly feel so uncomfortable? Why did she suddenly feel so angry? *Deep breath*, Kathryn, she told herself. *He's just making polite conversation. You've already asked him all about his business. He's just reciprocating.* "I still have a few clients. The commissions keep me from having to dip into my savings."

Anthony laughed incredulously. "That's a nice word for it. *Savings.* What, you retired at twenty-five? I did some quick calculations and you've got to have a *substantial* amount tucked away to justify a decision like that."

"My," Kathryn said, feeling a coolness descend over her, "you've certainly done a lot of research."

"Being a lawyer has its privileges," he said with a proud smile.

"Did you do this research on me just recently or ten months ago when I was first mentioned by Pattilou and George?"

Anthony looked at her with just a hint of concern. He frowned. "I'm sorry. You seem somewhat upset. You shouldn't feel offended that I did a background check on you. Lawyers have a tendency to be mistrustful of others." He gave her a self-deprecating smile. "I'm not sure if it's a quality that gets us into the profession or a characteristic we develop as a result of the profession." He leaned over conspiratorially and said, "Actually, you should be complimented."

"How so?"

"Well, I liked what I had originally heard about you from George and Pattilou, so I took the time to pursue further information. Not all girls I date get that level of attention, you know."

Just the potentially wealthy ones. "And what was it that Pattilou and George said about me that so intrigued you?"

Suddenly, he had that deer in the headlights look about him.

"Come on, Anthony," she cajoled, "it's not a hard question at all. I'm simply asking you to tell me *what specifically* was said about me that so sparked your interest? What could they have said that would have had you running to your computer to use your valuable time to do a background check on little 'ole me?"

He took the time to take a sip of his espresso and then just looked at her. A lawyer through and through, he wasn't going to do anything to incriminate himself further.

"Did they mention that Advancement Corporation seeks to empower skilled women so that they can become vital, productive participants in the business world? I like to say I make dreams come true."

Silence.

"No, huh? Did they mention that I use my own money as start up funds and devote my own time and skills to help this come to fruition? It's a personal goal to try to give back some of the blessings I've been fortunate enough to have received."

Silence.

"Not that either, huh? I don't suppose they mentioned this part, because I don't tend to spread it around, but perhaps you were intrigued with how I manage my budget. You see, all of my assets are completely tied up in this "new venture" as you called it or my retirement fund and as a result, I live a very ... frugal, I guess is a good word ... lifestyle."

Silence.

Kathryn forced herself to smile pleasantly as if suddenly realizing the correct answer. "Oh, *I know* what they must have mentioned! They must have said something like 'very successful, retired at only twenty-five, and now runs her own business.' That must have set off bells as someone worthy of your valuable time. Was that it?"

He was still silent when she gathered up her coat and walked out of the coffee house.

Normally, Adam didn't begin his day until about ten o'clock in the morning. He was a night owl, happy to work until one or two in the morning. Being an early riser had never been his strong suit. Consequently, looking for Miles at eight o'clock a.m. was an eye opening experience since he found Miles dressed in a Speedo, swimming laps in the indoor pool.

Adam had to admit that for an old guy he looked pretty good. And although Miles should have looked out of place without his butler getup, his crisp precise strokes still communicated a person in absolute command.

As Miles pulled himself up out of the pool and padded over to a towel he had carefully folded on a chair, Adam called out, "How many laps?"

True to form, Miles showed absolutely no surprise at Adam's presence, even though this was the first time both had been in the pool area at the same time. "I used to swim three miles, Sir. I rarely manage that these days though. I just do as much as I can."

"You swim every morning?"

"Most mornings, Sir. Keeps the arthritis at bay … among other things. I definitely notice if I skip a day." Even dripping wet from the pool there was not a hair out of place. Putting on a dark blue robe and tying the belt he said, "Is there something you need this early, Sir? Are you well? Have you had bad news? Is there imminent disaster on the horizon?"

"Something's bothering me, and since you are the cause of it I thought I'd seek you out."

Miles frowned. "I usually shower and then begin preparations for breakfast. Do you need me to provide an immediate solution to your problem or do I have time to dress?"

Adam scratched his unshaved chin and stretched. "You can do what you normally do. I'm going to swim a few laps myself and then I'll meet you in the kitchen. Say in an hour?"

"That would be fine, Sir."

The smell of French toast, eggs, and bacon beckoned Adam as he came up the hallway, leading from the pool, wrapped in his bathrobe. Adam spent a majority of his life in his office, ate most of his meals at his desk, met all visiting clients on its comfortable leather sofas, and occasionally spent the night sleeping on the matching leather recliner. It was his safety zone, his comfort area. He might own a twenty-seven room mansion with indoor movie theater and pool, but his office was what he considered home. Never had he eaten in the kitchen. "Mind if I join you?" Adam gestured to the kitchen table.

Miles turned, dressed in his modified butler uniform for his chef's role: jacket off, apron on, and sleeves rolled up. "Sir, this is your house."

"I know that. I was just being ..." Adam caught himself.

Miles lifted one eyebrow. "Polite, Sir? Was that what you were going to say?"

Choosing not to answer, Adam sat down at the table. Sun filtered in through the windows and outside the expansive lawn was meticulously cut with patterned variations of green. Not once in the eight years he had lived in this house had he ever walked out on the back lawn. "So you swim, shower, get dressed, cook breakfast ... what else do you do with your morning hours before I start hounding you?"

Miles turned back to the business of getting breakfast ready. "I make preparations for the day: verify the day's schedule, make necessary phone calls, complete necessary household responsibilities," turning over his shoulder he said, "laundry, food shopping," going back to get plates out from the cupboard, "and, of course, my devotions."

"Devotions?"

Miles took the time to load up both plates before answering. Setting down two plates on the table heaped high with food he finally said, "Bible study, Sir."

"You really do that every day?"

Miles smiled at him. "Swimming keeps my body supple, Sir. Bible study keeps my soul supple."

"Which leads me to the reason I sought you out this morning." Adam took a bite of fluffy eggs and chewed for a moment. "You said something a number of days ago that I can't seem to shake out of my head."

Miles did his silent response so Adam continued. "You talked about the school of people that don't have time to deal with the inconsequential things but instead had to make sure that when they got the opportunity to talk God talk that they spoke of the most important stuff. Well, I've been thinking and thinking and I can't seem to figure out amongst all that's packed in the Bible, what do they figure is most important?"

Miles polished off an entire piece of French toast before he finally answered. And before he even spoke, Adam knew it wasn't going to be the simple, straight answer he wanted. "It's the secret, Sir," Miles said in an overacted stage whisper and a smile, "of eternal life."

Adam stared at his butler. "You're kidding me."

Miles shook his head. "No, Sir, I absolutely am not. I am completely serious."

Adam leaned back in his chair and stared at Miles' serious, intent face. "You're not going to give me the simple answer so I can understand, are you?"

Miles took a sip of his coffee. *"The beginning of knowledge is the discovery of something we do not understand."* [33]

Adam rolled his eyes and pushed himself to his feet. "I should have known better than to come to you. You never have been able to give me what I really need."

Miles stood too and began clearing the table. "What is it you *really need*, Sir? Do you even know?"

Adam turned and stalked out of the kitchen.

———————————————

[33] Frank Herbert, 1920-1986

"*Sir.*" Miles said quietly. Adam stopped but did not turn around. "You are the type of man who must *see* before he believes, *touch* before he accepts, and *experience* before he embraces. It would do you *no good* to tell you what I believe. It would only give you an opportunity to doubt and ridicule. I do, sincerely with all my heart and soul, believe that the Most Important Information, the Secret of Eternal Life, is indeed contained within the Bible. I *have found* it. I *possess* it. I am *already living it.*"

Adam turned, a look of incredulity on his face and words of sarcasm on his tongue.

"*But you see, Sir,*" Miles said in a surprisingly loud voice giving Adam pause, "it is *my belief,* not yours. To your own ears this all sounds … ludicrous." Miles smiled at him. "Read that book again, Sir. It shouldn't take you too long. Pretend it's a heavy-duty business proposal that needs to be edited down to a fifty-page brief. What would *you* leave in, Sir? What would *you* feel was important enough for those fifty pages? Once you get that done, *then* decide if you believe it or not, Sir. If you come up with something you can embrace, then come back and have breakfast with me again."

Miles looked at him and nodded encouragingly. "*Then* we'll talk, Sir."

All truths are easy to understand once they are discovered;
the point is to discover them.[34]

Chapter Ten

Said aloud, at the start of each morning, as a prayer and a promise before going out for a morning run. "I arise today, through the strength of heaven: light of sun, radiance of moon, splendor of fire, speed of lightning, swiftness of wind, depth of sea, stability of earth, firmness of rock ...

"I arise today through God's strength to pilot me. God's might to uphold me, God's wisdom to guide me, God's eye to look before me, God's ear to hear me, God's word to speak for me, God's hand to guard me, God's way to lie before me, God's shield to protect me, God's host to save me ...[35]*"*

Kathryn walked briskly into the restaurant, scanning the visible tables while waiting for the hostess. Glancing at her watch she smiled and took a deep breath to get into her 'calm zone'. She was right on time, well

---

[34] Galileo Galilei, 1564-1642
[35] from *The Deer's Path*, St. Patrick, c.390-c.461

prepared, and completely in her element. She *loved* this part of her work. The wheeling and dealing, sewing up an agreement that made everyone satisfied. She was here to meet *the* Mr. Bishop of Bishop Pharmaceuticals. Her proposal had intrigued him enough to ask, via email, a number of questions that further clarified who she was and what she wanted to accomplish with Advancement Corporation. This meeting, face-to-face, would determine if there would be something more between their two companies besides Bishop's idle curiosity and Kathryn's awe.

It was exactly what she had been hoping to accomplish in the grand plan of her business life: to expand, grow, and broaden her influence. Yes, it was true that she had accomplished a lot in the past years since she had begun Advancement Corporation, but with another person or company willing to invest, she could double her influence. At one time, she had thought that she could have achieved this with LeGrande Corporation. Kathryn sighed and said a quick prayer for wisdom as she stepped up to the hostess' station. *Please, Lord, let this meeting end with more success than the LeGrande meeting.*

"Yes, Ma'am?" The hostess smiled politely.

"I'm meeting Mr. Bishop here for dinner and I don't know if he's arrived yet." Kathryn scanned the restaurant but only had a limited view.

"Mr. Bishop, at table sixteen, is waiting for a Ms. McFadden."

"Well," Kathryn smiled, "it seems like we are both on time."

Following the hostess, Kathryn reviewed the salient points that she wanted to bring forward first and foremost. "Mr. Bishop, Ms. McFadden has arrived."

"Great. Thanks, Anne."

Kathryn looked into the smiling face of Miles, Adam LeGrande's butler. He stood, walked around the table and pulled out her chair. "It's a pleasure to see you again, Ms. McFadden."

The hostess looked confused as Kathryn stood, staring at Miles, open mouthed with shock. When he arched his eyebrow in inquiry, she decided at least to sit down.

Was Adam behind all of this? A wave of anger, tightly woven with disappointment swept through Kathryn. She struggled with what to say and where to begin.

Miles seated himself back in his chair, readjusted his napkin on his lap, and smiled across the table at her. He was dressed in a tweed blazer, white shirt, and no tie. No white butler gloves, either. While there was no doubt in Kathryn's mind this was Miles, it was a completely different man who sat across from her. Polished but casual, proper but relaxed, he exuded an air of confident authority. After asking the waitress for unsweetened iced tea for both of them as well as an assorted appetizer plate, Miles smiled at Kathryn and said, "I apologize for the shock, Ms. McFadden. It was not my intention to be so … deceptive," he sighed, "but unfortunately meeting you like this was necessary."

"Are you here as Adam's representative?" She struggled with her anger and confusion.

Miles shook his head and smiled again. "No, Ms. McFadden. I'm here in my capacity as Chairman of the Board of Bishop Pharmaceuticals."

Kathryn shook her head and struggled to keep her voice calm and even. "You'll have to pardon my inability to comprehend all of this … Mr. Bishop. The last time we met was in your capacity as … Adam LeGrande's *butler*."

Nodding, Miles said, "Your perplexity is entirely appropriate, Ms. McFadden. Would it make you feel better were I to assure you that there are a number of other people who share your incredulity at my dual careers?" *No, not really …*

The waitress brought their drinks and appetizer plate and Miles served them both. Kathryn, usually in a rush to present and dazzle at these types of meetings, felt such a wave of uncertainty that she chose silence instead. Miles Bishop had orchestrated this entire meeting. Let him set the pace and the tone.

He did with an understanding smile. "Let me first assure you that all of our communication, right from the initial inquiry regarding Bishop's interest in investing in your company are all completely legitimate. Should you wish," he paused and took a sip of his iced tea, still smiling, *"should you be able to*, we could proceed with this meeting exactly as you anticipated it. I'm eager to hear what you have to say, what you have to show."

Miles looked at her inquiringly, waiting. *Oooookay ... She was a professional. Had been in far more awkward business situations with much less at stake.* Kathryn met Miles' gaze for a few moments and then reached down, opened her briefcase, and took out a number of file folders. *Here goes everything.* "I am Advancement Corporation, Mr. Bishop. Advancement Corporation is dedicated to discovering, empowering, promoting, and achieving business successes that in the typical world are regularly considered unworthy of industry time and money. I am not a charity. I am an astute businesswoman who wants financial success for both myself and the people I choose to represent. Advancement Corporation provides initial financial backing, advice, training, and unlimited support to people who show the right ..." Kathryn hesitated and then shrugged, "*spark* to warrant my time and money." As always, she got lost in her presentation. It was important for those who inquired about Advancement Corporation to understand that while she might be Advancement Corporation she was nothing without the talent, dedication, and commitment of those she represented. Using photographs, professional brochures, and solid examples of work well done, Kathryn worked to bring her company to life. Twenty minutes later, she smiled and shrugged. "I recognize how fortunate I am that I enjoy my job as much as I do. It's tremendously satisfying."

"Why do you need Bishop?" Miles asked. "Sounds like things are pretty good as they are. The reality is you don't even need funds. You have to admit there is a lot to be said for being able to work independently without others breathing down your neck watching and keeping track."

They both knew the answer, but Kathryn sensed that Miles wanted to hear how she was going to phrase it. "Yes, you're right about the independence. Part of my enjoyment of my job is being my own boss with no one to answer to. Bishop would have to be prepared to trust me in the way I run things because I'm *not* looking for a partner." She smiled at him and said with little apology, "I want your money but not your advice." He barked out a laugh at her abrupt honesty. Kathryn continued, "Bishop's financial support will make me less of a solicitor and more of a performer.

I want to widen my potential for accomplishing my goal which is making dreams come true. I'm doing amazingly well on the small scale. I'd like to see what I could do on a larger one. Bishop's financial backing would enable me to do that."

Kathryn smiled. "Please don't misunderstand me though, Mr. Bishop. I am a businesswoman first and a fairy godmother second. I'm willing to give you full financial accounting any way in which your company would require. Actually, I can provide you with anything you need to make sure you are comfortable with this business venture. By supporting my company, you receive financial tax deductions and continue to add to your excellent goodwill reputation. Bishop Pharmaceuticals has always been known for its generosity and concern for the world," she demurred, "and I would be honored if you found my company worthy of your support."

"I just can't offer you any advice," Miles said straight-faced.

Kathryn looked Miles directly in the eye. "Mr. Bishop, a good business person always knows when to take and when not to take advice. *Successful* business people never reach a point when sound advice is not welcome. I'd be happy to listen to anything you or your company thinks I need to know to improve. But I *will not* become your puppet. As much as I would welcome financial support from Bishop, I cannot have you under the impression that you have bought me with your money." She smiled. "*I* will choose just as carefully as you will."

Miles leaned forward. "Why? The financial documentation you provided in your proposal shows that you are financially secure and could live luxuriously for life. *You don't need to do this.* What compels you?"

Kathryn leaned back in her chair and crossed her arms. "What an odd question from a man who must assuredly be more financially secure than I could ever hope to be, but who is currently working as a *butler.*"

Miles leaned back and nodded his head in approval. "*Touché*, Ms. McFadden. *Touché.*"

Bishop Pharmaceuticals Makes Sweeping Changes

Changing of the guard at the nation's premier pharmaceutical company catches many by surprise

---

By Wendy Norgalis

BRIDGEWATER, January 19 – With eldest son James Brian Bishop by his side, Miles Althorpe Bishop made the stunning announcement today of his intended retirement from the thriving company that bears his name. "James has been working beside me for years," the elder Bishop explained. "This shift in power is nothing more than a formal announcement of the unofficial way of things here at Bishop. While James will assume my current titles of President and CEO, I will maintain my position as Chairman of the Board of Directors." Placing his arm around his son, Mr. Bishop stated, "I have every confidence in James that he will not only be able to assume all of my current responsibilities but will also be innovative and forward thinking in the direction in which he intends to take the company." When asked what the elder Bishop intended to do with his free time, he replied with a smile, "Enjoy a taste of anonymity."

Miles Bishop is no stranger to the limelight or the rumor mill. From his original explosion on the pharmaceutical scene with his creation and copyright of the AIDS treatment drug *Antiphason* to his much-scrutinized private life, Miles Bishop has not only basked in the limelight, but at times seemed to actively court it. Indeed, often the playboy lifestyle has been more a façade than that of the brilliant biochemist and businessman. Married four times, Bishop was once quoted as saying, "I've never met a woman that I haven't considered possessing." Critics have always maintained that marriages to the likes of actress Jizelle Landrieu, cosmetics heiress Mackenzie Brouche, state senator MaryAnn Clifford, and lastly the widow of banking magnate F.

William Frueh were all more strategic business alliances than true love affairs.

Many insiders question whether the loss of the senior Bishop's charisma and star quality at the forefront of the company will cause serious financial repercussions. It was Miles Bishop who brought little known Quest Pharmaceuticals onto the scene more than thirty-five years ago. Brilliant, savvy, and cunning he rose from entry-level employee at Quest to President, acquiring along the way - besides the company itself - numerous patents, unequaled power, and world-renowned prestige.

Those close to Miles Bishop question his ability to step away from both the challenges of the competitive pharmaceutical business and the ...

It had never occurred to Kathryn when Bishop Pharmaceuticals had originally contacted her that she needed to research the *personal* lives of the company heads. Live and learn, right?

Kathryn looked up from the Internet article she was reading and shook her head in amazement. *Miles? A ladies man? Married four times? 'Never met a woman that he hadn't considered possessing?'* Whoa. Accompanying the article - from approximately a year and a half ago - was a large black and white photo of Miles and his son James. Both handsome, distinguished looking men smiling into the camera. What was Miles doing serving as Adam LeGrande's butler? Kathryn continued to search the Internet, but after the date of this article, there was no publicity about anyone in Bishop Pharmaceuticals besides James. She found past pictures of Miles with all of his ex-wives, accounts of his fabulous wealth, descriptions of his multiple homes, and even details of his private jet. But after this article announcing his retirement it seemed, to all intents and purposes, as if Miles Bishop had simply dropped off the face of the earth.

And landed in Adam LeGrande's house dressed in butler duds. What game was Adam playing? Kathryn racked her brain trying to remember any references he made regarding his butler. Kathryn came up with an impression of vague dislike and impatience on Adam's part. A desire actually to have Miles leave his employ, in fact. That in itself didn't make any sense. Why did Adam keep Miles on as an employee if he was unhappy with his services? *He's only my butler to annoy me. I can't get away from him.* That was certainly an odd way to describe someone who worked for you, wasn't it? A wave of intense curiosity washed over her.

The ringing of Kathryn's office phone broke into her thoughts. "Kathryn McFadden."

"Ms. McFadden. Miles here, from LeGrande Corporation. At Mr. LeGrande's request, I have made this call. He was hoping you were available to speak with him?"

Miles. Adam LeGrande's butler. Miles Bishop, Chairman of the Board of Bishop Pharmaceuticals. Miles, ex-husband of Jizelle Landrieu. Kathryn clicked on the photo of she and Miles laughing at an after-party for the Academy Awards many years ago. *Newlyweds Miles and Jizelle Bishop enjoy the caviar and company at Morton's.*

Kathryn hesitated. How awkward was this? "I don't know whether I'm to address you as Miles or Mr. Bishop."

Kathryn *thought* she detected a slight smile in his response. "Calling me Mr. Bishop just might get me fired, Ms. McFadden. I would appreciate if you continued to address me as Miles."

That threw her off balance completely. "Mr. Bish-, I mean Miles, do you mean to tell me that Adam doesn't know that you're … Well, that he isn't aware that you …"

Miles interrupted her stuttering. "Please, Ms. McFadden. There is no cause for alarm. I am unaware as to the full extent of Mr. LeGrande's information regarding my identity. That is not so much a choice on *my part* but more of a decision on *his* part. He is often rash in his conclusions and rejected my initial offer of full disclosure regarding my background."

"Oh." She was at a loss for words.

"Are you willing to speak with Mr. LeGrande? I suspect your last conversation once again ended unfavorably, hence this flash and dazzle with his butler placing the call," Miles inquired patiently.

"Miles, why are you doing this?" The question poured out of her.

Miles was silent for a heartbeat. "Ah, I suspect, Ms. McFadden, that you have spent some time doing a bit of background research on me. Please, do not feel awkward. It is perfectly understandable that you would do some checking." He actually had the audacity to chuckle, a surprisingly pleasant sound. "Frankly, I would have been disappointed in you if you had not." Miles paused. "Your question is understandable. But unfortunately, you are asking the wrong person."

"I don't understand," Kathryn burst out with real frustration.

"The first step to getting the things you want out of life is this: Decide what you want.[36] That is the best I can give you right now, Ms. McFadden. But feel free to ask Mr. LeGrande these same questions. One moment, I'll connect you."

"Adam LeGrande," came Adam's crisp voice over the phone.

"Having your butler call me was smarmy."

"At least you didn't hang up on him."

Kathryn sighed. "Look, I'm sorry about that. It really was nothing you said *this time*," she purposely emphasized those two words. Pausing, she continued, "For once you really didn't deserve it. You had no idea, but you walked into one of *my* issues."

"Really. And here I thought I was just being cluelessly obnoxious and rude again," he sounded intrigued.

"So you had your butler call me?" Kathryn asked trying to keep the subject off herself.

"Yeah," he finally answered. "I wanted to know how your hot date was."

Hot date? Oh, yeah. Anthony Lombardo. She rolled her eyes. No way was she going to share *that* disaster with Adam. "Fine, fine. He was nice."

"Didn't bring his ax?"

"What?"

"You were worried that he was an ax murderer. Or at least fairly certain that he wasn't one, right?" Adam paused. "Are you alright?"

---

[36] Ben Stein, 1944 -

Pull yourself together, Kathryn. "Yeah, I'm fine." She took a deep breath. "No, he didn't bring his ax. He's a real estate and divorce lawyer with his own practice."

"A real estate and divorce lawyer?" Adam laughed into the phone. "Wow, that cleans up both angles. He can get a pile of money out of them for divorce fees and then collect some additional cash when they divide up all the assets. What an angle."

Kathryn said with little enthusiasm, "Yeah, well, he does encourage them to seek counseling if they haven't already. Even has a friend he refers them to."

"If he's my kind of guy, he'll even get a finder's fee for the referral." At her stony silence Adam said, "Have dinner with me tonight."

Kathryn couldn't help it. "Going to send your butler to pick me up?"

"Would that earn me any points?"

"*No.*"

He sighed over the phone, a loud, exaggerated burst of frustration. "Come on, Kathryn. I'm trying here. Do you know that I have had more casual, non-business, no hidden agenda conversations with you than anyone else in my entire life? You might not be impressed with my progress, but I sure as hell am." His voice turned cajoling. "I even went to all the trouble to find out what God called the first man and woman he created. I have the right answer now."

"You sure?"

"Absolutely."

"Okay, you get the answer right this time, and I'll go out to dinner with you."

Quick on the uptake he said, "I get to drive. That way if I piss you off it will be more difficult for you to leave abruptly."

She laughed, a delicious low throaty sound in his ear. "I'll make sure I have enough money for a cab ride then."

"I can't stop that, now can I?"

This is a huge mistake, Kathryn thought. There was no doubt in her mind that Adam LeGrande had figured out the correct answer to the question this time. "I'm afraid I'm going to regret this. Big time."

"I'll promise to be on my best behavior."

"That doesn't make me feel even *slightly* less hesitant ..."

She hadn't said no, had she? Adam dove in. "God called the first male and female creation 'Adam'. Or, depending on the translation 'human' or 'human being' or even 'man'. Genesis 5:2. That's the verse with the answer. It was Adam who later on, after they were expelled from the garden, renamed the female 'Eve.' Eve means 'the mother of all living things.' And you know, I've been thinking about that. Adam could have named her a whole slew of other names that weren't as loving or complimentary. After all, the woman did start the whole thing." His voice rose and took on a desperate pitch for a moment. "And I know! I know! Before you start yelling or hanging up on me, Adam could have taken control of the situation - or at least his own behavior - and said no, but he didn't, did he? So I believe they're both culpable, okay? But, I think that the fact that Adam named her 'Eve' shows a level of love there that gets missed sometimes, don't you think?"

Kathryn sat at her desk with the phone held to her ear and her mouth hanging wide open. She was absolutely speechless.

"Kathryn? Are you still there? Hello?"

Cradling her forehead in her hand, she said into the phone, "What time will you be picking me up tonight?"

A very satisfied male whoop filled her ear. "Score One for Adam LeGrande! I'll pick you up at six."

Anger makes you smaller, while forgiveness forces you to grow beyond what you were.[37]

Chapter Eleven

(Underlined in Sheila Docherty's copy of <u>Hitchhiker's Guide to the Galaxy</u> by Douglas Adams) "It is known that there is an infinite number of worlds, simply because there is an infinite amount of space for them to be in. However, not every one of them is inhabited. Therefore, there must be a finite number of inhabited worlds. Any finite number divided by infinity is as near to nothing as makes no odds, so the average population of all the planets in the universe can be said to be zero. From this it follows that the population of the universe is also zero, and that any people you may meet from time to time are merely the product of a deranged imagination."[38]

He drove a Porsche Boxster. Of course. Kathryn hadn't noticed it before, but it was hard to ignore when she had to fold herself into it. Funny, with all her wealth, fancy transportation had never intrigued her. House, garden, picket fence, curtains, full refrigerator, pictures of friends

---

[37] Cherie Carter-Scott, *If Love Is A Game, These Are The Rules*
[38] Douglas Adams, 1952-2001, *Hitchhiker's Guide To The Galaxy*

and family all around, now that was critical. But transportation? Nope, didn't even register on her radar.

He drove fast, too, with that air of confidence that someone owning a $65,000 car would be expected to have. "Do you get a lot of speeding tickets?" Kathryn asked as they roared down the interstate to, according to Adam, a 'surprise' destination.

Adam grinned at her, his eyes obscured by dark sunglasses. "Well, there's a difference, you see, between *getting* speeding tickets and getting *pulled over* for speeding. Do you see a distinction in the two?"

Kathryn rolled her eyes. "Forget it. I already have my answer."

He laughed. "Actually, I have a superb driving record. You would be proud."

They talked about business mostly. Adam seemed happy guiding the conversation and Kathryn was more than willing to keep things safe and professional. In the end, over the course of the hour drive, Adam managed to get out of her pretty much the entire presentation about Advancement Corporation that he had missed at the very first disastrous meeting.

"You know your stuff," he finally said as they wove in and out of the streets of Philadelphia. It was a statement, rather than a compliment and she was surprised at how pleased she felt to receive his affirmation. Turning into a parking lot, he folded his sunglasses, looked at her and said, "Here we are." The smug expression on his face made Kathryn look carefully at her surroundings. A harbor side was visible with boats of every imaginable shape and size. Adam grinned when she looked back at him questioningly. "You may have cab fair, but it won't do you any good once we're at sea."

Adam took her hand and led her toward an enormous yacht, lit up like a Christmas tree and bobbing gently at the dock. "Welcome aboard the *May's Flowers*, Sir," said the uniformed gentlemen at the bottom of the gangway. "Right on time. We set sail in approximately fifteen minutes if that suits your schedule."

"That will be fine," Adam said as he dragged Kathryn up the gangway.

"Tell me this is yours," she said in wonder as she gazed around at the gleaming teak wood and brass accents.

"Okay, it's mine," he glanced over his shoulder as he continued to drag her along the deck, "but I'm only saying that because you told me to. It really belongs to a business associate of mine. He offered to let me borrow it anytime, but this is the first time I've taken him up on it. He's trying to impress me with his wealth and generosity, I suppose." He stopped abruptly and she almost bumped into him. "Hey, is this a babe magnet kind of thing? Should I pick one of these up? Do you think it would get me a little more action?" Adam gave her a wicked smile.

Kathryn cocked her head to one side. "You don't know how to deal with people unless you're annoying them or dazzling them, do you?"

His smile dimmed a notch or two. "That's about what sums me up, Katty-girl. Since the day I was born."

The entire yacht was theirs for the evening. Kathryn counted approximately six wait staff not including those running the boat. "Is Miles somewhere running the show?" she couldn't resist asking.

Nonplussed, he said, "Nah, he's got the night off. Probably out chasing the Mayor."

"Miles is dating the Mayor?!" A kaleidoscope of pictures that she'd looked at on the Internet whirled through Kathryn's head of Miles with his various wives.

"Yeah, can you believe it? Not only are they dating, they attend church together, too." Adam laughed and shook his head. "I've seen Miles in a Speedo, which should be disturbing enough, but the thought of him holding hands and doing kissy-face with June Willoughby really gives me the creeps."

Toward the back of the boat was a huge open area with deep cushioned bench seats that you could curl up on and relax as you enjoyed the view. Adam pulled Kathryn down on the couch next to him and immediately a waiter brought them both glasses of white wine and a platter of assorted hors d'oeuvres.

"You have a rather interesting relationship with Miles, Adam. How long has he been working for you?" Kathryn watched Adam's expression intently.

He shrugged. "A little over a year. I have a ... reputation," he gave her a wry smile, "of being difficult to work for." Adam rolled his eyes at the ridiculousness of the accusation that made Kathryn laugh out loud. "Consequently, I offer top salaries and excellent benefits to lure the greedy and insensible. Miles is my sixth personal assistant in ten years. And my first butler." Adam shook his head and rolled his eyes. "I'm still not exactly sure how I ended up with a guy following me around with white gloves like Lurch from the Addam's Family. You know, he only call's me 'Sir' because he knows how much it pisses me off. He's very passive-aggressive." He shrugged. "A few more months and he'll set a record for staying power. Right after Miles started working for me the chef and the chauffer both quit, and Miles took over those jobs, too. He was happy to do the cooking, and since I rarely entertain, it has worked so far. When I am forced to have some kind of function at the house we have it catered. As for the driving," he gave another careless shrug, "he's the one who knows where and when I've got to be somewhere. Why shouldn't he just drive me there anyway?"

"Why do you dislike him so?" A silent waiter came and refilled their wine glasses, and Kathryn heard shouted directions as the boat was made ready to sail.

Adam gave her an impatient look. "He's shifty, manipulating, pompous, and in general a pain in my ass. He works hard to piss me off, show me up, or put me in my place as often as possible."

Kathryn smiled and stood up, walking to the rail to watch the action on the dock. "Oh, now I understand," she said with a twinkle in her eye. "You put up with him because he reminds you so much of yourself."

Following her to the rail, he stared at her intently for a moment. "You really think so?"

His serious expression made Kathryn burst out laughing. "Yes. Very much so."

The boat engines roared far below them and with amazing swiftness they were heading down the Delaware River. Adam seemed content to stand by her side and enjoy the evening, and perhaps contemplate her honest observations regarding the similarities between himself and his butler. Shortly, the sun would set, and it promised to be a glorious late spring night. "This is lovely," Kathryn felt compelled to say, "thanks for the invitation."

"Jury's still out on whether you're going to want to swim to shore in search of a cab though," Adam said quietly. Taking her elbow he murmured, "Come on. I'm hungry. Let's see what they're feeding us tonight."

The meal was sumptuous. Seafood at it's finest: shrimp, lobster, and flaky flounder fillet. Again conversation veered toward business, but this time Adam shared with her his business side.

"So," Kathryn said as she pushed back her plate, determined not to eat another delicious bite, "it seems like you always wanted to be a ..." she tapped her chin in pretend thought, "... how did the magazine article I read describe you? Oh yes, a 'business whiz and a financial genius.' Your parents must be very proud."

It was said innocently enough. Adam knew it, but it didn't stop him from saying rather bitterly, "Nah. I was a perpetual disappointment to my mother until the day she died, and my father never gave a sh-, er, a rat's ass about me. Until I became fantastically wealthy." He made a disgusted face. "How predictable." He gave her his 'I'm tough and don't need anybody' look.

She had paused with her water glass midway between the table and her mouth. "Oh. I suppose I should apologize for entering into a conversational danger zone." Kathryn placed her water glass down on the table without drinking and gave him a smile. "Between my comment earlier about you and Miles and now this, maybe you'll be the one swimming for shore hoping to catch a cab."

The attempt at humor relaxed him. Adam shook his head. "No, really, apology not necessary. I'm usually not so sensitive." He stopped and frowned. "No, that's actually a lie. I think I'm always sensitive about that topic. I just deal with it by never having personal, casual conversations with anyone, that's all."

"Who do you have, Adam?"

He attempted humor at her serious expression. "Miles."

Kathryn studied him intently and then finally said, "I know the truth about him, you know."

She rendered him absolutely speechless. Kathryn watched a myriad of emotions flash across his face, but he remained completely silent.

"Why, Adam? Why are the two of you playing this bizarre game?"

He shrugged defensively. "He started it."

"Do you hear how you sound?"

His tone emphasized his exasperation. "He sought a position in my life. I offered him one. He took it." He got up from the table and wandered over to the large windows, looking out at the beautiful evening lights glittering along the intercoastal waterway. "He can leave anytime he wants. In the mean time, I'll take advantage of his relatively inexpensive but effective labor."

"Why would a man like Miles Bishop seek a position as your personal assistant and then morph himself into your butler?!" Kathryn came and stood beside Adam and looked at his profile. "It makes absolutely no sense. What does he gain from this? He certainly doesn't need the job."

"I don't know about that. The salary and benefits are pretty good." Sarcasm dripped from his every word. He turned and faced Kathryn, both hands thrust into his pockets. "He thinks to convince me of his sincerity. It's a waiting game. I never win the day to day games he puts me through," Adam smiled a smile that held no humor, "but this waiting game, I Will Win."

Reaching out, Kathryn rested her hand on his tense arm studying his face. "This is a lot more than just a dislike," Kathryn murmured, standing close to him and looking into his eyes, "this is more like hate."

"Oh yeah," he nodded in complete agreement, "it's a lot like hate."

With the interruption of the waiter bringing dessert, they both allowed the conversation to steer towards safer waters. Sitting back outside looking up at the stars, Adam asked, "Can I ask you a question?"

"Sure," Kathryn said. She was comfortably curled up, enjoying the solitude of the night and the delicious sweet tea she was sipping.

"If you had to edit the Bible down to just, say, fifty pages, what do you think would be the most important stuff to keep?"

"Is this a trick question?" She watched him intently.

He shook his head. "Nope. I'm going to do my best to listen, absorb, and refrain from sarcastic and crude remarks."

"*Really.*" There was absolute disbelief in her voice.

Adam chuckled. "Really. I promise to be good. Let's give you a high sign if I go over the mark at all in what is considered acceptable behavior. If I start annoying you, just slap me on the back of the head. Or give me a big, smackin', wet kiss. I won't tell you which one I'd prefer."

"Nor will I," she responded primly.

He laughed.

Kathryn frowned in concentration. "Well, I understand - I think - what you're asking, but taking anything out of context from the Bible can be very dangerous. For me, part of the beauty of the Bible is how it is so cohesive, so interconnected. Did you appreciate that as you read it? Written over the course of hundreds of years, by numerous authors, it still has a cohesion that is absolutely stunning."

Kathryn shifted, setting her empty teacup down. Adam smiled to himself watching her in the muted boat light getting into her 'zone.' "But were I to have to decide what is the most important part of the Bible, it would have to be the account of Christ's time on earth. All of the Old Testament anticipates His coming, and all of the New Testament is the accounting of His impact." She smiled at Adam. "So, in my humble opinion, the life and teachings of Christ would have to be in those fifty pages."

"I read it again, you know," he said quietly. "You said that I should consider why I was reading it and what I was hoping to learn. So the second time I read through it I tried that."

"Did it make a difference?"

"Yes and no," Adam answered truthfully. "I read it the second time wondering what all the hype was about. Even if this was fictional," he glanced at her sitting quietly in the shadows, "don't get angry," when she smiled he continued, "there had to be something pretty fantastic about the book for it to be around all these years, right?"

The waiter came and refilled their tea and coffee cups. Both of them declined any more dessert so the dishes were all efficiently removed. Adam continued, "There are a lot of good lessons to be learned. I'll give you that. Lessons about honesty, and commitment, strength of character and obedience. I got a better handle on God this time. He came across as a very strict parent, and everyone else came across as hugely annoying, disobedient children."

Kathryn nodded. "Yup, I agree. He doesn't get referred to as 'Our Father who art in heaven' for nothing."

"So I got that, okay? But now you say that the parts about Christ are the most important. I'm no dummy. I realized that as I read through it. But that's the part I really don't get. I can't believe that all this Jesus stuff is for real. For me, it's the hardest part to swallow."

"Why do you say that?" There wasn't anger or a confrontational tone in her voice. Adam guessed he was still safe.

"He's just … I don't know, too perfect, I guess. Loving, wise, patient… And forgiving. That's the hardest to swallow. I mean, come on, the guy's hanging on a cross and he asks for forgiveness for the ones that put him there? How can anyone believe that?"

Kathryn was silent for long moments, obviously gathering her thoughts. Finally, she said, "Does it make sense to you if I said that I need to believe that about Him?" Adam watched her bite her lower lip and frown in concentration. "I mean," she said, leaning forward, "if He can forgive those people, then I don't think that there's anything I personally could do that would make me irredeemable, you know? No matter how badly I mess up, if I can bring myself just to ask for forgiveness, I know I can have it."

Kathryn sighed, stood up and walked over to stand at the rail. With her back to him she spoke. "You can read the Bible and just absorb it as a fantasy story. You can read it and absorb it as a basis for philosophical discussion. Or you can read it and choose to believe it. That's the beauty of God's style. No one can say that He forces us into anything. He put us in the garden, gave us the rules, and then let us choose. We failed. So He gave us a new scenario. He gave us the Ten Commandments for new rules and let us choose. And we failed again. So He gave us the newest scenario - which He had promised all along from the moment that Adam and Eve sinned in the Garden. He sent His Son. Along with Jesus came a new set of rules. And He lets us choose again. Will we fail again?" Without turning around she shook her head vigorously, "I certainly don't want to."

She shrugged, still not facing him. "It's a personal decision, Adam. You just have to decide if you are going to believe it or not. It takes faith, which for me grew into love. I choose to believe all of this. You may wonder why. I'm an intelligent, capable, confident woman." Kathryn turned around and smiled at Adam, still sitting on the couch. "What you don't realize is I'm what you see *because* of my faith. Not *in spite* of it."

Adam stood and walked over to stand next to her at the rail. While they had been talking, the yacht had turned around and begun its slow progress back to Philadelphia. He looked out into the inky nighttime darkness, admiring the occasional twinkle of lights visible along the coast. "I hear what you're telling me, Kathryn. It's powerful, truly it is. But I'll go back to forgiveness. I'm someone who never forgets a slight. I'm truly gifted at remembering and retaliating. It's both a business and a personal mentality, ingrained in me from as far back as I can remember. I just can't do it."

Kathryn exclaimed animatedly, "But that's the beauty of it! Don't you see? That's the crux of Christ's message! Accepting Him, believing Him, and confessing that you can't do it in your own power! It reinvents you. Some call it rebirth. The Bible says that *'what this means is that those who become Christians become new persons. They are not the same anymore, for the old life is gone. A new life has begun!'* [39]" She looked down at her tightly clasped hands as if embarrassed by her passionate explanation. She took a deep breath. "It's important to me, as you can see."

Adam reached out and touched her face making her look up at him. "I can see that. But it can't be for me. It would be absolutely impossible for me to have even the smallest level of forgiveness." He shook his head in frustration. "All roads lead back to Miles it seems."

"Miles?!" Kathryn looked at him in confusion.

He smiled and nodded. "Yeah. You said you knew the truth about him. You know, I never asked you how you found out."

All roads lead to Miles ... Impossible to have even the smallest level of forgiveness ... Suddenly Kathryn was unsure of what truth she actually knew. Frowning, she said hesitantly, "Miles told me."

"Miles!" Adam's face registered profound surprise. "I can't believe he told you such private information. When did this happen?"

"We met for dinner last week to discuss business."

Adam laughed incredulously. "And over a business dinner he felt compelled to share with you his claim that he's my long lost father?!"

"YOUR FATHER!" she exploded.

"Yeah, my father. Some guy, huh? Doesn't see fit to show up when I was cold, hungry, and neglected. No, he conveniently waits until I'm fantastically wealthy and world renown. Then he shows up thinking I'm going to willingly embrace, forgive," that word was emphasized with real venom, "and share. I told him that the only position that was open in my life was for a butler. *Which was a complete joke.* I sarcastically told him if he was interested, I'd hire him at the going rate and nothing more. He showed up the next day dressed in his butler clothes, and he's been driving me crazy ever since."

"Have you talked with him?"

"Sure," he said defensively, "I talk with him every damn day. More than I'd like, actually."

---

[39] 2 Corinthians 5:17, New Living Translations

Kathryn gave him an impatient look. "You know that's not what I'm talking about. I mean, have you really and truly sat down and had a serious discussion about all of this. You need to do this. For yourself and for Miles."

Adam shook his head. "You don't understand, Kathryn. It isn't that simple." His voice had an anguished sound to it.

Gently, Kathryn said, "You know what one of my good friends told me just a few weeks ago? She said anything that really matters is never easy. I'll tell you honestly that she told me this in regard to my personal life, which could also be referred to as a Complete Disaster. She challenged me because she knew that deep down, a satisfying personal life is something that I not only desire but that I need." Kathryn threw her hands up. "So here I am, even though I swore I would never date again, dealing with lonely, traveling, married men and greedy divorce/real estate attorneys. Sweating and fretting over how badly I can screw my life up this time around." She glared at Adam. "But I'm doing it. Because my wise friends see that void in my life. Because deep down it's something I truly long for. Because if I try hard enough and keep myself focused on what's good and right, then maybe the Lord will bless me with someone special."

Kathryn took a step closer to Adam and poked him in the chest with emphasis. "I asked you earlier this evening who you had. You gave me a flip answer. I don't think you have anyone in your life. And I don't care what you say to me, you cannot convince me that you're happy about that situation." She finished with her hands on her hips. Taking a deep, calming breath she spoke in a voice low and full of emotion, "This man has devoted over a year of his life to be close to you in the only manner you offered him. He has done his job efficiently, put up with your numerous idiosyncrasies, and exhibited a staying power that very shortly will put him above all the rest. It may be impossible for you to forgive. It may be hard for you to deal with the whys and the wherefores of your past. But you'd better figure out just why Miles is doing all of this. I'll tell you with the utmost of confidence he's not doing it for the money."

In the midst of her speech Adam had had to look away, unable to bear the intensity. When he finally looked back he was amazed to see tears making slow tracks down her face.

"I didn't realize," Kathryn began hesitantly on the drive home, "that I didn't know the whole truth about your relationship with Miles." While there had not been silence between the two of them as they finished the boat trip and docked, it had been awkward. "I had no intention of causing you to reveal such private information. I'm sorry."

Adam shook his head, dismissing her apology. "That's the way Miles operates, Kathryn. I told you he was shifty. Manipulative, too." He turned and looked at her briefly, his face illuminated by the car headlights. "What truth did you think you knew then?" Adam asked.

"About Bishop Pharmaceuticals."

"What? How he's supposedly Chairman of the Board, ex-president and ex-CEO?"

Kathryn couldn't hide her surprise. "You don't believe him?"

"I don't care." His knuckles flashed white as they gripped the steering wheel.

"Okay. End of this discussion, I think. Please, though, understand that I'm sorry and feel very awkward for the way this misunderstanding played out."

"It played out exactly the way that Miles wanted it to, Kathryn. Welcome to my world."

Maria had left the front porch light on. Standing at Kathryn's front door, he said, "I feel like a teenager coming home from a date; nervous that the parents are peeking through the living room curtains making sure I don't make an inappropriate move."

"Done that often, I suppose," she smiled.

Adam's mouth twisted in a wry grin. "Done that never. I told you that. I just watched television occasionally, and that's how it always seems to play out."

Kathryn reached up and palmed Adam's cheek. "I had a lovely evening. You were well behaved and there was never one time when I checked out how far it would be to swim to shore." She chuckled. "We've certainly come a long way, you and I."

"Not as far as I'd like to go," Adam murmured as he pulled her carefully into a firm embrace and kissed her. He may have claimed to have no experience with committed relationships, but he certainly knew how to kiss. While one arm held her close against him, his other hand reached up to cup the back of her head and keep her just where he wanted her.

Kathryn worked her other hand up so that she was holding his face in her hands. Eventually, she forced them apart. Taking a steadying breath she said, "I think I'll say goodnight now." When he started to say something she recognized the gleam in his eye and hastily put a finger against his lips. "Now don't go and ruin your good record for the evening, okay? Just say good-night."

He stared at her, obviously debating his options. When he kissed her fingers she removed her hand. "Goodnight, Katty-girl," he said and walked away off into the evening.

Do not fear death so much but rather the inadequate life.[40]

Chapter Twelve

(Said with incredulous disbelief.) "That's all you have to say? 'So?' Do women come up to you on a daily basis and inform you that they are pregnant with your child, Miles?"

(Casual, disinterested shrug.) "I'm a powerful man, Sheila. People have all kinds of agendas in an attempt to obtain a piece of me." (Sardonic smile.) "You should feel honored that you have such a ... substantial ... piece of me to claim."

"I guess I'll see what your new little wife, Mackenzie, thinks of the fact that her husband can't keep it in his pants."

(Laughter.) "Darling, that's why she married me."

"Well?" Pattilou asked. She'd phoned first thing Thursday morning demanding a report about Kathryn's date with Anthony Lombardo. "I can't wait until tonight to hear all the details." She has no idea, Kathryn thought to herself.

---

[40] Bertolt Brecht, 1898-1956

"He was nice."

"Nice good or nice bad?" Pattilou said impatiently.

Kathryn sighed and let her silence speak for herself.

"Oh, no," Pattilou said. "What did he do?"

"Before or after he asked me for stock tip information and practically asked me directly what my net worth was?"

"He didn't."

"I think he qualifies as strike two in the dating scene for me. At least I got dinner out of this one, huh?" Kathryn chuckled. "It was particularly cruel because from the start he seemed really nice. Things fell apart over coffee." She was silent for a minute. "Maybe I was just over reacting ..."

Pattilou sighed deeply over the phone. "Don't do that, Kathryn. Go with your gut. Your gut tells you something is not right, you go with it, okay? Just because George and I thought he was nice doesn't mean he wasn't really scum. Heck, I met him only twice. Everyone but Charles Manson can hold it together for that brief a time." She started to chuckle. "Hey, why don't I give April a call? Her stepbrother is sounding better and better."

"Very funny. Don't you dare. This just goes to prove, yet again, that I am, and continue to be, a looser magnet." Kathryn sighed. "Can I ask you a question though?" Kathryn was still in her pajamas, sipping tea, and reading the paper at the kitchen table.

"Sure."

"Well, you're usually very private about your life, so if I get too personal, tell me okay?"

"You want to know about me and George."

"Well, yeah. How did you know he was The One?"

"I'm still not sure," Pattilou chuckled.

"Oh, come on! You two are adorable together and you know it. I don't think I know any other couple who complete each other as well as you two. I, well, I never really had a good example of marriage to watch until I met you. I know my Gran was happily married to her husband for many years, but he was already dead when she took me in. And I have only bad memories of my real mother and father. Those are filed in the 'what not to do' section of my brain. My foster mother and father were never around long enough for me to have any kind of memories of them at all." She hesitated, "I just had Gran."

"So, what do you want to know?"

Kathryn sighed. "Dating is terrifying. Not the actual date, but the implications of the entire process. I mean, you're shopping around for someone you want to live with for the rest of your life. Then I look around at all the failed marriages. Even in Bible study, so many of the women are unhappy with the men they're married to. I'm smart enough to realize that being a Christian doesn't guarantee me a happily-ever-after kind of life. But, how'd you and George do it?"

"I think you have the completely wrong mindset, Kat."

"What do you mean?"

Pattilou sighed, taking time to get her thoughts together. "You're putting too much pressure on yourself if you scrutinize every date as a possible life partner. No wonder you've been happily out of the dating scene for so long." She chuckled. "I didn't particularly like George at all when I first met him. And I know I drove him crazy. If I was analyzing him based on your standards, we never would have had even a first date."

"You're kidding. You didn't hear smarmy background music and get all fluttery and ga-ga over him?" Kathryn hesitated. "I'm kidding you know."

Laughing, Pattilou said, "Yeah, I know. No, he showed up at work as an assistant to the assistant to the head architect who was going to do remodeling at the office. He made every effort to try to impress and make himself appear more important than he really was, and I made every effort to continue to remind him of his actual place in the real order of things. I had a blast, verbally and mentally sparring with him. I'm two years older than he, did you know that?"

"No!"

"Yeah. I called him 'young man'." She chuckled at the memory. "I was all of twenty-four, and he was only twenty-two. Every time the poor guy showed up I gave him a hard time one way or the other. I corrected his spelling on one of his memos, and I pointed out that he had a poppy seed stuck between his two front teeth once. The poor guy got more and more insecure with each visit to the office. He so brought out the worst in me."

"I can't believe this," Kathryn murmured.

"Oh, believe it. One day, after about four weeks of this, I came down into the parking garage at the end of the day and there he was, leaning against my car. He had on a dark blue suit and a white shirt with some red and green patterned tie. I'd pointed out earlier that day that the tie didn't go with the suit and offered to take him shopping sometime and help him improve his wardrobe.

"I gave him a big, flirty grin and said, 'Hey, you ready for me to take you shopping?'" Pattilou got quiet.

"And?" Kathryn prompted, her head full of a young Pattilou and a young George facing off in a parking garage.

"He grabbed me and gave me a kiss that practically knocked my socks off. Long and sweet, slow and sure." Pattilou sighed a dreamy, schoolgirl sigh. "When he finished kissing me he said, 'Pattilou, you just keep right on teasing me, and I'm going to keep right on kissing you, all right?'" She giggled. "Sounded like a good plan to me! We were married within the year and I've been teasing him and he's been kissing me for close to thirty years."

"But that doesn't tell me anything," Kathryn said.

"Look, if I had a secret formula for attracting the right guy I'd be a millionaire, Kathryn, okay? I can only tell you what worked for us. Surprisingly, we turned out to have some really important stuff in common. First and foremost, we both had a Godly perception about life. You know, believing He was in control and He should be the focus of our life. That was major and has been major to everything that we're about as a couple. Because of that, we matched with what was important to us: family, commitment, values." Pattilou paused. "But there was that initial spark, that initial attraction. I can't put a finger on it, but George stood out in the crowd for me. From day one when I was determined to put him in his place, then on consecutive days when I delighted in tormenting him, and then in those final days when I couldn't wait to see his cute face and have him give me a wink and smile as he walked through the office. I believe, at least for George and me, that it was God's push. That little internal voice that said, 'Take note of that one.' George felt the same way, too, he said. It was a big office full of lots of young men and women, but we only had eyes for each other.

"One day I realized I couldn't imagine life without him. Didn't even want to try. He completed me. We were both better together than apart." Pattilou laughed. "The rest is history."

"Thanks for telling me this."

"All this is very personal, Kat. You can't listen to my story and then go out and try to duplicate it. That's guaranteed failure. But you can hear what I told you contributed to our success: God, similar values, being better together than apart. I don't think anyone should compromise in any of those areas ever. Marriage is for a long time. In the heat of the moment, you may think those things don't matter, but trust me, they do. George and I have our rough moments. I'd be lying if I told you differently. But the rough areas are more manageable when you have a good foundation to stand on." Pattilou teased, "Gee, one lousy date with Anthony and I've got little miss 'I Don't Want To Have A Personal Life' asking me questions about marriage and happily ever after!"

"Well," Kathryn said, preparing for the inevitable explosion, "I also went out on a date with Adam LeGrande last night." She couldn't help but tease her friend. "You know, he's got a lot of potential ..."

"LeGrande Incorporated."

"Mr. Bishop, this is Kathryn McFadden. I'd like to schedule some time in which we could talk privately."

"Business or pleasure, Ms. McFadden?"

"It's of a personal nature, Mr. Bishop."

"I see. I also note the formality in the way you are addressing me."

"When would be a good time, Mr. Bishop?"

"Saturday's tend to be lighter for me. Would you be interested in meeting for lunch?"

"That would be fine. Do you have a place in mind?"

As Kathryn sat down at The Dinner Hour, waiting for Miles' arrival, she was forced to concede that perhaps some of Adam's perceptions of Miles were accurate. Unlike what she had anticipated, the restaurant was a greasy spoon diner with Formica countertops and plastic booth seats. Flipping through the numerous laminated pages of the menu, she struggled to maintain her focus. She was here to end her part in whatever game Miles was playing. And he *was* playing a game, dribbling out just enough information and just enough mystery with just enough open encouragement to achieve his agenda. Trouble was, Kathryn wasn't sure what Miles' agenda was. She just knew that she had unwittingly played a part in it, and she was not happy about it.

"The souvlaki is the best in the state here," came Miles' well-modulated voice from above her. Kathryn glanced up as he slid into the opposite seat in the booth. His jeans and buttoned down white shirt were surprisingly casual and a subtle scent of cologne wafted across the table. He had a quiet air about him that nonetheless spoke of power, culture, and wealth. He smiled at Kathryn and said, "Lamb at its most succulent, fresh baked pita bread, and a sadziki sauce that is to die for. I've offered the chef a substantial amount of cash to reveal the recipe, but alas, he has refused. I've found it most frustrating that I've been unable to replicate it." At Kathryn's somber expression and deep silence, Miles sighed. "You are annoyed with me."

"I do not like being used."

"It was never my intention for you to feel so, Ms. McFadden. I am a very patient man, but Adam is more … obstinate … than I had anticipated."

"Why are you doing this, Mr. Bishop? What is your ultimate goal?"

Miles arched a surprised eyebrow. "But surely that is more than obvious. I'll ask you a question that should help you arrive at the answer: what would you do to have the opportunity to speak with your Grandmother once again after all these years?"

Kathryn started. How had the conversation suddenly turned to her grandmother? Kathryn heard Adam's voice saying, 'He's shifty, manipulating, pompous, and in general a pain in my ass.' "What does my Grandmother have to do with any of this?"

"Would you do me the courtesy of humoring me for just a moment or two? I will in the end do my utmost to answer all of your questions and alleviate your anger."

She sighed with resignation. "I'd do anything to have the opportunity to speak with Gran again."

"Why?"

"Because I miss her: her wisdom, her love, her companionship."

"This opportunity would be worth *anything?*"

The intensity of Miles' expression made Kathryn turn away. She sighed deeply. Okay. She got it.

The two of them were silent until the waitress arrived to take their orders. Miles ordered his souvlaki, Kathryn ordered a chef salad. "Not a souvlaki fan?" Miles inquired.

"I would appreciate it, Mr. Bishop, if in the future when you need my help, you would be up front about it. Rather than ..." Kathryn caught herself.

He smiled. "Adam likes to refer to me as 'shifty'. I prefer 'prayerfully manipulative.'" He grinned at her. When she failed to respond, he sighed. "Very well, Ms. McFadden. You wish me to 'spill my guts' or 'pour out my heart' or 'bare my soul', hmmm?"

Shaking her head, she quickly responded. "No, Mr. Bishop. I want just what I've asked for. Honesty. No deception. A sincere request for assistance if that's what you'd like. Just no more games."

"I don't play games, really," Miles said. "I pray, a lot, and try to follow my inner voice." He gave her a wry grin. "Lately, it's taken me on quite a unique journey." The waitress brought their order and Miles took a bite of a French fry. "Take you for instance. I simply prayed for some help. And, presto! you showed up."

"I didn't just magically appear on the doorstep, Mr. Bishop. There was a significant trail that led to that … disastrous … first meeting with Adam."

Miles had the temerity to roll his eyes. "Yes, I was dismayed at that setback." Then he shocked Kathryn with a seductive wink. "But it worked out in the end, didn't it?" He shrugged. "In retrospect, I realized that had you been the typical businesswoman you would have swallowed your outrage, sucked up your dislike, and plowed on with the meeting just to get the opportunity to work with LeGrande, Inc. Which would have been even more disastrous. But you're not typical. You left the great Adam LeGrande, boy wonder and mega billionaire, high and dry with 'egg on his face.' You couldn't have behaved more perfectly to get his attention."

"I didn't want his attention!" she shouted and two customers turned to look at her.

Miles chuckled and reached across the table to pat her hand consolingly. "I know. I know." He composed his expression and then said, "Do you know the only thing that intrigues Adam LeGrande? A problem. Something he can't understand or master. I know you simply saw a rude, egotistical man that first day. But what he saw in you was a beautiful, opinionated, unattainable woman. I had recognized those qualities in you the first time I'd seen you and was absolutely delighted, in the end, when they were so vividly displayed for Adam on your very first meeting."

Kathryn frowned in puzzlement. "When did you first see me?"

"I became aware of you when your Teach Me program began its tutorial program at LeGrande's downtown office. Whether you realize it or not you are very hard to miss, Ms. McFadden, even when you make significant attempts to remain in the background. You have vitality, a sparkle about you. I made some inquiries …"

"What do you mean 'inquiries'?" Kathryn interrupted.

"The usual things: marital status, financial state, general background history …"

"And I met with your satisfaction?" she said heatedly.

Miles nodded, unfazed by her tone. "Better than I could have imagined." Despite her outraged expression he continued, "You have remarkable staying power with the men you become involved with. Just like everything in your life; you latch on and are determined to succeed in what you set out to do. That's what Adam needs. Someone who's not going to be put off by his extremely insufferable exterior and who will make the effort to get to know that real man on the inside.

"Then June mentioned you regarding Computer Dynamics, and it was too perfect an opportunity to pass up. I knew if Adam agreed to mentor Ms. Gonzalez, you two would eventually have to meet." When she went to speak, he held up his hands. "But you must understand, Ms. McFadden, not once have I worried or stressed over any of this. I have planted ideas and suggestions, manipulated circumstances here and there, and then prayed about everything. But then it is all out of my hands. If it is meant to happen, then the Lord will make it happen."

"MAKE WHAT HAPPEN?!!!" Kathryn all but shouted. "The only thing you're accomplishing right now is driving home Adam's point that you are nothing but a pain in his ... behind," she finished lamely.

Miles chuckled. "That is my ultimate gratification, you know, that he can't ignore me. I'm in his face day in and day out. He's too stubborn to fire me." Suddenly serious, he said, "And too proud to ask the right questions."

"And that's where I come in?" she burst out. "You just instinctively knew that I would be so curious, so intrusive, so aggressive that I would ask all the questions that Adam's stubbornly refused to?"

"You're here now, aren't you?" he said gently. "Involving yourself in a situation that, technically, you have nothing to do with. Why are you doing this Kathryn? Why are you using your valuable time to meet with me and discuss Adam LeGrande's relationship with me?"

She opened her mouth and closed it, twice, before she came up with the answer. "Because, despite everything, I care about him. He's an abrasive, annoying, egotistical nightmare, but," she shrugged, closed her eyes, put her head in her hands, and groaned, "he's got potential."

"Which leads you exactly to where I want you to be led, God willing. I want my son to be alone no longer. I want my son to have someone to love and care for him. I want my son to embrace life and know what joy is. I want my son to come to know God and the amazing things He can do." Miles reached out and took Kathryn's hand. She looked up at him and saw tears in his eyes. "Do you know, every time I call him "sir", in my heart I'm calling him "son"? At the far end of this long list of things I have for Adam is a desire for him to forgive me, get to know me, and come to love me the way I love him. But at the rate we're going, I don't think that's going to happen."

"Why?" she asked trying to be flip for once. "You going somewhere soon?"

He released her hand and helped himself to another French fry. "Actually, yes I am. I'm dying."

Long moments passed before Miles finally spoke. "Would you be willing to go for a walk with me?" he asked. Kathryn realized he was standing by the side of the booth with his hand extended.

"Oh ... of course," she stumbled getting out of the booth and he took her elbow to guide her.

Miles was his usually charming self with the receptionist, calling her by name, as he paid the bill and added a generous tip for the waitress.

"You really do come here often, don't you?" she asked as they stepped out into the bright sunshine.

He looked surprised. "Yes, I told you they have the best souvlaki in the state." He studied her for a moment. "I don't lie, Kathryn. I don't think I've been dishonest with you once." He nudged her jokingly and murmured under his breath, "I will admit to being evasive, occasionally. You ask very good questions. I find it fun to spar with you."

"Mr. Bishop ... Miles ..."

He chuckled. "The familiarity ratio goes up once my death becomes imminent, huh?"

"That's not funny."

"Death is more universal than life; everyone dies but not everyone lives.[41]*"*

Kathryn sighed, giving him an impatient look. Miles gestured to a bench that overlooked a nearby park. "Will you sit so I can tell you my story?"

Once they were settled, with Miles looking off into the distance and Kathryn sitting stiffly beside him, he began to speak. It was not Miles the butler speaking, and perhaps, Kathryn suspected, it was not even Miles the 'brilliant scientist and businessman" talking. She glanced at his profile as he sat beside her, more casual and relaxed than she had ever seen him. He was a handsome man. Just like his son.

"I was an awful man for most of my life. Impressive in all I did, I managed to be impressively awful as well. I knew it and just about everyone else knew it, too. Very confident, full of myself, driven … Adam … takes after me in more ways than appearance.

"I can honestly tell you that I don't think I've ever been in love." He shrugged. "Came close a few times, but love is a choice, and I always had other things much more important to concentrate on.

"I was pretty impressed with myself. Had very much a King Midas quality: magic in science, business, …" he glanced at her and rolled his eyes, "women." He looked back out at nothing in particular. Kathryn found that watching him was much more interesting than the mundane scenery. "You've done your homework and I'm sure you know the count. Four wives, four failed marriages. There was speculation that my marriages were more career moves than love matches. That was accurate. With my third wife, Mary Ann, I added the children, James and Edward." He looked at her again. "King names." His gaze flickered, and he turned away. He reached up and rubbed his face with one hand. "I was as good a father as I was a husband which in a word was 'lousy.'

"No goodness, no loyalty, no faithfulness, no love … I met Sheila Docherty in a bar. She was a beautiful woman on the make. I knew it but enjoyed what she was willing to give despite that fact. I'd just gotten married to wife number two, Mackenzie Brouche. Bishop Pharmaceuticals

---

[41] A. Sachs

developed a very popular line of hypoallergenic make-up products during our time together." This time he looked directly at Kathryn and just let her see. His expression was wide open, no façade, and no illusions. Just a man filled with loathing and regret.

"When Sheila confronted me with her pregnancy …" Miles shrugged, "… I just blew her off. Laughed in her face. Belittled her and knew how to provide enough threats to keep her silent. I sent her money on occasion over the years. I knew that the kid received absolutely none of it. I had files documenting his appearance and apparent neglect. I did nothing about it. I was sending her money, wasn't I? What was I supposed to do, start babysitting her every move?"

He leaned forward, resting his forearms on his thighs, examining his perfectly manicured hands. "The kid was smart. Just like me and then some. What irony. My two claimed sons are steady, solid, not brilliant boys. My bastard son is a certified genius. Soon as Sheila clued in to Adam's potential, things improved in some ways for the boy. She never knew but much of the financial support that came her way in the form of scholarships, amenities, and outright cash was through me. She thought it was private funding because of the boy's brilliance." He shrugged. "Worked for all involved. The kid managed to get legally emancipated after her death at sixteen. Good move. Began to set the world on fire and I sat back and watched." He nodded his head, pride in his voice. "It was a great show.

"I had a bout with testicular cancer when I was in my late thirties. Kept it all quiet and hush–hush not wanting it to affect business. Had my right testicle and my stomach lymph nodes removed. Years ago, recovery from testicular cancer was not as promising as it is today, but I beat the odds and made a complete recovery. Ten years ago I was diagnosed with prostate cancer. Initial biopsies showed I was already in stage four with a fast growing tumor and a real party of irregular prostate cells. Did the whole chemo route that time." Miles reached over and touched her forearm and grinned. "I always thought one of the wives wished all this on me. I earned it you know."

At Kathryn's somber face, he reached up and tapped her under the chin. "Smile Kathryn, this story has a happy ending, you know." At her continued solemn expression he finally sighed and looked away.

"There was a woman who was doing chemo treatments on the same schedule I was. Breast cancer. We used to sit and chat, compare doctors and medicines. She was always eager to hear my wealth of information on all the different medications. Surprisingly, I was eager to hear all of her talk about God." Miles turned again to look at Kathryn and arched his eyebrow. "See where the happy ending comes in?" At her hesitant nod, he continued. "I made a profession of faith sitting beside that young woman while we both got pumped full of toxic medications designed hopefully to kill just the bad cells in each of us and none of the good ones.

"She was twenty-nine years old, Kathryn. Twenty-nine. Didn't know anything about the world and living, and yet taught me the secret of eternal life and then some." He swallowed with difficulty and was silent for long moments. "She died," he said after a time.

Miles chuckled bitterly. "My fourth wife, Jennifer, put up with all of my foibles for a few years. She was a very troubled woman, and I did nothing to help. But when I 'found God,' that was the straw that broke the proverbial camel's back. She … left … me, and for the first time in my life, I began the process of creating something worthwhile for all the years I've spent on earth.

"I'm proud to say that I have a pretty solid relationship with most of my children now. They've turned out quite fine, despite my influence." He turned and winked at Kathryn. "The only one left is … Adam. And, as would be expected, he's been my biggest … challenge. I want a relationship with him, too.

"I've got stage two prostate now. They can't do chemo because I've done that once already. In addition, I'm at a tremendous disadvantage because of the testicular cancer years ago. They've removed a number of lymph nodes already … Had radiation therapy right after I resigned from Bishop, and James took over. They've got me doing hormonal treatment now." He smiled at Kathryn. "It's buying me some precious time. I want … time to fix what needs to be fixed with Adam."

"You don't always get everything you wish for, Miles," Kathryn said quietly.

"Seems to me you speak from experience," he said just as softly.

Kathryn shrugged. "Don't you think that everyone is forced to deal with difficulties over the course of life: trials, tribulations? I mean, we're not supposed to have a 'happily ever after' life. We're supposed to stay true to the course, focused on God and His plan for our lives, and learn from our ... experiences," she finished lamely.

"My research into your background included your abandonment by your parents." Miles took her hand. "Talk about 'learning from experiences'," he said wryly.

Kathryn forced a casual shrug. "I never even knew their names," she said. Sighing, she elaborated. "I don't even know my real name." She gave Miles a bitter smile. "For a long time I wanted that information. Passionately. I'm not sure what I would have done with it or exactly why it was so important, but ..." Kathryn shrugged again. "That's an example of something that you must eventually put aside or it consumes you in a way that is not ... positive. Just acknowledge God's wisdom and greater understanding about something in which you cannot see the whole picture. I no longer agonize over my ... namelessness. No longer feel like a nameless ... nothing ..." She smiled at Miles. "God has filled that hole," she said sincerely.

Miles nodded in understanding. "I've come to terms with the fact that I may not ever be able to settle things between Adam and me. Life just doesn't work that way. I know that. But in a lot of ways he's more messed up than I ever was, and that haunts me. Thanks to my neglect and his mother's ..." he shrugged, "well, his mother. Maybe, somehow, someway, I can negate the bad I've done ... his mother and I have done. Ease some of the sorrow and the pain. Explain things that need explaining. Affirm things that need to be affirmed. I pray that I'll have the opportunity to do this. So, I started thinking that if I couldn't make some kind of progress myself, maybe I'd try to arrange to have someone else take over in my stead."

"You could tell Adam the truth about your health," she said quietly.

Miles shook his head vigorously. "No, absolutely not. I'm not going to play the pity card. Ever. And I forbid you to tell Adam about my health."

Kathryn arched her eyebrows in surprise. "You *forbid* me? It's a little bit late in the game for you to second guess or try to control how this thing is going to play out."

Miles sighed. "Point taken. So, I'll ask you. Please. Don't say anything. If Adam decides to ... speak with me ... I want it because he's curious, or vaguely open, or even so angry he's got to finally let it all out. But I don't want guilt or pity to drive him. Please?"

Slowly, Kathryn nodded her acquiescence.

Miles sat back up on the park bench and looked directly at Kathryn. He extended his arms across the back of the bench and crossed his legs, the picture of casual elegance. When Kathryn remained silent, he waggled his eyebrows at her. "End of story."

Kathryn frowned and shook her head still not clear. "So let me get this straight. If things don't work out the way you want, you'd like me to ..."

Miles interrupted her, nodding his head, "Save him. Any way you can."

The truth that makes men free is for the most part
the truth which men prefer not to hear.[42]

Chapter Thirteen

"I appreciate you finding the time in your busy schedule to see me."

"Hey, just call me Mr. Nice Guy, okay?"

"I'd prefer to call you 'son'."

(Bitter laughter.) "Yeah. How convenient. Wasn't that article in Business Today informative about my company breaking into the Fortune 500 list of up and coming companies along with the detailed accounting of my net worth? You'll excuse me if I don't jump on the 'happily ever after bandwagon' so we can go riding off into the sunset."

"I don't suppose admitting my culpability and assuring you that I have no interest in your financial holdings would make any difference."

"Absolutely none whatsoever."

"I see. So, there is no room in your life right now for a father?"

"None. But I do have an opening for a butler. I've never had one and I'm beginning to think that with my level of prestige and fortune, it would be appropriate to

---

[42] Herbert Agar, 1897-1980

add one to my household staff. You know, the kind of guy who walks around all day wearing a suit and white gloves saying, 'May I get you anything else, Sir?' Salary and benefits are excellent. Except for a butler, I've got everything else *I could wish for."*

"Miles!"

"Sir?"

"How come my lunch date with Datatron was cancelled? It's been set up for months."

"Mr. Wilshire's assistant called and requested rescheduling the meeting. Seems as if Mr. Wilshire, a double black diamond ski trail, and a tree did not mix well. If you look ahead three weeks from today, in your Blackberry, you will see that the meeting has been rescheduled. In addition, you will have to go to Mr. Wilshire's home office as he will still be recuperating, Sir."

Adam studied the expressionless face of Miles, The World's Most Manipulative Butler. Something was going to have to give with this bizarre relationship. It was reaching the point that Miles' presence alone, was starting to annoy Adam. Putting his chin in his hand and adopting his 'I'm really sincerely interested' expression he said, "How's the mayor, Miles? Things heating up satisfactorily for you?"

"How's Ms. McFadden, Sir? Managing to avoid her arranging for your death?"

Adam leaned back in his desk chair and grinned. "Hmmm, I don't usually get a rise out of you, Miles. And I think that response was perhaps just a hint of a rise. Seems like Mayor Willoughby might just be a perfect subject for me to use to ruffle your perfectly coiffed hair."

"Was the dinner the other night with Ms. McFadden up to your standards, Sir?"

"My standard is you and your cooking, Miles. Are you fishing for a compliment?"

"Hardly, Sir. The *May's Flowers* has an excellent gourmet chef on staff. I couldn't begin to compare my culinary skills with hers."

Adam stood up and walked toward Miles. "How do you know the chef on the *May's Flowers* is a woman?" he murmured suddenly with deep suspicion in his voice.

Miles expression was purposefully blank. "Those of us in the service industry tend to know one another, Sir. It's a remarkably small world. You'd be surprised."

Crossing his arms, Adam said, "You told me that Elijah Corliss of General Infusion owned the *May's Flowers*."

Miles shook his head. "No, Sir. If I remember correctly, I stated that Elijah Corliss, of General Infusion, was interested in establishing a favorable business alliance with you regarding some government contracts he's been made privy, too. I observed personally, Sir, that he seemed rather desperately inclined to take advantage of your already solid business inroads within the military sector. I also pointed out that the *May's Flowers*, a luxury yacht anchored in Philadelphia, had been made available for you at your convenience."

"Who owns the *May's Flowers*, Miles?"

"I am not at liberty to say, Sir," Miles said coolly, turning to go.

"I know a number of people who work for the Pennsylvania DMV, Miles. I can find out in a matter of minutes!" Adam said to Miles departing back.

"You do that, then, Sir. You do that."

"Kathryn McFadden."

"Have you eaten dinner yet?"

Kathryn gave an exasperated sigh. "Hello, Adam. And no, I haven't already eaten dinner. It's only five-thirty. I don't usually quit for the day until at least seven-thirty."

"I'm sitting on your front porch with a bucket of moo-goo-gai-pan. Could that induce you to end things a little early today?"

There was silence at Kathryn's end while she walked to the front room, pulled back the curtains in the front room, and stared at Adam sitting on one of her wicker chairs talking on his cell phone. "It really is moo-goo-gai-pan and not some of that horrible tofu you brought last time?" she finally said.

"Yeah, it is.   May I please come in, Kathryn?"   He looked unbelievably forlorn sitting on the front porch all by himself.

Kathryn cut the connection and went over to open the front door. "You're going to have to give me about forty-five minutes.   I've got a conference call in two minutes."

"Sure.   I'll just riffle through your personal effects while you're busy," he said handing her the delicious smelling bag of food and then wandering over to examine the books on her bookshelf.   When she made no move, he turned and said, "Go on.   Finish up.   I'm happy waiting."

"Are you okay?" Kathryn finally asked.

He shook his head.   "No," and went back to studying her books.

The conference call actually took an hour, but Kathryn was very pleased with the results.   The Teach Me mentoring program was going to be picked up by another major corporation thanks in part to its amazing success with LeGrande, Inc. and the favorable word of mouth it had generated.   In an amazing stroke of genius, Kathryn had also managed to get the corporation to allow Maria's company, Computer Dynamics, to provide an online program that would allow direct communication between the company and the involved schools.   Things had gone even better than she had prayed.

She found Adam sprawled on her living room couch reading *Paul, Women and Wives: Marriage and Women's Ministry in the Letters of Paul.*   He looked up when she entered the room.   "Is this part of the She-Woman-Man-Haters Club required reading?"

"What are you talking about?" she asked as she collapsed into her favorite chair.

"The Little Rascals on television used to have a 'He-Man-Woman-Haters Club.'   I always thought that you'd probably be president of the complimentary women version of the club."

Frowning, she asked, "What gave you that impression?   Have I ever given you cause to think that I hate men?"

"Well, you certainly weren't very kind to me when you first met me," he said in a slightly defensive tone.

"Adam," she said laughing, "you weren't a very pleasant person. Do I need to remind you of some specific examples?"

He sat up, closing the book, and tossing it on the coffee table. "Please, spare us both." Adam gestured toward the book. "Why do you have that one in your library then?"

Kathryn shrugged. "Another one of the books I enjoy in my study of the Bible. If you're going to embrace the Bible, I don't believe you can pick and choose what you like and what you don't like. I believe it's got to be all or nothing. You only weaken your whole credibility argument when you say stuff like, 'I passionately believe in this passage, but I choose not to embrace this one.' For some Christian women, Paul is very controversial. He advises women to be silent in the churches, to not instruct men, to ask their husbands at home if they have questions, to wear hats in church ..."

Adam looked down at the book on the table and then gave Kathryn a wicked grin. "My kind of man."

Rolling her eyes, Kathryn stood and headed for the kitchen. "You're so cliché." Speaking to Adam as he followed, she said, "Rather than dismiss Paul, I chose to do a bit of research and figure out where he was coming from and what the state of the churches were for those recipients of his letters." She carefully spooned the moo-goo-gai-pan into a microwaveable dish, slid it into the oven, and punched in the time and temperature. "I found, that given the circumstances and the culture of the times, Paul was right in his advice to both the men and the women." She winked at him as she got out plates and cutlery, handing them to Adam to set the table. "I think, if I was truly in the ... She-Woman-Man-Haters Club," she looked at him questioningly to see if she'd gotten the name right and he smiled and nodded, "that I wouldn't have been able to admit that. Don't you think?"

"Yeah, I've got to give you credit for the admission," he said as he got down glasses from the cupboard, adding ice and iced tea to each.

"So, why aren't you okay?"

Sitting down at the table, Adam said, "I'm either going to have to fire Miles or kill him. I was hoping you'd help me make the wise decision."

Kathryn chose to ignore him. It was the easiest solution and besides, controversial topics like dismissal and murder tended to interfere with the sheer pleasure of moo-goo-gai-pan. Later, sitting at the kitchen table, among the remains of the meal and sipping green tea, Adam finally said, "Are you going to help me?"

She sighed and looked pointedly at Adam. "You know what the wisest decision is, and it has nothing to do with either of the two choices you've voiced."

"I'm not going to talk to him, Kathryn. That's what he's been angling for all along. If I talk to him, he wins."

"Did it ever occur to you that if you talk to him you could both win?" At his closed expression Kathryn retorted, "See, I knew you didn't really want my opinion. You're already shutting me out." When he opened his mouth to say something, Kathryn pointed a finger at him and said, "Don't patronize me, Adam LeGrande. I never have been and never will be a 'yes person'." Adam couldn't help it and started to chuckle at her politically correct term, which made her glare at him all the more. "Don't come into my house asking for my opinion about wise decisions when you know darn well that you're not going to take any of the advice I throw your way. *Honesty*, Adam. That's what you need more of in your life. Not games."

He slumped down in the kitchen chair and rested his head on the back of the seat. With eyes closed he said, "I can't deal with honesty. It hurts too much."

"Why don't you tell me what's happened? What has Miles done this time?"

He lifted his head off the back of the chair and said, "You know the yacht we were on? *May's Flowers?*"

"Yes ..."

"Guess who owns it."

"You told me it was some business associate who was trying to impress you."

Adam shook his head. "No, that was what Miles manipulated me into thinking. That's not the truth though."

"Uh-oh."

Adam stared at her for a moment. *"May's Flowers* is Miles' yacht. I've just spent the better part of the afternoon doing research on him. Much more than the standard references check the personnel department did to verify all of his references when he applied. *This time I* did the searching. The man's filthy rich. Is a real ladies man – married four times ..."

"I tried to tell you that night ..."

Adam continued as if she hadn't spoken. "He's got four homes: in Paris, London, San Francisco, and Key Biscayne. Besides the yacht, he has his own private jet and supposedly one of the largest privately owned collection of vintage Corvettes in the United States." As he spoke he seemed more and more upset. He swallowed. "He's got two sons and one step-daughter whom he legally adopted during his fourth marriage ..."

"You're wrong about some of that information," Kathryn interrupted gently.

"What?"

"He's got three sons, not two."

Adam propelled himself out of his chair to stand at the kitchen sink and look out into her back yard. "Do you ever go out to your garden?" he asked as if it was a perfectly appropriate question. "I've never gone out to mine. Not once."

Kathryn sighed. "Are you happy, Adam? It may sound corny, but if you had one wish, what would it be?"

He turned, leaned against the sink, and crossed his arms. "To see you naked."

Kathryn shook her head and chuckled at the absurdity of it all. "Nope, can't do it. You can't distract or annoy me anymore. I've got your number."

"Oh yeah? What's my number?"

She stood up and began to clear away the dishes and garbage from the table. "Your number is one. Solitary. Alone. Separate. Not connected with anyone or anything. When anyone gets too close, whether intentionally or accidentally, you strike out in numerous ways to reestablish distance. Actually, you behave the way you do as a constant defense. Kind of like an inborn security system." She set dishes on the counter and threw the garbage in the trash, coming to stand directly in front of him. "Go ahead, try and deny it."

Adam pushed up off the sink and took a step toward her, crowding her against the utility island in the middle of the kitchen. Stretching out his arms, he placed them on the counter on either side of her, trapping her. "If that's so true, how come I keep seeking you out for company, Katty-girl?" he said in a low voice.

He addled her with his closeness. She smelled his subtle aftershave, looked into his handsome face, and with a rush, remembered the kiss just a few nights ago. "Because you live to be unpredictable and contrary," she said in as businesslike a tone as she could muster as her heart practically pounded out of her chest and a slow blush crept up her neck.

"Nah," he said slowly shaking his head and moving in even closer, "that's not the reason. I told you why. That night on your porch. Remember?"

Kathryn shook her head. She could barely remember her own name let alone a conversation that happened weeks ago.

As if he couldn't wait another moment, he leaned in and kissed her. Pulling back only slightly, he said softly, "You've managed to see the real me." Kiss again. "You don't see my money," kiss "or my power." Long kiss. "I like that you don't take the crap I dish out so well." Kiss. "I like how you're just as quick as I am with comebacks so that I never feel that I have the upper hand." Long kiss again. "In fact, I like every damn thing about you, Katty-girl." And with that, he pulled her into his arms and this time she did forget her name.

"Oh, whoa. Excuuuuuuse me," Maria said with very little actual apology in her voice.

Kathryn tried to jump out of Adam's arms, but he held on tight. "Really, *really* bad timing, Maria Gonzalez. It's taken me weeks to get this far." He seemed casual and at ease and not at all bothered by the fact that he'd just been caught necking like a fourteen-year-old in the kitchen.

At Kathryn's continued attempts to break free, Adam finally sighed deeply in frustration and released her. He resumed his casual stance leaning against the kitchen sink with his arms crossed against his chest while Kathryn made every effort to look constructive and not mortified. She suspected she failed miserably.

"Should I leave and come back in a while?" Maria asked.

"NO," Kathryn said.

"YES," Adam said a little bit louder.

Maria laughed at both of them. "I've got truckloads of work to do, so I think I can make you both happy. I'm going to go and get lost in my computer which should make Kathryn happy with my presence and, at the same time, Adam happy with my total obliviousness." She grinned and waved a hand airily at them. "Please continue. Pretend I wasn't even here."

Kathryn groaned in embarrassment while Adam gave her a lazy grin. "I like that woman's style. I should try to do some business with her." He made to move toward Kathryn and she held up her hand like a traffic cop.

"Stop right there. Don't come any closer. My brain goes to … mush … when you get too close. I've got to work on self-preservation here." She gave him a determined look. "You were here because of Miles. Stop trying to change the subject."

"So, what's your advice, Katty-girl," he spoke softly and walked slowly toward her, crowding her in once again, leaving her hand resting against his chest.

She took a steadying breath and her hand clenched his shirt. "You should know, since you think you have full disclosure on Miles, that he's played matchmaker here between us, as well. This," she motioned between him and her, "is just what he's hoping for."

Adam was silent for a moment, digesting what she was telling him. "Finally, after all this time," he said with a wicked smile as he lowered his head for another kiss, "I've got a reason to be glad he works for me."

Adam broke the kiss after a time and held her in a firm embrace. Kathryn struggled to get her head and her heart in order and then finally gave up and enjoyed the pleasure of being in his arms. "I'm not going to forgive him, Kathryn."

"That's not what you need to do."

"We're not going to become a best-buddy dad and son team."

"I don't think anyone is expecting that."

"I can't promise to keep my temper nor be polite."

That comment made Kathryn laugh out loud. "Oh, darn. I really thought I could at least count on that. You do so well in both of those areas."

That made him snort with laughter. He was silent for a long time and then finally said, "I want you to be there when I talk to him."

"This is not my business, Adam! This is between you and Miles."

"Okay, then just answer this question for me: do you honestly think that without your presence in our lives these last five weeks I would be standing here contemplating anything except my extreme dislike of my butler?"

"No," she said quietly after a time.

"And answer this, has Miles, or has he not, purposely involved you in this 'business' between him and me?"

"Yes," she said in a very resigned tone.

"So, it's my turn to involve you. If I talk to him, you have to be there. Look at it this way. It will keep us both from killing each other."

"Only if Miles is okay with it."

Adam pulled back and looked at her. They stared at each other for long moments and then, finally, Adam rolled his eyes. "Oh, he'll be okay with it. And you know it."

"Well, I say you give him a chance. He's come a long way from the Mega Disaster he was at that first business meeting. I'm starting to like his style," Lydia said. "Besides," she added with a wicked gleam in her eye, "based on the kiss Maria described to me, I think you've already made your decision, haven't you, Kat?"

"Kiss?" Meredith said looking over at Lydia and then back at Kathryn. "How come this kiss wasn't included in our weekly installment of 'For The Love Of Kathryn'?"

"Oh, ha-ha. Is nothing private?" Kathryn said.

"Whoa," Meredith said with a grin, "look at that blush!"

"Let's look at this logically," said Lydia. She began to keep count on her fingers. "We know he's not married. Better yet, he's not even divorced. In the scheme of things, sometimes a perpetual bachelor can be a drawback, you know with the whole commitment phobia thing, but right now, let's assume his single status is simply a positive."

"He can't possibly be interested in your money," Meredith volunteered. "He's got too much of his own."

"And if he starts asking you for stock tips," Pattilou groaned and rolled her eyes, "at least he's got enough of his own money to play with. Another positive."

Audrey nodded. "And he's gainfully employed and, although he struck out significantly at the start, has redeemed himself. He's agreed to mentor Computer Dynamics, consistently giving good references for the Teach Me mentoring program, and has made every effort to understand what Advancement Corporation is about."

"On paper, this guy seems pretty darn good. Don't forget. He's handsome and drives a Porsche," Meredith added. Kathryn wondered if she was serious or not. "And it sure sounds like he's a great kisser."

Kathryn groaned and got up to cut herself a piece of pie. Turning to address the group, leaning against the kitchen counter covered with all the desserts, she said through gritted teeth, "He believes the Bible is a fairy tale. He's never managed a committed relationship *in his life*. He's a loner who has lived his whole life without the benefit of love. He's obnoxious, overbearing, and unbelievably rude. He's ..." She felt herself quieting, realizing that the picture she was painting of Adam wasn't entirely accurate anymore. Yes, he was all those things but he'd shown a genuine curiosity about the Bible. He'd admitted his failure with relationships and expressed a desire to change. And lately, the obnoxious, overbearing, and unbelievably rude side of him had kind of taken a back seat … She had a flash of him saying in his deep voice, 'I like every damn thing about you, Katty-girl.' She felt a blush slowly creep up her neck.

"He's what, Kat?" Gwen said gently.

Kathryn moaned and said, "He has a lot of potential."

"Sounds like your eyes are wide open on this one, Kat," Gwen said. "Sounds like you have your head screwed on straight with a very discerning heart. I don't hear one instance where you've compromised what's important to you just to keep this man in your life. In fact, I hear that you've been pretty darn emphatic about what you need, expect, want, and are unwilling to compromise on, and it has … intrigued him. Am I right?"

Kathryn looked at her friends sitting quietly on the big wrap around sofa staring at her intently. Slowly she nodded.

"Anything you regret so far? Anything you wish you could take back or redo?" Pattilou asked.

Kathryn shook her head no.

Pattilou grinned. "So far, so good. And, just for the record, they all have potential, honey. Just some more than others."

Audrey said with a completely straight face, but there was a mischievous glint in her eye, "Well, we could always get April to set you up with her stepbrother." She turned to April. "Your stepbrother still available?

April shrugged. Tonight April was wearing her long hair loose, except for an elaborate single braid extending out of the side of her head like a fountain. Although she wasn't wearing any rubber bracelets to fiddle with, she was wearing three-inch long dangle earrings that were an excellent substitute.

"I continue to maintain that I'm best off without a personal life," Kathryn said. "This acquaintance I have with Adam is just another one of my tests. Maybe it's the final quiz or something, because I just can't believe it's as cut and dried as you all seem to be making it out to be."

"You've got to admit that God's talking to you about him," April said quietly.

All heads swiveled to April. "Go ahead, let's hear what you've got to say," Audrey said with some trepidation.

"Well, there's no such thing as coincidence, right?" At everyone's nod, April continued. "You've had the really bad first meeting, the country club meeting where he spilled soda on you, the fight over Maria Gonzalez and her company, then that night at the restaurant where he dumped a whole pile of food and drinks all over you by accident." April looked around at the group. "That's an awful lot of times that they keep 'accidentally' meeting each other isn't it?"

"It's always scary when she starts making a lot of sense," Audrey mumbled and Pattilou gave her a shove.

"Then he shows up with the Chinese food, and Kathryn sends him the Bible and now they're talking on the phone a lot... Meanwhile, Kathryn's not having any luck with meeting any nice guys - and now we're all praying about that - not just me. The next thing we know, Kathryn's going on a date with Adam on board the *May's Flowers*." April stopped and frowned. "Why did you go with him if you don't want to be dating anyone? I don't get that ..."

Everyone turned various curious expressions to Kathryn, who made every effort to appear suddenly blasé. Unfortunately, she could feel the blush creeping up her neck. Hesitantly, she volunteered, "I sort of lost a bet ..."

"A bet?" Audrey exploded.

Meredith started to laugh. "Oh, this is priceless. You went out on a date with Adam because you *lost?*" She fell back on the sofa laughing hysterically.

"A bet," April repeated to herself and then shrugged. "So, again, it's no coincidence that you lost this bet, right?" She didn't wait for anyone to answer as she was deep into her train of thought, "and now everyone's thinking you should give him a chance and you do admit that you've got the hots for him."

"I never said that!" Kathryn exploded as everyone fell about in various stages of laughter.

"Oh, I don't know," said Lydia, trying to pull herself together, "you have used words like 'potential', 'handsome', 'intriguing' ... those could all add up to 'hot' I think."

Meredith's puzzled frown was overshadowed by her grin, "Maybe she said 'hot' and we just forgot that one ..." and then burst into laughing again.

"I didn't mean to tease you, Kat," April said quietly. "I just wanted you to see things the way I've been seeing them these last few weeks. For two people who are just 'acquaintances', you seem to be spending an awful lot of time together. That's all."

"Out of the mouths of babes," Audrey said in wonder as she wiped away the tears of laughter.

Sensing that Kathryn was at the end of her rope, Gwen turned everyone's attention towards April, "What are those brochures you've been clutching through dinner?"

April looked down at them, still in her hand. "I've had a lot on my mind this week and I wanted to talk to you all about something."

"You okay, honey?" Gwen asked.

April sighed. "My stepfather has offered to pay for me to go to nanny school. He says it's an excellent paying job and the fact that I love kids and pets so much might make me an excellent candidate."

"How do you feel about that?" Kathryn asked, happy to have the focus off her for once.

April shrugged. "I think I'd like to be a nanny. I think I'd be really good at it, too. I *am* good at taking care of children. I'm always being asked to baby sit, and I love helping out at church with the kids." She paused. "I'd have to give away my dogs, though. I don't know if I'd be able to keep coming here and I would sure miss everyone. That's scary."

Audrey piped up. "Why don't you just go take a look at the school before you get all up tight about it?" She rolled her eyes. "It's not like you've got anything big here that would stop you from getting away for a few days to go visit the school."

Meredith said thoughtfully, "Or, would your stepfather spring for an apartment off campus while you go to school there? You could bring your dogs then."

Kathryn offered, "Would you like me to make a few calls about the school and the living options?"

"Sure," April smiled, looking a bit hopeful. "I'd appreciate that, Kat."

Some things have to be believed to be seen.[43]

Chapter Fourteen

(Said with immense frustration and not a small bit of annoyance.) "This is absolutely ridiculous! When is this charade going to end? Do you know what people are saying? Edward and I have done our damnedest to keep this as quiet as possible and still they're talking!"

"I didn't ask you to keep this quiet, James. I don't care who knows. (Said with sarcasm and a bit of self-loathing.) I've never been a slave to public opinion. You know that."

(Sigh.) "So, when people ask me how you are doing and what you are up to, I'm just supposed to say, 'Oh, he's doing just fine. He's spending his remaining time on earth being a BUTLER'?"

(Said patiently, but firmly.) "This is more important to me than public opinion, James. You know that. He's my son. I know I was a lousy father for you and Edward, but my failure is far greater with Adam. It took you and I a while to get things settled. Can't you understand that I crave the same relationship with this man

[43] Ralph Hodgson, 1871-1962

that I have with you and Edward? Can you honestly tell me I should give up and just have a party the final moments of my life?"

(Said with resignation.) "What do you need, Dad. Tell me and I'll do it or get it or make it happen."

"Anything?"

(Completely resigned now.) "Yes, anything."

"Come to church with me on Sunday."

(Groan.) "Oh, great. I walked right into that one, didn't I? Did anyone ever tell you you're amazingly underhanded? I might even go so far as to call you 'shifty'."

(Chuckling.) "More than a few have, Son."

"LeGrande Incorporated."

"Hi, Miles, this is Kathryn McFadden."

"Hello, Ms. McFadden. And how are you today?"

"I'm fine. I'm calling with a request."

"I'm happy to be of service to you in any way I can."

"Could I arrange to have a lunch meeting with Adam, perhaps this Sunday?"

"Is this business or pleasure, Ms. McFadden? You see, Sunday is traditionally my day off and Mr. LeGrande is usually on his own."

"Actually, I think it's a little bit of everything." Kathryn resisted the urge to give more information than necessary, enjoying the chance to give Miles a bit of his own medicine.

"I see. Very well. Where shall I arrange this luncheon? Do you have a particular restaurant in mind?"

"Well, I was hoping we could have lunch on the back patio at the house. Is that possible?"

"It is not customary for Mr. LeGrande to eat outside on the patio. In fact, to the best of my knowledge, I cannot recall him ever stepping foot outside onto his property."

"I know. I'm thinking it might be time for him to branch out a bit."

"Luncheon here would require my presence, Ms. McFadden, since I am not only Mr. LeGrande's butler, I am also the chef."

"Yes, I know. Could you manage this for once? Please?"

After a pause Miles asked, "Is there something I should know, Ms. McFadden?"

"Maybe. Maybe not."

"I see." There was a significant pause once again. Finally, Miles said, "I attend church on Sunday mornings. Lunch would have to be later than usual. Perhaps as late as one-thirty."

"That would be fine. I attend church as well, so I wouldn't be able to get over there until about twelve-thirty or twelve-forty-five."

"Do you have a particular menu in mind, may I ask?"

"Nope. Actually I don't think there will be that much eating, in the end, so don't go overboard."

"Is that so?"

"Yup. That's so."

"Are you being purposely vague because you find it amusing or because you find it necessary?"

"Uh-huh."

"I see ... Tell me, Ms. McFadden, is Mr. LeGrande aware of this lunch plan or do I need to inform him?"

"Oh, you need to inform him, of course, Miles."

"Very well, Ms. McFadden."

"Thanks, Miles."

"Sir, Ms. McFadden called this morning and scheduled a luncheon date with you on Sunday."

Adam looked up frowning. "Sunday? Why Sunday?"

"It was not my place to question her choice of day, Sir. She simply requested me to schedule a luncheon date. Here. Out on the patio."

"*Outside? On the patio?*"

"Yes, Sir. I informed her of your aversion to all things natural, but she felt it was time for you to 'branch out a bit' I believe was how she put it."

Adam settled back in his chair. "Sunday is your day off. Am I going to have to order pizza? That's not exactly the way to impress a woman, you know."

"Ms. McFadden gave me the distinct impression that she wished me to be present, Sir. I assured her I would be willing to prepare something as long as the timing didn't conflict with church."

"Did you tell her she was cramping your style with the mayor? Don't you usually get some action after church? I should give her a call and tell her that …"

"That will not be necessary, Sir. As it happens, Mayor Willoughby is out of town this weekend."

"Ahh. High and dry, huh, Miles?"

"Is there something in particular you wish me to prepare for Sunday, Sir?"

"Nah, I'll leave it up to you," Adam said with complete disinterest.

"Very well, Sir."

"Good afternoon, Ms. McFadden. Right on time, I see. Mr. LeGrande, is, as usual, in his office." Kathryn followed Miles through the main hallway.

"I'm getting a little deja-vu here, Miles," she murmured.

"Those who cannot remember the past are condemned to repeat it," [44] Miles said cryptically. Kathryn waited patiently as Miles knocked on the office door and entered without waiting for a response. When moments passed without Miles announcing her, she peaked around him. The office was empty.

"Where is he, Miles?"

---

[44] George Santayana, 1863-1952

"I have no idea, Ms. McFadden. He's never anywhere but here." He actually sounded puzzled.

"Is that door open over there?" Kathryn observed as she stepped into the room and looked around. The last time she had been here she hadn't actually taken much time to admire the surroundings. She was too busy stifling the urge to kill.

Miles walked past her to stand in front of the French doors, one of which was open. "He's out in the garden," Miles said with wonder in his voice.

"Well, give a yell and let him know I'm here."

"Ms. McFadden," Miles said giving her a look of complete distain, "butlers *do not* yell," and stepped out into the garden.

"Gee, Miles," Adam said as they reentered the study moments later, "I know it's not my style, but if I'd realized that simply walking outside in my own garden would bother you so, I would have done it months ago."

"I just don't understand your rationale for going outside, Sir, when you knew full well that Ms. McFadden would be arriving at any moment. Your last meeting here, might I remind you, Sir, was abysmal. You certainly do not want a repeat performance."

"Well," Adam said, looking around, "where is she then? I thought you said she was waiting in the office? Did you scare her off?"

"Sir, I escorted Ms. McFadden here to your office. That's when I discovered you were not at your desk. It never occurred to me that I needed to instruct Ms. McFadden about where she should wait until our return."

Adam arched an eyebrow at his butler. "Messed that one up, didn't you?"

In retrospect, Kathryn wished that she could have had a photograph of both Miles' and Adam's expressions when she appeared at the door of the study. "Mr. LeGrande, Mr. Bishop, luncheon will be served on the back patio." She'd purposely dressed in a plain black skirt and a crisp white top with low heel shoes. With her hair pulled back in a no-nonsense pony-tail, one of Miles' apron's tied around her waist and, as a spur of the moment afterthought, a white linen cloth draped over her arm in place of gloves, she hoped she looked like the female version of Miles.

Adam was the first to recover with a slow, knowing grin creasing his face. "Well, well, well, Miles. Looks like you have some competition." Crossing his arms he sat down on the end of his desk. "What's for lunch, Katty-girl?"

"Sir," Kathryn said, struggling to keep her voice well modulated and the hysterical giggle deep in her throat, "I would prefer that you address me properly. 'Kathryn' will be fine. And in answer to your question, it appears that lunch will be ham and cheddar quiche with asparagus and a garden salad."

"And fresh orange wedges," Miles couldn't help but add, looking thoroughly perplexed.

"Sounds delicious," Adam said, enjoying Miles' confusion. "Lead the way. *Kathryn.*"

Miles had outdone himself with the table set for two: crystal, silver, china, and fresh flowers. Kathryn turned and gestured to the table. "If you'll have a seat, Sirs, I'll bring some iced tea."

"Table's only set for two, Kathryn. If Miles and I have a seat, there won't be a place for you." Adam looked at Miles and then back at Kathryn. "And there's no way I'd choose him over you. Even if you are dressed up in a 'D for dog' ugly outfit." He softened the comment with a wink.

"Sir," Kathryn said with a straight face, "the *help* never eats with the employer."

"Which is exactly why I am unable to sit down at this table, Ms. McFadden," Miles finally said.

Kathryn looked directly at Adam and waited. He didn't disappoint her. "Miles, you're fired. Now sit down like my … what are you? A butler-ess? Is that what I should call you?"

"I prefer 'majordomo'," Kathryn said with a slight smile.

Adam looked at Miles and then pulled out a cushioned patio chair and sat down. "Have a seat, Miles. I'm hungry and I'd like my majordomo to serve us." As Kathryn turned and headed into the kitchen, Adam watched her until she disappeared inside. He grinned wickedly at Miles.

"She's significantly better looking than you are even in those foolish butler clothes. If she hangs around long enough, maybe I can get her to wear a French maid's costume."

Adam sat while Miles stood, both staring at each other. *Patience, patience,* Adam thought, *you just might win the waiting game this time.*

Slowly, Miles removed his gloves and shoved them into his jacket pocket. Then he unbuttoned his coat, slipped it off and draped it across the back of the patio chair. Lastly, he loosened his tie and unbuttoned the top button of his dress shirt. Pulling out the chair, he finally sat down, and remained silent. Finally, Miles arched his eyebrows at Adam.

Kathryn brought out two plates of garden salad, dressing, a basket of fresh Italian bread, and a small dish of butter. Rushing back inside, she came out with a large pitcher of iced tea and filled both glasses. She stood for a moment watching both men, taking note of Miles' change in appearance and Adam's deceptively casual posture. "I see conversation is flowing freely," she said sarcastically.

Adam shrugged his shoulders looking out into the back garden, and Miles continued to stare at his son, expressionless.

"You know what?" She finally asked, leaning in so that both of them were forced to glance at her briefly. "You two can't be father and son. *You've got to be identical twins.*" Rolling her eyes, she stalked off into the kitchen.

"Doesn't hide her temper and exasperation as well as I do," Miles finally murmured.

"Yeah, but at least she doesn't rattle off annoying quotes all the time," Adam shot back.

Miles inclined his head. "You do have a point there, I suppose."

"Did a full background check on you the other day."

Miles rolled his eyes. "*It's about time.* Are you that lax with all your personal employees?" He shook his head in disgust.

"You're going to criticize *me?*" Adam said incredulously.

Miles shrugged. "Why not? I don't have to worry about *my job* anymore. And something tells me you're not going to give me good references, whether I keep my mouth shut or not."

"Stop it, Frick and Frack. Just stop it right now," Kathryn said from the kitchen doorway. She walked slowly toward them. Her voice rose to a fevered pitch. "When I last left you, you were both playing the 'I'm going to be silent longer than you' game. *Now,* you're both arguing about Miles' butler references?!"

"Miles," Kathryn said looking at him while gesturing to Adam. "This is your son, Adam LeGrande. He's a brilliant man with a chip on his shoulder the size of Cincinnati. You own much of it, unfortunately. But he's a *grown man*, Miles. He's going to sit here and listen to whatever you have to say." She glared at Adam for a moment and then looked back at Miles. "What you have in your favor, Miles, is your determination, despite insurmountable odds, to right a past wrong."

"Adam," she said, looking at him intensely while she pointed at Miles, "this is your father, Miles Bishop. *Your father.* Think back into your head and your heart and remember the time when you were a little boy and must have been dreaming of an image of the ultimate father. *Then take a look at what's sitting across from you.* A man who's literally dropped everything to try to retrieve something that is more precious, by far, than anything else in his life up until now. *You.*" She straightened up, smoothed her hair and adjusted her apron. Taking a deep breath she said, "The quiche will be ready in five minutes," and stalked off into the kitchen.

Miles chuckled briefly and then shook his head. "I had no idea how perfect she was when I met her."

"Don't you mean when you started manipulating her?"

Miles shrugged. "Call it whatever you like, Son."

"Don't call me that."

"What are you going to do if I refuse, Adam? Fire me again?"

"Get up and walk away from this table."

Miles glanced toward the kitchen at Kathryn bending down to take the quiche out of the oven. "Wonder how your majordomo's going to react to that." His lips twitching with humor.

Adam glanced into the kitchen, and Kathryn, holding the quiche with two potholders, looked out at him. Even from where they were sitting on the patio, both men could see her narrow her eyes filled with annoyance. He sighed. "I don't think I care to find out."

"Was there a time in your life that you dreamed of the ultimate father?" Miles asked quietly.

The silence hung between them, heavy and mournful. Adam's mind flashed with images of his mother's neglect, his classmate's scorn, his own desperation and loneliness. He'd spent a lot of time in his own head, pondering the way of things, tearing apart new discoveries, and applying them to different venues. And yeah, there were many times when he'd dreamed of a … father. Sheila had never revealed any information other than how completely unwanted he had been. Adam had a flash that made his gut clench and his heart race. Had Miles even known of him back then? He looked Miles directly in the eye. He was doing his 'I can wait forever face'. "Yeah," Adam said at last, shrugging like it was no big deal, "I had my own fantasy father thing going for a while." He studied Miles' face. "The only thing Sheila ever told me of you was that you didn't want me. Was that true?"

Miles' face drained of color and a look of real pain flashed across his face. He seemed to struggle with himself for a moment and then he said, without breaking Adam's gaze, "Yes. That's true. When your mother came and told me she was pregnant with you I offered her a substantial amount of money to go away and not come back. She took it." When Adam showed no reaction, Miles said, "I don't suppose you believe me, but there is nothing in my life that I regret more than that conversation."

Adam shrugged, his 'I couldn't care less face' carefully in place. "Well, it sure shows me what a lousy businessman you were back then. You could have saved a substantial amount of money by offering to take me off her hands. I'm sure she would have done *that* for a whole lot less than what you ended up paying in the end. She always made it perfectly clear how she would have preferred me *not* in her life either."

Another pause, loaded with unsaid words. "I'm sorry I left you with her."

Another shrug. "I managed." Adam threw his arms out wide. "Look how far I've come. Pretty impressive considering."

"Yes," Miles nodded, "very impressive. Considering."

"So, why the big turnaround, huh? Why all of a sudden do you show up on my doorstep? At first I thought you were after my money. That would have made perfect sense to me. Or you were interested in tapping into my business influence in some way. Recently, I've thought you had some vendetta against me and were trying to drive me insane for some misguided attempt at revenge. I just can't wrap my head around it. You *didn't* want me and you were willing to pay a huge amount of money to accomplish that, and then years later you have this magnanimous turnaround and want to have some kind of relationship. What, are you dying? Do you need a kidney or bone marrow or something?"

"Adam!" Kathryn said in horrified tones, "I can't believe you'd say such a thing." She placed a quiche on the table along with a covered dish of asparagus tips.

Giving her a sideways glance, Adam said, "What happened to "Sir", Kathryn? Usually I don't allow the help to be so familiar."

Placing her hands on her hips she said, "Oh, that's how it's going. Things are getting difficult so you're falling into your 'nasty, obnoxious, and downright rude' persona." Walking back into the kitchen she returned moments later with serving utensils and a dish of orange wedges. "I'd say, Miles, if he's getting nasty then you must be on the right track."

When she went to walk away, Adam grabbed her arm. "Stay, Kathryn. I want you here."

"Miles?" she asked.

Miles nodded. "You're more than welcome to stay, Ms. McFadden."

Turning, she dragged over another chair, settled it by the table, and sat down. Adam, without asking her, reached over and dragged the chair close enough to him that he could drape his arm across the back of it. When she turned to look at him he gave her his 'don't mess with me expression' which caused her to roll her eyes.

"So, how's it going?" Kathryn finally asked in the ensuing silence. "You should both know that if you force me to sit out here it is not in my nature to remain a silent observer. Take it or leave it." At their continued silence, she sighed. "How much ground have you two covered?"

"Miles has admitted he never wanted me and paid my mother a truckload of money to get us to disappear."

Kathryn looked at Miles' pained expression. "I give you credit, Miles. I don't know if I would have had the courage to admit something like that." She looked at Adam. "He could have lied, you know. There's certainly no one to prove him wrong."

Adam's gaze flickered at Miles. Miles looked thoughtfully at Kathryn. Kathryn sighed and looked at Adam. "What have you admitted?"

"He admitted that he'd dreamed of a father figure," Miles said quietly.

Kathryn looked at Adam, searching his face. "Honesty. Painful stuff, huh?" she whispered and reached over to take his hand.

She looked at both of them. "So, Miles. Did life run smoothly once you cleared up the mess with Adam and his mother?"

Miles looked at her. "No, Kathryn. My life has never run smoothly to the best of my recollection."

"How so, Miles?" At his intense stare but continued silence, Kathryn leaned forward and said fiercely. "Here's your chance, Miles. Grab it while you can. What did you say to me a while back? *This opportunity would be worth anything'?"* She turned and glanced over her shoulder at Adam sitting stiffly next to her then back at Miles. Tension radiated up her arm as Adam continued to hold on tightly to her hand. In a loud stage whisper she said to Miles, *"Don't mess this up."*

There were long moments of silence as the three of them sat in the beautiful early summer afternoon. Finally, Miles took a deep breath and began to speak. "Adam, I am a gigantic failure in every area that counts: family, integrity, honesty, love. By the time I realized this, most of my life had passed me by in a flurry of inconsequential things that for the longest time I thought were ..." he hesitated and then closed his eyes as if in intense pain, "worth the sacrifice."

Forcing his eyes open, Miles looked at his son. "It may sound trite, but I found God, Adam. The secret of eternal life. And with it the knowledge that put my whole sorry life into stark, honest perspective. Suddenly, things that had been important to me no longer held any sway, things that I had been dismissive about, even scornful, became huge, unbearable voids that I realized I could never replace." Tears formed in his eyes and he made no effort to hide them or stop them. "I became determined, energized, committed … that wherever I had failed I would work until my last breath to repair.

"I have a good relationship now with your half-brothers, James and Edward. They know who you are and what I've been doing this past year even though they think I've lost my mind to have been serving as your butler." He laughed mirthlessly. "They have supported me, encouraged me, and listened to me even though they don't always understand me.

"I was unable to salvage my last marriage. Surprisingly, the fact that I found God was something my wife couldn't cope with … she'd struggled with many things over the course of our marriage, including me. We parted … I have been uninvolved romantically since then. Despite what you assume, my relationship with June Willoughby has been based on friendship, not romance. I have been very honest with her about that. The time in my life for romance is long over.

"Most of my personal financial assets have been given or directed toward worthy charities. I live comfortably, but no longer in the appalling luxury I once considered my right." He smiled at Adam. "Living here has been quite nice, actually."

Miles stretched out his arms. "So, here I am, Adam. God is teaching me patience, humility, love …" He smiled again. "I find myself intensely proud of you, even when you are annoying, offensive, and dictatorial. I've had more enjoyment than you ever could imagine working here for you. At least I've had a chance to spend time with you and get to know you and …" he shrugged, "sharpen my wits and spar with you." He leaned forward toward Adam, a fresh trail of tears spilling down his cheeks. *"It is absolutely better than nothing."*

There was silence when Miles finished talking. Even the birds and the early summer bugs seemed to be quiet. When Miles reached out and picked up his glass of iced tea to take a sip, Kathryn couldn't help herself and took to a sip of Adam's glass. She risked a glance at Adam and he was gazing off into the garden in stony silence.

"My parents abandoned me at five while attending a Grateful Dead concert," she blurted out. "They'd been trying to lose me for a couple of years," she laughed a high, slightly hysterical laugh, "but I was pretty good at keeping up with them. Through the foster care system, I was adopted by a very nice couple who were killed in a car crash four months after my adoption was final. I was raised by my adoptive father's mother. I called her Gran. I am the woman I am because of her love and care. She taught me what was important, what was worth forgetting, and what was worth fighting for."

She took a deep breath, trying to still her unsteady voice. "I always had *piles* of dreams about what a *real* dad would be like, since I never had a father figure of any kind. He would be tall and laugh a lot. He would pick me up and swing me high over his head whenever he came home from work. He would wear," she felt herself blushing, "loafers with very, very shiny pennies in them and would always smell good. He would never shout, never hit, and always want to hold my hand *tightly* whenever we went out somewhere. We would live in a house with curtains on the windows and flowers in the garden and I would have a bedroom with a *real bed* and a pair of black patent leather shoes with black bows on the front. And he would call me," Kathryn realized that both men were staring at her intently, "Kitten." She helped herself to another sip of Adam's iced tea, now thoroughly mortified by her outburst. "I don't think I've ever told anyone about my dad dream before," she said quietly. "Not even Gran."

"When did Gran die, Kathryn?" Miles asked quietly.

"When I was just twenty. I had fifteen wonderful years with her." She looked at Miles. "She always said that the two best gifts God ever gave her were me first and extra time second."

Miles nodded in complete understanding.

Kathryn looked at Adam, who was still staring intently at her, still holding her hand. "*I wish*," she said in the barest of whispers, "that my father had wanted a relationship with me when I was born rather than choosing to abandon me. *I wish* that my adoptive father had not died before I got to know him and love him. *I wish* that my Gran was still alive today to see what good things I'm doing with my God-given talents and money." She shrugged. "I don't think I ever wished that my real father would show up on my doorstep announcing who he was and willingly serve as my butler for a year just to be near me. *But I wouldn't turn it down.*"

There is no revenge so complete as forgiveness.[45]

Chapter Fifteen

"What's your name, honey?"

(Shrugs shoulders.)

"Just a first name will do. Is it Beth? You look pretty enough to be a 'Beth'."

(Shakes head vigorously. Begins swinging legs rapidly. Clutches paper bag tightly.)

"Those are nice flip-flops. Do you know blue is my favorite color?"

"My Momma took them from the store. I wored them out when the man wasn't lookin'. I wanted the panties with the flowers on them, too, but Momma said there was no time."

"I see. What's in your bag? Will you please show me?"

"My collection. Poppa says I gots too much junk. So I can only keep what I can carry in this bag. If I pick little things, then I can have more of 'em." *(Opens up bag and carefully dumps contents on desk.)*

"My, my! Look at this excellent collection of ... beer bottle caps. Wow. Do you know how many you have altogether?"

---

[45] Josh Billings, 1818-1885

(Nods proudly.) "I can count real good. Twenty-seven. Four gold ones, twelve silver ones, one blue one, and ten black ones with a green dot. I play games with them."

"Maybe we should put your name on the bag so if you misplace it, then whoever finds it will know to return it to you."

(Shakes head.) "You don't need no name to get lost or found. I don't always have a name and up until now I hardly ever got lost. You just need to hold on very, very tight and not ever let go. (Shakes head vigorously again and frowns.) You can't let go. Not even for a minute." (Sighs in resignation.) "I letted go of Momma's skirt. Now they're gone for good."

"Her skirt?"

(Nods head.) "Uh-huh. Momma said if I wanted to stay with her and Poppa I had to keep up on my own or I was gonna be on my own. I lost my flip flop in that big crowd and I stopped to put it back on and Momma kept going and I couldn't hold on to her skirt and ..." (Sighs.)

"Here, let me help you get your ... collection ... back in your bag."

"You're a nice man. You wanna call me Katy? That's one of my favoritest names."

"What do you want from me, Miles? I think you're hoping for things that I'm not capable of giving."

Kathryn turned to Adam. "What are you incapable of giving?"

Adam searched her face and realized she was serious. "Kathryn, you've been around me on and off for six weeks. You've got to have a pretty good impression of what I'm all about. You've seen me at just about my worst, and I've shared some of my personal demons with you." At her blank expression, Adam turned impatiently to Miles and said, "I'm incapable of forgiving. Anyone. Anything."

Miles nodded like Adam had just changed the time for dinner. "All right."

The answer was totally unexpected. Adam would have expected something more clever. Perhaps a quote or two on the perils of latent anger and the inability to forgive.

"Have you forgiven me?" Kathryn asked, drawing Adam's attention back to her.

Adam looked at her in complete confusion and was stunned to realize that she was again serious. "I have nothing to forgive you for!"

She rolled her eyes. "Of course you do! Not four weeks ago you called me the most abrasive, unyielding, holier-than-thou person you had ever met in all your life. It just about devastated me, but the reality was you were accurate. Do you still have that opinion of me?"

Letting out a blast of frustrated air, Adam said, "Of course not! Lately I've been thinking that ..." he caught himself and glanced quickly at Miles and then at Kathryn.

"Thinking what?" Miles asked.

"None of your damned business," Adam growled at him. This whole scene was getting way out of hand. Time to cut losses and move on. He made to stand up but Kathryn stopped him by placing her hand on his tense arm.

"You also said," Kathryn persisted, "that I was completely unlikable."

"Ahh, jeeze," Adam moaned, finally letting go of Kathryn's hand and cradling his head in his hands.

"You certainly covered all the bases fast," Miles observed.

Adam looked up and glared at Miles. "I told you ..."

Kathryn's hand on Adam's arm tightened. She glanced at Miles, "You are not helping here," she admonished. "Adam," she spoke quietly, but he refused to look at her, feeling a lot more satisfied glaring his hatred at his father. "I know you don't think that way about me anymore, but you certainly did at one point. You can't deny it. What I'm trying to get across is that at some point over the course of this ... relationship we have," that got Adam to look at her sharply, "whether you realize it or not, you forgave me for things I said and did that were 'holier-than-thou, unyielding, and abrasive.' Forgiveness is a precious, precious thing. And we all have capacity for it. Some just use it more frequently than others."

"Okay," Adam said hotly looking at Miles and feeling an anger of a proportion he never remembered experiencing before, "maybe I've got the capacity to forgive, but I sure as hell don't have the capacity to forget."

"I wouldn't expect you to," Miles murmured quietly. "I certainly never will."

Throwing his arms out wide, Adam shouted, "So what exactly do you want from me then? Let's hear it. Sum it up. Spit it out."

"I know," Kathryn said as she drew a deep breath, stood and began gathering up the uneaten meal. Reaching over she touched Miles on the shoulder. "He wants two things, Adam. One you can give him and one God can." Miles looked at Kathryn and both of their eyes filled with tears. Finally she looked at Adam. "Miles would like you simply to give him a chance. And he'd like God to give him a little more time."

"Oh, and I'm giving you my notice," Kathryn said as she picked up the remaining dishes off the patio table. "I'm not cut out for this majordomo stuff and definitely not for the chef part. I've already burned my hand on the quiche plate."

"Gee, I was hoping to move you out of the butler clothes into a very nice, very short French maid's uniform," Adam said, feeling much better in comfortable conversational territory.

"Yeah, I bet you were," she huffed and stalked away.

"I'd be willing to stay until you found an assistant to replace me," Miles offered.

Adam stared at him. "Will you lose the butler duds and the annoying quotes?"

Miles allowed a slight smile. "I can give in on the clothing. Keeping those gloves white was a real chore. But the quotation inclination has been with me all my life. That will be significantly harder."

Adam stared at Miles, who looked back at him with a bland expression. Waiting. Always waiting. Adam sighed. "Okay. We'll give it a try."

"I can't believe it!! This is way better than any soap opera I've ever watched," Meredith said with a real amazement in her voice. "Never in a million years would I have thought to do something like that."

"You really dressed up like a butler and served them lunch?" Even April was stunned.

"Yeah," Kathryn said, "but nobody ate anything at all and I was the one who drank Adam's iced tea."

April frowned. "I don't think real butlers are supposed to do that."

Audrey rolled her eyes and Kathryn tried not to laugh.

"So, spill it," Lydia demanded. "Let's hear the entire account. Including any kissing."

Kathryn sighed, rolling her eyes in frustration. "There was no kissing. Don't you understand? It was a very intense, very emotional time! And, I'm sorry, I can't tell you anything specific. It's very private. I shouldn't have even been there but Adam insisted and Miles said it was fine with him. I've told you all I can right now. I played butler while Miles and Adam talked. The fact that the two of them actually had a dialogue, other than Adam ordering Miles around and Miles saying, "Yes, Sir, no, Sir" every five minutes, is huge."

"There's much more to this relationship than just employee and employer, isn't there?" Pattilou asked.

"Yes," Kathryn said quietly, "much more. I've only shared this with you because I'd like you all to keep them in your prayers. Big time. This is the first step on a very long road."

"I bet you did more than serve lunch, Kat," Gwen said quietly, almost to herself. "I'll bet you initiated the whole thing." Kathryn gave her very wise friend a wink.

"Well, I know for certain that there's no way you would have been able to keep your mouth shut," Audrey said emphatically. "No. Way. And I'll bet you were stellar with what you decided to say, too."

"Thanks, Audrey," Kathryn murmured.

"I call 'em like I see 'em, good and bad," Audrey pointed out.

Kathryn did laugh then. "Well, I assisted in something that needed to be done, with both actions and words. Heaven knows how long it would have taken those two to sit down and finally talk if I hadn't."

"So, we're not going to get to know anything? I feel like I'm reading a mystery novel," Meredith groaned.

"Yeah," Kathryn said under her breath as she rolled her eyes, "we'll call it *The Butler Did It*."

"It was a huge compliment that both men wanted you there," Pattilou observed. "For someone who claims not to do so well with personal relationships, I'd say you're very much in demand. I hope you're taking note of that."

"Have you and Adam acknowledged that there is something special going on between you two yet?" Lydia asked, taking a sip of her coffee. "You can at least tell us that."

"Will you all stop this?" Kathryn hastily said, "Adam's got a lot more important things on his mind than his dating schedule." As an afterthought she added, "And so do I. We're friends, okay? He's sought my help and advice, I've responded as best I could. I think I've made a positive contribution and I'm pleased with that."

"Relationships have started on a heck of a lot less than what you've just described, Kat," Pattilou said. "Actions really do speak louder than words. And what you're telling about Adam LeGrande says a heck of a lot."

"It seems pretty obvious to me," April said with a sigh. "You might not have found your prince yet, but you're not hanging out with a frog anymore either."

"Well said, April," Gwen grinned.

"You'd better start thinking about someone else to fix your stepbrother up with, huh?" Meredith teased.

"You know, we're always calling him "your stepbrother," Lydia observed. "What's his name?"

April stared at Lydia for long moments without responding.

"Earth to April," Audrey finally said.

"Ah," April said, "I've never been formally introduced to him, you know."

"Tell me you don't know his name," Audrey said with an edge of impatience. She turned to Gwen. "That would be the topper to everything she's ever done so far."

"I know his name, it's just … well, my stepfather asked me not to spread it around."

Now April had everyone's undivided attention.

"Why would he do something like that?" Pattilou asked puzzled.

"Yeah, that sounds sinister … shifty even," Lydia said.

"Shifty?!" Kathryn murmured frowning. Suddenly, she looked at April. "April, what's your stepfather's name?"

April looked directly at Kathryn. "I call him 'Dad'. I've been doing that for years." She sighed. "But that's not what you're asking, is it?"

Kathryn shook her head.

"Well, my stepfather was married to my mom, Jennifer, for about three years. I was about eleven when they got married. My real dad died of a heart attack, you know. Just keeled over at his desk at the bank. His secretary found him. I loved my dad a lot and was pretty upset when he died. My mom," April sighed and looked at Gwen, "she was really beautiful and always dressed up really nice. But she was always sad and it made me pretty sad, too. It was always hard to please her, even before my dad died, but it was way worse afterwards. I just never seemed to measure up or say or do the right thing. When my stepfather started dating my mom, things got happier again for a while. When they got married, I was glad." She shrugged and looked at the group. "My mom got happy for a while.

"But then my stepfather got cancer and my mom," she fiddled with the yellow fringe on her shawl, "started saying stuff about being cursed and how bad luck followed her wherever she went and when was she going to be cut a break. I remember her screaming that her whole life had been nothing but one misery after another. My stepfather," she frowned, deep in thought, "was really different after the cancer. I mean, he was nice to me before, but after the cancer he was a changed man. He tried real hard to talk and keep my mom calm, tried to reassure both of us that the cancer was taken care of. I remember him always rejecting Mom's constant claim of bad luck. He talked for the first time ever about God and faith and trust." April looked at the silent women around her. "You'd think that the fact that he didn't die from the cancer and became even nicer afterwards would have been great but it wasn't ... Not for my mom anyway."

April was silent for long, long moments. "My mom killed herself. She took lots of sleeping pills one night." The ladies looked at each other. No one had known. Slowly, each one of them moved over closer to April and touched her somehow: her shoulder, her hand, her knee, the top of her head. "That's when my stepfather legally adopted me. Up until then, he wasn't my real dad, just the man my mom was married to. But I didn't really have anyone else and he said he'd be proud if I let him legally claim me as his daughter." She sighed and gave them all a tremulous smile. "So I did." Earnestly she said, "My stepfather is a really nice man."

"And his name is Miles Bishop, isn't it, April?" Kathryn said softly.

"Yeah," she nodded. "He always encouraged me to keep a 'low profile' - that's what he called it - when it came to the fact that my real father was pretty rich because of all the banks his family owned and I was the only child and when I turn thirty I get like a really big trust fund." April looked at Kathryn. "Then, you know, my stepfather is pretty rich. My two stepbrothers, Edward and James are rich, too, but not as much as my stepbrother, Adam. My stepfather said that there are a lot of people out there who would only want to be friends with me because of my money and that I should always be careful."

April gave them a brilliant smile. "It never ever mattered who I was with you guys. You love me just for what I am. Just like my stepfather. He likes to hear all my stories about you and he says he sleeps better at night knowing that I have all of you close to talk to and hang out with. He always tells me that he likes 'my style' and my 'free spirit way of looking at things'." She studied the fringe in her lap. "He bought me this shawl ..." she said absently. "He also," she took a deep breath, "says that there was nothing he or I could have done to make my mom any happier or to have stopped her from ... well, you know."

Kathryn looked up at all the serious, silent faces, then back at April. "So you've known all along about Miles and Adam and … me?"

"Oh yeah," April nodded, looking at Kathryn. "My stepfather," she swallowed, "his cancer came back. That's why he stopped working at his other job and let James take over, and that's why he's at Adam's now. He's real worried about Adam and is trying to do as much as he can. He knew about you, because I tell him about all of you. He wanted to know if you were married or dating and," she looked at Gwen, "I was already praying, you know, about Kathryn being alone. Well, when I said that I knew you weren't dating anyone and I was praying about *exactly that* he said that he'd already met you at some meeting at Adam's work and had really been impressed with you." April glanced at Kathryn. "We kind of made a prayer pact about you and about Adam. Not that you two would end up together but that the Lord would provide opportunities for the two of you to get to know each other."

April looked at all of her Bible study friends and smiled tentatively. "Hasn't it been cool the way God's been answering our prayers?"

Audrey chuckled at Kathryn's stunned expression. "Absolutely *amazing.*"

"How are you doing?" Kathryn finally asked Adam as they sat on the bench outside the local ice cream parlor. She didn't need to elaborate; they both knew what she was specifically referring to. They'd just finished a casual meal and now were enjoying the restaurant's claim to fame: homemade ice cream. Throughout dinner they had both studiously avoided mentioning Miles. Instead, they had talked about what had happened over the course of the past week - *since* Sunday: each other's work, the weather, and even, when they had gotten somewhat desperate, Kathryn's Bible study compatriots. That had guaranteed a few laughs. Kathryn's gentle probing had been unable to reveal how much or how little Adam knew about his stepsister, April. Given all of the things he'd had thrown at him this past week, *and* the fact that he'd spent an entire week working with Miles, his father, rather than Miles, his butler, Kathryn felt it was prudent not to provide anymore surprising or shocking family information. At this time.

"He's the most patient man I know," Adam said in frustration. It was obviously not a compliment, either. "Sometimes I wish Miles would just haul off and punch me. Then I'd know how to deal with everything."

"Sure, then you'd punch him back, throw him out, and that would be the end of your relationship with him."

Adam looked at her pointedly. *"Exactly.* Instead, he's just as efficient as ever, without all the butler clothes and the "sirs" being thrown at me every five seconds." He shook his head in disgust. "If he wasn't a multimillionaire and my father to boot, he'd be the perfect business assistant."

"You know, he told me that every time he called you 'sir' he was calling you 'son' in his head."

"Don't tell me that stuff, Kathryn. *It doesn't help.* Honest it doesn't."

"I'm sorry."

Adam leaned over and put his arm around her. "Can we talk about a different subject?"

"Okay."

"You referred to 'this relationship' we have between us last Sunday. Care to elaborate?"

Looking at him this close, his huge green eyes framed with dark long auburn lashes staring intently at her, she responded the best way she knew how. "Absolutely not."

"Why not?"

She took a lick of her ice cream, to stall for a moment, and then said, "Why do we need to discuss anything? I don't see a need."

"So, if I attend this stupid country club get-together Miles says I have to go to on Sunday and the usual thing happens where some intelligent and highly ambitious young woman tries to pick me up, and I'm in the mood, it's okay if I just ... let her?"

Kathryn swallowed and shrugged. "If you're in the mood ..."

"Course, if I had some attractive, brown haired, brown-eyed fantasy scenario woman on my arm, well then, that might keep the other women at bay, you know. But then, that fantasy woman would have to put up with all the gossip and scandal of being seen out in public *in a nonprofessional setting* with me." He popped the rest of his cone in his mouth and crunched it. Reaching up, he twirled a piece of hair that had come loose from her hair clip around his finger.

"Maybe that same woman already has an escort for the country club function."

He grinned, whispering in her ear. "You have all the classic body language when you lie, Katty-girl. You look away," he reached up to capture her chin and turn her head so she was once again facing him, "you smile, but it doesn't reach your eyes," he reached up to touch her lips briefly and then the outside edges of her eyes, "and you work to keep some object between the two of us," he said with a grin when she determinedly brought the last of her ice cream to her mouth and popped it in. Kathryn crunched her cone, smiled brilliantly and looked him straight in the eye. "Come on, will you brave the gossip and go with me to the country club thing? You know how much I hate to go. It would be fun if I had you nearby to grope and tease and try to fluster."

"Wow, that sounds like so much fun," she managed once she had swallowed.

"Do you remember on Sunday when I started to say that 'lately I had been thinking' and then I never finished?" She nodded tentatively. "I was going to say, but I chose not to because of *the audience* at the time, that lately I had been thinking that I would like to really get to know you. *Really know you.* But I realize, I mean, it makes perfect sense that *you* would have to feel the same way about me. You're on my mind all the time, Kathryn. In business situations, I catch myself before I say harsh things sometimes because I can hear your voice in my head or I can imagine an expression on your face. You have *no idea* how many times a day I *don't* call you. I'm so inept at this whole 'relationship thing' that I don't want to come across as a stalker or anything!"

He reached up and cupped her cheek. "I'm trying here, Katty-girl. You've seen some really bad examples of how I can be, so at least I don't have to worry that you're ill informed. Then you said something on Sunday and I thought maybe, *just maybe*, you're feeling similar things about me? I know you seem to dislike this word because you hung up on me the last time I used it, but don't you think the two of us have *potential* to have some kind of a romantic relationship? I promise to do my best to be tolerable. And you can correct me whenever you see me getting out of hand. And whenever I …"

Kathryn kissed him to shut him up. It was easier and much more enjoyable. He sat very, very still while she reached up and touched his face, letting her hands and then her arms wrap around his neck. Finally, when he seemed certain that she wasn't going to be scared away, he reciprocated and wrapped his arms around her.

Driving her home, Adam said, "Now about the dress you're going to wear to this shindig on Sunday. Do you have *anything* low cut? Or short? Or tight? Tight would be good. I *love spandex* …"

"Church is at ten fifteen a.m. Sunday," Kathryn pointed out.

"*Huh?*"

"You heard me. You want a relationship, you want to get to *know me*," she glanced at him out of the corner of her eye, "you want to find out if I even *own* any spandex, you'd better embrace the whole picture, Sweetheart."

"You want me to go to church with you?" He sounded mildly horrified.

Kathryn thought about it. At first she'd just been teasing him, trying to counteract his comments about her wardrobe. But she might as well be honest. She looked at him. "Yeah, I'd like you to go to church with me. No one I've ever been involved with before has done it."

That got him. "Really? Why not?"

She sighed. "I don't know. Probably a little bit my fault. I never took a stand or expressed the desire. Part of it their fault; they just weren't interested."

"I'll go to church with you if you want."

"*Really?*"

Adam shrugged. "Yeah. That way I can see what all the hype is about. See if I can figure out what the big deal is." He grinned an evil grin. "See how much I can misbehave in a place of holiness."

"Oh great," she said, already seriously beginning to doubt the wisdom of this entire relationship, "just the attitude I was hoping for."

Pray that your loneliness may spur you into finding
something to live for, great enough to die for.[46]

Chapter Sixteen

(Shakes head and tries hard not to cry. Sighs.) "I couldn't make her happy. I tried to be good. I tried to dress nice. I know I'm not very pretty, but I tried always to keep my hair neat like she wanted me to. I used to draw her pictures when I was little but ..."

"April. Listen to me. I know you loved your mother. No one doubts that. No one. But sometimes, people get so sad that there is nothing anyone can do. Nothing at all. It's just the way of things and not something that you need to carry with you to weigh you down." (Smile.) "This is a special day! Today you officially become my daughter! My One and Only One! Remember I told you I had a surprise for you? Remember I said we were going to go out to a special restaurant for lunch to celebrate?"

(Nods head curiously and looks around at the sights where they have just parked. Get out of car and take Miles' hand.)

"Wow, are we going on that boat ... Dad?"

---

[46] Dag Hammarskjold, 1905-1961

"Yes. But first you have to see something." (Walks to the back of the boat.)
Do you see the boat's name?"

"May's Flowers."

"Right. Today is the start of new things, April. April's showers will become
May's Flowers. *Have you heard that saying? We, you and I, are going to take this*
very sad time of tears and loneliness over your Mom's death, and we're going to make a
new start today. Today, we are officially father and daughter. Today, we're going to let
the sadness bloom into something pretty and bright. Just like you."

"I want to sit in the back."

"What, you think God can't see you back there?" Kathryn teased.

"Forget God, I don't want the preacher getting any ideas. Places
that rely on donations tend to go nuts when I show up. For all I know,
he'll take one look at me and invite me up on stage."

"Number one, the minister is a 'she'. Number two, it's called the
altar, not the stage."

"The minister is a woman?"

"Yes," Kathryn smiled at him. "And also the covert president of
the She-Woman-Man-Haters Club, Religious Chapter."

"Is that why you chose this church?"

"I chose this church because they embrace sound Biblical doctrine
and preach the truth. The original minister, Reverend Samuel Invers,
recently retired. Pastor Kiloski has been here just two years. I like her a lot,
not because of her gender, but because of her sincerity, knowledge, and
overall wonderful personality."

"Hrmph," he said as he settled himself next to her in the very last
pew and began to glance through the bulletin.

"Do we have to go through *all* of this stuff before we get sprung?!"
he whispered in her ear, purposely getting close and giving her a delicious
shiver. He seemed to read her mind because before she could respond he
added, "Hey, I like this whole close whispering thing. I think I'm going to
talk like this to you the whole service," and then he kissed her lightly on the
ear.

"Behave, Adam.

"Maybe," he murmured again, far too close, "you should say 'down boy' instead."

They sang hymns, chuckled at the antics of the children during the children's sermon, shared Kathryn's Bible during the scripture reading, sat through the sermon, and then received the minister's final blessing before they left. It wasn't until they were in the car driving toward Adam's house that Kathryn said, "Well?"

"You know what my favorite part was?"

"I'm afraid."

Adam shook his head. "No, don't be. I'm serious. My favorite part was the last thing the minister said about before, and behind ..." He frowned and shook his head. "Darn, I wanted to remember that."

Kathryn grinned. "The Lord go with you: before you to prepare your path, behind you to encourage you, beside you to befriend you, above you to watch over you, beneath you in trouble times to carry you, and, most importantly, within you, giving His abiding love and peace now and forevermore."

"Yeah! That part. I liked that. I never thought about God being that constantly present before. God's always been this big impersonal entity for me that people build churches for and fight wars over."

"God's been very personal to me. I'm a different person because of it." She glanced at Adam as he zipped along the side streets. "That doesn't mean I'm smarter or better or even less inclined to make mistakes. It just means I've got a special support, a unique defense, and a superior resource."

"I can't picture you much different than you already are, Kathryn," Adam said doubtfully. "I think you've always been perky, fun loving, and smart."

She looked at him pointedly. "You're wrong. Very wrong. I was a very angry person in my late teens and early twenties. Bitter about how my parents abandoned me - I didn't even have a name! - and angry with God for taking away my adoptive parents who seemed so much a dream come true. Then Gran got diagnosed with a reoccurrence of her cancer and I was," she sighed and looked out the window, "enraged. A lot of my determination to succeed was fueled by that. The anger morphed into hatred and bitterness. Finally depression."

"I can't believe what you're telling me!" Adam finally said glancing in her direction but she continued to look out the car passenger window.

"Oh, believe it," she said quietly. "I searched for … happiness, peace, contentment … *something good* in all sorts of bizarre places: men, work, money, power. For a while there, I was really ripping up the pavement in my quest. Gran tried to talk me down to the right plain. Tried to get me to listen to reason. I loved her with all my heart so I tried to please her at least on the surface. I went to church, said the right things when I was around her, told her the stories that she wanted to hear. But she was a really smart woman, Adam. She knew exactly what I was doing. She never stopped loving me but she wasn't happy with me by a long shot."

"How did your Gran get you to change your mind? How did she make you see things her way?"

Kathryn turned and looked at Adam. "*She died.*" Then she went back to looking out the window.

They rode in silence for a while. Finally Kathryn said in a voice choked with emotion. "After Gran died I realized I had two choices. I could keep doing what I was doing, heading where I was heading - feeling angry, and empty, and bitter and … *miserable*. Or, I could try to make a change." There was a long pause. "I could *finally* hear what Gran had been saying and *really believe it*. I chose to make a change. I gave up the fight. Put it all in God's hands. Asked Him to take control of my life and make me into the woman he wanted me to be."

Adam glanced at her after a time. "That's it?" Adam said. "You just made a decision to change? Just 'poof!' and like some magic formula you're the happy, loving Kathryn I see right now?" They slowly entered the gates of his property and drove up the long, winding driveway.

"*I wish.*" Shaking her head, Kathryn said, "Not by a long shot. I made the *decision* that day, but it's been a long road to where I am today. I am thankful to God for His constant love, patience, persistence, and forgiveness. I made most of my money in the market during the years after

Gran died. I started to attend church because *I* wanted to, and I read the Bible, studied, and learned. I kept making mistakes with guys for a long time after Gran died, too." She made a sad, moan. *"I was so terribly lonely.* I thought that if I could just get married and have a family, I wouldn't feel so alone. But I didn't have my head or my heart straight. I didn't know what I needed to make myself *right*, so how could I choose somebody else to spend my life with who was right? I got within six weeks of marrying someone but called it off in the end. That's why I haven't been dating for almost six years."

"*Six years!*"

She laughed at the incredulous tone of his voice. "Yup. Six years." Kathryn smiled at Adam. They were parked in the garage now sitting in the cool dimness. "One good decision led to another, though. I quit working on Wall Street, stopped living in the city, moved out here to the suburbs, and started Advancement Corporation. These last few years I've felt happier - with myself and with my life - than I ever have. There's a peace that surrounds me that I realize was what I was searching for."

Glaring at Adam she said, "Until I met you and you insulted me and upset me enough that I talked about you to the Bible study ladies and they made some ... observations ... about certain voids in my life."

"Like?"

"Like one made a suggestion that I become a nun."

That made him burst out laughing.

"Keep laughing, buddy, that's my life: a huge comedy," Kathryn said but she gave him a sweet smile.

"Come inside. We'll see if there's anything to eat, okay?" Adam unfolded himself from the car and came around to hold the door for her and help her out. "Keep talking. This is a great story."

"That's pretty much it." She held both arms out in the garage. "Here I am."

Adam crowded her against his car, wrapping his arms around her waist. Kathryn automatically embraced him and he smiled into her upturned face. "I'm glad you're here. I'm even glad about your 'nun status'." She made a rude noise in the back of her throat. He couldn't resist and kissed her. Against her lips he murmured, "Maybe these good choices you've been making will rub off on me."

She reached up to touch his face. "You think so? I'd like you to have peace, happiness, contentment … You give the impression that demons chase you wherever you go." She smoothed his hair, pushing down the ever-present cowlick at the back of his head. "Just understand what I'm telling you, okay? *I* didn't make the change, *I* made the decision. God caused the changes in me."

"You're still talking God and I'm trying to get you into a romantic mood."

"I'm always in a romantic mood when I'm around you," she said honestly.

"Oh?" He suddenly seemed fantastically intrigued.

She grinned at him. "Why are you so surprised? Because I don't throw myself at you?"

Adam studied her. "Actually, you're the opposite of any woman I've ever considered being involved with. Because you've *never* thrown yourself at me. Because you blew me off that first meeting because I was so obnoxious. Because you give the distinct impression that when you spend time with me, it's not because you *need* to, it's simply because you *want* to." He reached up to touch her hair, the side of her face, and let his hand finally rest in the curve of her neck. "I shouldn't be surprised at all if you confess that you've been madly in love with me all this time."

Kathryn gave an outraged gasp and pushed to get out of his arms as she laughed and said in a haughty tone, "You *wish* I was in love with you, Adam LeGrande. You should be so fortunate."

He stilled her with another kiss, prolonging it until she sighed against his mouth and wound her arms around his neck once again. Finally, he murmured against her mouth, *"Yes, I should be so lucky, Katty-girl."*

"Well, say *something.*"

Adam walked slowly around Kathryn, taking in the whole picture.

The moss green silk, luxuriously draping off the shoulder and pooling at her feet felt delicious against her skin. She was wearing Gran's pearl choker and earrings to complete the look. Kathryn grinned at Adam's speechlessness. Obviously he liked what he saw. "Sorry it's not spandex," she teased.

"If I attempt to make suggestions regarding your wardrobe ever again, you have my permission to start hitting me with a blunt object and continue to hit me until I'm silent, okay?"

Kathryn smiled, picking up her small purse and wrap. "You don't look too shabby yourself, you know."

"A tux, is a tux, is a tux, Kathryn," Adam said dismissively. Reaching out to take Kathryn's hand, he said, "Come on. I think this is the first time in forever that I've actually looked forward to going to a function at the country club."

It was a Cinderella evening: beautiful gowns, ballroom dancing, and a handsome prince to dance attendance on Kathryn. There was fun and laughter and a general lightheartedness as she twirled across the floor with Adam. From the corner of her eye, Kathryn saw Miles looking dashing and kingly himself in his tux dancing with Mayor Willoughby. "Did you know that Miles would be here this evening?" she asked Adam.

He glanced over in the direction she indicated and stared at Miles dancing with the Mayor. "Yeah, he told me." Twirling Kathryn around, he said, "You know, June knew."

"Really?" Part of her was surprised, but she was forced to admit that part of her was not. She thought about what she had just discovered about April only this week and wondered what Adam knew, if anything, about Miles' health. "I'm beginning to think that no one really knows the whole picture of who Miles Bishop is."

Adam frowned at her. "Uh-oh, that sounds suspicious." He guided her to the bar to get them drinks after the dance had ended.

Kathryn shrugged. "We've all got secrets, don't we?"

"Something tells me you've got secrets that *I* should know," Adam gave her a penetrating look.

"Adam! Adam! Come quickly! Something's wrong with Miles!" June Willoughby called to them as she worked her way towards them across the dance floor. Adam gave Kathryn a 'now what?' look as he walked toward the mayor.

Miles was sitting in one of the country club's offices, holding some bottled water. His bow tie had been undone and the top buttons of his dress shirt had been loosened. He looked ashen, and very angry. "I told you," he said impatiently to June, "that I didn't need you to get him, June."

"Well," she responded crisply, "it's a good thing that I make my *own* decisions about important matters."

"Miles," Kathryn said, kneeling down beside him, "what can we do?"

Glancing up at Adam standing in the doorway he said through gritted teeth, "Get him out of here."

Kathryn glanced at Adam and then back to Miles. "What are you hiding this week?" Adam asked Miles.

The silence in the room was telling, and everyone looked at everyone else while no one spoke. "Perhaps," Kathryn spoke quietly to Miles, "although it may not be the appropriate time to explain the full situation, it is time to say *something*."

Miles closed his eyes, taking shallow breaths as beads of sweat appeared on his upper lip. It was the first time in Adam's recollection that Miles did not look calm, cool, and collected. Flipping open his cell phone, Adam dialed rapidly. "I need an ambulance," he said looking Miles directly in the eye, challenging him to try and stop him, "at the Wickfield Country Club. Immediately." Closing his phone, Adam said curtly, "*Tell me.*"

How had the two of them worked with each other for over a year and not seen the resemblance? Kathryn wondered as she stood and looked at father and son glaring determinedly at each other. It was impossible for her, now that she knew so much, not to see how similar they were in looks, mannerisms, and mostly, their stubborn personalities.

Once again closing his eyes Miles said, "My guess is that you need to hold out only about two more months before you win this waiting game between us, Son. By then, I'll be out of your life permanently."

Adam, never the soul of patience, approached the nurses' station at the hospital after pacing back and forth in the hospital waiting room for little more than half an hour. "I'd like an update on Miles Bishop."

The nurse looked up from her computer screen, "Hospital policy forbids the release of any patient information except for immediate family. And Mr. Bishop has further stipulated that he wanted," she glanced over at her computer, moving her mouse and clicking through a few screens, "his exact conditions were 'no one but specified immediate family'. He listed three sons and a stepdaughter by name. Are you family?"

They stared at each other for moments, and the nurse gave him an impatient look. "It's not a difficult question, young man, you either are or you aren't."

Little does she know. Damn him. Even from a hospital bed Miles was still playing his games.

"I'm his son." It was the most difficult collection of words he had ever uttered in his life.

She glanced at the screen and looked back at him. "Name?"

"Adam LeGrande"

She arched an eyebrow in skepticism, as if to say, *Are you sure?* Adam stared at her with his 'don't mess with me' face. "You can go in to see him. He is in cubicle twenty-two, down the hallway, make a right, then a quick left. It will be on your right."

"Thanks."

Kathryn had insisted on coming to the hospital and sat waiting for Adam to return with an update. He stared at her sitting on the hard plastic chair in her silk gown and pearls and felt … what? Desire? Compassion? *Love?* A wave of longing washed over him as he stood there staring at her. For a simple life. An uncomplicated future. The ability to have a casual, uncomplicated relationship with a woman. *To have a real love affair.* He mentally rolled his eyes at himself. What did he know about love? Normalcy? Compassion? What business did he have thinking of those things in regard to this beautiful woman walking slowly toward him her face a mask of concern?

"Adam?" Kathryn closed the small distance to stand in front of him, reaching up to put a cool hand against his cheek. "Are you okay? What's the update?"

"I told the nurse I was his son. That's why I can go in. He specified only family."

She gave him a tender smile and sighed. "How did it feel? Admitting?"

She always asks good questions. Nothing ever flusters her. She makes every complication smoother. "It didn't kill me."

Kathryn laughed. "That's a relief." Her hand slid down his chest to his arm and grasped his hand.

"You knew about all this." It was a statement, not a question and he struggled to keep any negative tone out of his voice.

She nodded and sighed. "Yes, Miles told me." Her eyes filled with tears. "It is difficult being in the middle of you two. You've both come to be … special … to me."

"Oh great," he tried some wry humor, "I'm just as special to you as my father is. Yippee."

It worked because she chuckled. "Well, you *are* a better kisser." At his incredulous expression she laughed out loud. "Go. You need to do this, Adam. Go talk to him. I'll be here waiting, drinking this fabulous coffee, and reading this magazine from last summer." She smiled at him. "Don't worry, I haven't read this edition." When he continued to stand there looking at her, she said quietly, *"You need to do this."*

"Yeah, I know."

"And if it makes you feel any better, Miles isn't any happier with these circumstances than you are."

She had a point.

As he turned to walk away she caught his arm, stood up on tiptoe, and kissed his cheek. "I'll pray things go smoothly," she whispered.

Nah, he thought as he walked down the hallway, *pray for a miracle.*

Miles appeared to be asleep when Adam entered the small cubicle. A nurse was reading the monitors and recording information on the chart she held in her hand. She smiled at Adam as he entered and said quietly, "He's been given some morphine for the pain and has dozed off."

"What's next?"

"His doctor's on the way. He'll be admitted just to reevaluate his medications and get the pain under control again." Her expression was full of concern. "This is to be expected and shouldn't cause you more concern than I'm sure you're already dealing with. We'll get things readjusted and he'll be able go back home with you."

"Thanks." Adam pulled a chair up to the side of Miles' bed and sat as the nurse quietly left the room.

"I called James. You don't have to stay," Miles said without opening his eyes.

"Kathryn and I are here. We'll wait. Make sure you get settled."

Miles sighed. "They're admitting me?"

"You didn't really think they'd just dope you up with morphine and send you home did you?"

Cracking one eye, it's pupil dilated and unfocused, Miles said, "I've insisted on it before. Donations from my company have built a majority of this new emergency wing. They'd parade a string of dancing girls through here if I asked."

"That might be worth seeing."

Closing his eye and sighing, Miles murmured, "Nah, there's better stuff to ask for."

"You're dying."

Eyes still closed, Miles responded as Adam expected. "So are you, I'm just going to go a bit quicker." At Adam's frustrated sigh, Miles elaborated. "Prostate cancer. Had testicular years ago, prostate ten years ago and now the prostate's reoccurred again. Fair to say, three strikes and I'm out. Last year the doctors gave me less than a year." He gave a satisfied grunt. "Beat that, but it looks like not by much."

"And you chose to spend your last year working *as my butler?*" Adam murmured sarcastically.

Still with his eyes shut, Miles ground out through clenched teeth, "No, you idiot. I chose to spend the last year of my life trying to get to know my son. *Have you been listening to a single word I've said to you?*" The words poured out in a furious, frustrated whisper.

"Always so *noble*."

"Always so stubborn."

"Always so sure of your superiority!"

"Always so sure of your righteous indignation!"

"Wow. I can really feel the love in here," came a sarcastic male voice from the doorway. Adam rose and turned to look at a tall, handsome, dark haired man dressed in jeans and a sweatshirt. He made no move to enter the room, just leaned against the door jam, arms crossed, taking in the scene.

"James, tell the nurses, *and the doctor* when he gets here, that I'm not staying overnight," Miles ordered from the bed, still with his eyes closed.

James pushed himself off the edge of the doorway and walked over to his father's bedside. "Gee, you look just terrific."

"I mean it, James."

"I know you do," James said mildly, making absolutely no move to speak to anyone. "I called Edward. And April."

Frustration and anger rolled off of Miles in waves. He opened his eyes and struggled to focus. "I don't want them here. Especially April. She'll get upset. Call them and tell them …"

"Will you be quiet?" James cut into Miles' string of new orders. "I called, told them the situation *as I understood it*, and promised to call them back should they need to come. Okay? *Just like you've always insisted.*" He glanced up at Adam and then back at his father. "Man, you're uptight. It must be the company, huh?"

"The company's … *just fine*," Miles said through gritted teeth.

"Then it's the pain," James said matter of factly. "Which is the perfect reason why you should stay overnight and get everything checked out and reevaluated."

"That's what the nurse said should be done," Adam volunteered.

"Yeah," James said nodding and giving Adam a dark look, "that's usually par for the course. Unfortunately, that doesn't mean that the patient will cooperate. Usually he insists on *getting back to work*. Butler duties are apparently *very pressing*."

"*James* ..."Miles commanded.

"You've been in here like this while you've been working for me?!" Adam said incredulously looking down at Miles.

"He's *dying*, man!" James shouted at Adam. "Supposedly he has got just months left ..."

"Keep proving them wrong, don't I?" Miles interjected mildly from the bed.

James continued shouting, ignoring his father's comments. "... and yet he continues to be the same stubborn, annoying ..."

"James, this is your half-brother Adam. He claims I'm shifty and manipulative," Miles interjected with a slight smile. Adam had a sudden flash that perhaps he was enjoying all of this.

"... *pain in my ass*," James continued clearly furious. "He's got his *own* agenda that *must* be completed at all costs, *despite* what anyone else says or advises ... doctors, nurses, family, friends ..."

Miles reached up to take James' hand. "I'm okay, Son. Just take a deep breath. They increased my pain meds last time I saw the doctor, but it makes me so darn tired and, well, there was the dance tonight at the country club and I thought maybe I could get by on the old dose but," he paused, "it was a pipe dream. I acknowledge it was foolish. June's become like a mother hen lately. If she'd just let me take a pain pill I would have been fine but she went and got Adam and ..." he shrugged, blinking slowly, "here I am in the hospital on morphine." He looked at James. "And *going home tonight* as soon as the damn doctor shows up and I tell him so."

"What do you need to inform me of *this time*, Miles?" came a long-suffering voice from the doorway. A man, clearly a doctor even though he was dressed in a pair of casual trousers, button down shirt, and a sport coat, came walking into the room.

"Martin," James said nodding his head in greeting. He indicated Adam with another nod. "Adam LeGrande, Dr. Martin Oates." Martin nodded a greeting and moved to look at Miles' chart.

"Where'd they drag you from this time, Martin?" Miles said, clearly annoyed again.

Martin shrugged, flipping through the chart. "Oh, you know I just sit out in the parking lot reading the paper waiting for the next time you show up, Miles. Need to appear dedicated and concerned about you so that you'll leave me all your money when you kick it."

"Fat chance you snake oil salesman. You're not getting a dime from me, and before I die I'm going to have your license revoked," Miles said as he closed his eyes once again. "And I'm not staying in this torture pit. You either sign the release papers or I'll walk out of here anyway."

James rolled his eyes and stepped back so that Dr. Oates could have complete access to Miles. At Adam's questioning glance he shook his head. "Don't let them snow you. They've been best friends for years."

The truth is more important than the facts.[47]

Chapter Seventeen

Dear Son,

In case you're curious, I have discovered the most difficult task in the world: writing the final communication to someone you love.

And I do love you. Never doubt that, please. As I write this, things are still completely unresolved between us and yet, as you read this, all opportunities on my part to remedy the situation will have been extinguished. I chose not to disappoint you and will get in the last word with this letter. (Please smile.)

It is my earnest prayer that you will, over the remaining years of your life, at least reach a point where you believe in my sincerity. That is my final prayer; my 'last request' of God, shall we say. And while you have had ample evidence to prove my many heinous faults, I would hope that over this past year you will see that I have at least made a sincere effort to become a different person.

I want for you what I never achieved in my lifetime: contentment in wise decisions, joy in achieving a greatness that would be pleasing to God and, last but not

---

[47] Frank Lloyd Wright, 1869-1959

least, true love. All of those are within your reach, Adam. And no one is more deserving of the fulfillment that goes along with those accomplishments.

I leave you with the assurance that my greatest accomplishments in life will always be my children: you, James, Edward, and April. Truly I have done at least four things right.

With sincere love and boundless pride in the man that you are.

Your father, Miles Bishop

P.S. *One last quote before I go. Can't resist. "What lies behind us and what lies before us are tiny matters compared to what lies within us.*[48]*"*

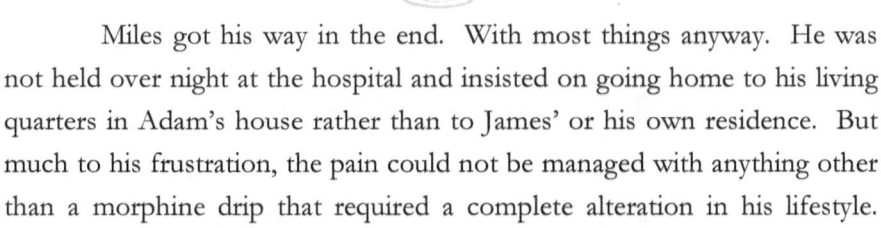

Miles got his way in the end. With most things anyway. He was not held over night at the hospital and insisted on going home to his living quarters in Adam's house rather than to James' or his own residence. But much to his frustration, the pain could not be managed with anything other than a morphine drip that required a complete alteration in his lifestyle. And wonder of all wonders, Miles was a *very* cranky patient.

"Miles, the new nurse is here. Be nice to her, okay? It's not her fault that you're in pain and crabby as hell," Adam admonished from the doorway. Over these last four days their roles had effectively been reversed. No one was unhappier about this than Miles.

"I do not need a nursemaid, nor do I need this infernal intravenous drip!"

"You do!" Adam shouted, tired of having the same conversation over and over again. "Your pain is no longer manageable with oral medication! You know that better than anyone! I'm not qualified to monitor and deal with your medical needs, and I sure as hell am not going to give you a sponge bath! *So get over it, okay?*"

"I cannot tolerate a stranger hovering by my bed invading my privacy. And the pain medication gives me nightmares and causes constant confusion. Surely there has to be something else."

---

[48] Ralph Waldo Emerson, 1803-1882

"Don't you think that Martin would have provided it if there was?" Adam said quietly. "Do you want me to speak to another doctor?"

But Miles refused to answer, glaring at the young nurse as she entered the room with confident steps. Obviously she'd dealt with difficult patients before, as she was completely unfazed with her nonexistent welcome. "How are you today, Mr. Bishop?"

"You're fired," Miles announced in what had become his perpetual stance, lying rigid, eyes closed, teeth clenched.

"I pay for your services, Janine," Adam reminded the young woman. "When in doubt about anything, come and talk to me. You know where my office is, and the door is always open. Even if I'm on the phone, just come right in. And if he gets fresh or rude you have my permission to slap him."

Janine chuckled. "Mr. Bishop is going to be a perfectly polite gentleman today, aren't you?" she said with a smile as she picked up Miles' wrist, looked at her watch and proceeded to take his pulse.

"My gentlemanly skills went out the door with my freedom," he groused.

"How long will you be here Janine?" Adam asked.

"I'll be here through ten tonight, Mr. LeGrande. Marnie will be here through six tomorrow morning. I think Alex is on for the morning shift."

"Yeah, that's fine.

"Who's Alex? *Another* stranger in my room?"

"You'll like Alex, Mr. Bishop. He's about six foot six, black as night, and *loves* to give sponge baths," she said with a wink at Adam.

Adam left Janine to her job while he went to try and concentrate on his own. His life no longer felt like his, and this was only the fourth day. So much for privacy and seclusion with nurses in and out at all hours. In addition, there was the stress of having to meet Edward, James' brother (he could not come to terms with the relationship in any other way) as well as April, Miles' adopted daughter. While Edward was a slightly shorter, slightly younger version of James, April came across as rather bohemian and flighty, introducing an entirely new style and appearance: bizarre. Was there anyone else in the world that wore so much jewelry – all of it horribly costume - in such quantities that it appeared difficult to move? It had been an awkward situation made absolutely impossible by the fact that *Miles was dying*, the ultimate card he had to play in this game of his. Check and mate. Dead and done.

Suddenly, everything seemed completely out of control. The house was in complete disarray. No one was cooking, managing, arranging, or scheduling. Between trying to do what needed to be done professionally and feeling obligated to do those things that needed to be done regarding Miles, Adam had absolutely no time to properly search for, interview, screen, train, and hire a replacement for Miles.

The wisdom of having Miles residing *here* in this house was significantly in question. But what could he do? Throw the guy out, morphine drip and all? How to win friends and influence people. He could see Kathryn frowning at him and could just imagine what she'd have to say about it all.

He sighed, putting his head in his hands. To top everything off, he wasn't sleeping much at all. Couldn't shut his brain off and when he finally did doze off he was plagued with tense, harrowing nightmares. During the chaos of the day he could escape the personal issues he was trying to avoid, but at night, lying in bed, he couldn't avoid the thoughts. This was no longer a battle of wills between himself and his annoying butler with an endless time frame and a personal goal of the 'one who could hold out the longer'. It was already very obvious who was going to hold out longer. Technically, Adam had the championship in the bag. The irony of his 'victory' was made even more galling by the fact that Miles was *still* manipulating him.

The guy's still in your house. Chances are he's going to die here, too. Talk about the ultimate guilt trip and the mother of all forms of manipulation.

The telephone rang and Adam reached to answer it. "LeGrande."

"Hi, Mr. LeGrande? This is Marnie Jackson. The night nurse? I can't make it tonight. My son's got a stomach bug and I'm not feeling too well either. I'm going to call the service when I hang up with you, but I just wanted you to know."

"Don't bother calling the service, Marnie. You don't do any serious medical stuff during the night, do you?"

"Well, no. Alex will come in the morning and administer the meds, do the bathing and stuff. I just kind of babysit through the night. But someone should be around, just in case Mr. Bishop needs anything ..."

"Yeah, I'll do it. I'm not sleeping anyway. I'll drag my laptop in and sit in the corner and work."

"Are you sure? They've always got people available on standby."

"Yeah, I'm sure." *Not.*

"Hey, Crabby. You wore that butler uniform all those months, you're not going to make me get into some white nurses suit are you?"

"What are you talking about, Adam? Where's my new keeper? She's late. Good employees are always punctual. You should fire this one. I don't want anyone handling my medical care that can't even arrive on time."

"I'm it, Crabby. The night nurse called in sick so I said I'd cover. Brought my lap top and figured I'd get some much needed work done without all of the nine million distractions I've been dealing with these past few days."

Miles sighed and shifted in bed. "Good help is hard to find."

"Tell me about it." Adam walked over to Miles' bedside. "You comfortable? I need to get you anything? How about sitting up for a bit?"

Miles shifted again. "I don't need anything that you can give me."

Pulling up a chair, Adam said, "Am I supposed to guess what that means or are you going to elaborate?"

"I want more time, damn it. And I don't think I'm going to get it." He looked down at the book lying face down in his lap, and fiddled with his reading glasses. "I'm not ready yet."

"How's the pain?"

Miles held up his arm. "Right now it's significant. Right now I wish I could ..." he bit back what he was saying and started again. "If I use the pump," he waved the arm with the intravenous tubing, "I can dull the pain and my brain and become a senseless, drooling, imbecile who's too out of it to know the pain is driving him nuts. If I don't use the pump, then I'm coherent, nasty, and in such agony I know exactly why wild animals chew their own limbs off to escape traps." He glared at Adam. "That a good enough description?"

"Yeah, that gives me a good idea," Adam paused. This was going to be one long night if things kept up like this. "What are you reading?"

"Some book about God. You won't like it."

"Says who?"

"After I die, you can speed read through it like you did the Bible, okay? I'll leave it to you in my will."

Adam leaned over and read the cover. *The Purpose Driven Life*[49]. "Any good?"

Miles looked at him, sighed and shifted again. "Not as good as the Bible, but the guy makes some very good points. Look, I was thinking," Miles began, "I don't want your final memories of me to be wasting away back here in my rooms like a piece of rotting garbage. When I insisted on coming back here I thought I'd bounce back like I've done other times. Edward wants me to come stay with him and his wife. I think it might be a good idea."

Adam leaned back in his chair, crossed his arms, and narrowed his eyes. "Let him and the little woman watch you waste away instead, huh? Let them have those wonderful, final memories?" Adam knew that wasn't the best thing to say, but this whole up close and personal stuff was difficult enough with Kathryn. And he liked Kathryn. With Miles *it was absolutely impossible.*

Miles closed his eyes and unconsciously began to rock back and forth. His skin had a grayish cast to it and a sheen of sweat appeared on his upper lip. Adam suddenly had an overwhelming desire to *get out*. What was he thinking, volunteering to sit through the night with a terminally ill person *he didn't even like?* His brain frantically flipped through his options. Unable

---

[49] Rick Warren, *The Purpose Driven Life*

to sit there a moment longer doing nothing, Adam finally ground out, "Will you use the damn pump?" He got up and walked around to the other side of the bed. Hell, if Miles wouldn't push the button, he would. The button was obvious, as it was gripped in Miles' hand. Unused.

Looking up into Miles' face he found his father looking at him intently, pain glazing over his eyes. "Use the button, Miles," Adam said quietly. "I'll read or sing or bang on pots so that you can stay grounded and not get lost and confused, okay?" Adam made a move to pick up the book in Miles' lap, but Miles shook his head. "I could read you the latest prospectus on a company I'm thinking of investing in," Adam tried a bit of sarcastic humor. Heck, it had always worked for him before. "That's guaranteed to bore you to … sleep."

Miles managed a grunt and finally moved his thumb to the pump button and pushed. "My Bible's on the nightstand, if you could stand that. Psalm 51. My favorite."

Oh, great.

At least the infernal rocking back and forth ceased as soon as Miles had pushed the button. Adam found the book, well worn and loaded with papers and notes and bookmarks, on the bedside table. He'd remembered the psalms, full of lah-dee-dah songs of praise and Godly love. Somewhere in the middle … It was easy to find in the end because it was book marked.

"Have mercy on me, O God, according to your unfailing love, according to your great compassion blot out my transgressions. Wash away all my iniquity and cleanse me from my sin. For I know my transgressions, and my sin is always before me.[50]*"* Adam stopped and looked up at Miles lying quietly. "Oh, this is real cheerful stuff, Miles. I read much more of this, *I'm* going to be crying."

"It's good stuff, Adam. King David wrote it." He took a shaky breath. "Me and King David," he held up his hand with his fingers crossed, "we're like this."

"You telling me you're just like King David? The guy who killed Goliath with the sling when he was a kid and was the great king of Israel?"

---

[50] Psalm 51:1-3, New International Version

You have to give the guy credit, Adam thought, *even lying on his deathbed he's still got plenty of arrogance.*

Miles nodded. "Me and David. Like two peas in a pod. Same kind of terrific husband, same kind of terrific father. Started the same. Looks like we're going to end the same… We're practically … twins." He was silent for long moments, his breathing steady as he drifted off into sleep. Adam observed that his color was better. Miles twitched in his sleep and murmured incoherently. *The pain medication gives me nightmares.*

Looking down at the Bible in his lap, Adam said aloud, "Well, if you're so much like King David, maybe I'll read you his story out loud." He began flipping through the pages and finally, after lots of frustrated searching came upon the first heading that mentioned David in first Samuel. He began to read out loud, noting that once he began to speak Miles seemed quieter, more peaceful. *Great, this was going to be one very long night.*

At four a.m., Adam gave his voice a break, wandering over to Miles' small efficiency kitchenette, and helped himself to a cold soda from the fridge. How could he have read that story, *two times before,* and not been moved by it? His head was full of images, vividly swirling in a kaleidoscope of colors. David's shining promise and goodness at the start of his life. David's courage with Goliath. David's friendship with Jonathan. David's forbearance with Saul. David's skill in the taking of Jerusalem. David's joy in his God as he danced before the Ark of the Covenant as it was brought into Jerusalem for the first time.

Then came David's slow downfall into the quagmire of his vast success and power. There were David's many wives and his obvious failure to ever find true love with any of them. Those that stood out in Adam's mind included his politically motivated marriage to Saul's daughter, Michal, and his obsession with Bathsheba that led to her rape. It had to have been rape and nothing else, which then led to the calculated murder of her husband so that David could cover up his sin.

The account of David's complete failure in his role as a father was harsh and unforgiving. He'd chosen to do absolutely nothing regarding the numerous tragedies his children had been faced with including incest, murder, revenge, and betrayal. That led ultimately to the execution of his beloved son, Absalom. Adam had actually been moved to tears as he had read the part where David, in finding out that Absalom had truly been killed sobbed, *"O my son Absalom! My son, my son Absalom! If only I had died instead of you—O Absalom, my son, my son!* [51]*"*. This sorrow was despite Absalom having raised an army and attempted to claim the throne for his own, and still David had mourned his death.

David died with his personal life in chaos, his sons and his wives fighting over who would be his successor as he lay in bed being comforted by a young virgin who slept with him just to keep him warm. *What a way to go.*

Sipping on his soda, Adam went quickly to his office to get the Bible that Kathryn had sent him. Maybe this translation wasn't as powerful? Maybe that's why he'd missed all this in the first two times he had read it? He sat down and reread Psalm 51 aloud. *The whole thing.*

"Against you, and you alone, have I sinned, I have done what is evil in your sight. You will be proved right in what you say, and your judgment against me is just. For I was born a sinner — yes, from the moment my mother conceived me. But you desire honesty from the heart, so you can teach me to be wise in my inmost being. Purify me from my sins, and I will be clean; wash me, and I will be whiter than snow. [52]*"*

No, the translation was just as powerful, just as condemning, just as vivid.

Adam looked at Miles breathing rapidly and beginning to move restlessly. He was in pain again. How long did the morphine last? The nurses had told him that it was impossible for Miles' to overdose, that it was all carefully controlled. It had been close to five hours since Miles had medicated himself. Three hours until the nurse came. He took another sip of soda. Miles murmured in his sleep, frowned, and shifted again restlessly. Better keep reading.

"O give me back my joy again; you have broken me — now let me rejoice. Don't keep looking at my sins. Remove the stain of my guilt. Create in me a clean

---

[51] 2 Samuel 18:33, New International Version
[52] Psalm 51:4-7, New Living Translation

heart, O God. Renew a right spirit within me. Do not banish me from your presence, and don't take your Holy Spirit from me. Restore to me again the joy of your salvation and make me willing to obey you.[53] "

The most incredible quality about King David, as far as Adam was concerned, was his determination each and every time he failed, to get back on the right track with God. That complete acceptance of his own blame. He looked over at Miles' Bible and reread Psalm 51 again in the different translation. Along the margin was a notation written in Miles' own hand: I Samuel 13:14. Adam flipped through the pages. He was getting pretty good at navigating his way through all of the books of the Bible. Carefully underlined by Miles was the following phrase that Adam read aloud, *"For the Lord has sought out a man after his own heart.[54]* "

"My personal goal," Miles said in a scratchy voice.

"Here, take a sip of this." Adam put the Bibles down and walked over to the side of the bed and brought a cup with a straw to Miles' lips. He drank deeply. When he was finished, Adam said, "Use the pump again."

"In a minute. It's a game I play. How long can I go. Only thing I have to amuse myself with lately. That and being nasty to the nurses." He sighed. "What time …?"

"About four-thirty."

"You've been here reading the whole time." It was a statement, not a question.

"Were you awake all this time?" Adam found that hard to believe.

"No, but it's the best sleep I've had in a while and it must have been because you were here talking." Pause. "What have you been reading beside first Samuel?"

"I read about David."

"Ahh, my Biblical twin," Miles made what appeared to be a gargantuan effort to roll on his side while Adam stood there feeling completely useless.

---

[53] Psalm 51:8-12, New Living Translation
[54] I Samuel 13:14a, New Living Translation

"Can I help …?"

"No, I can do it." He was completely gray again and sweating. No rocking yet, though.

"Do the pump," Adam urged.

"In a minute. Remember my game …"

Adam gave a frustrated sigh.

"It's reassuring to know that I can still annoy you …"

"I think I believe that you … really are sincere about all this," Adam felt compelled to say. It was the closest he felt he could come to the impossible topic of forgiveness.

"Sincere about what?" The rocking started for a few moments and then, as if realizing what he was doing, Miles forced himself to stop. He stared intently at Adam, forcing himself to stay focused.

"The whole 'I'm a changed man' spiel you keep throwing at me. The 'I don't want anything but to get to know you' crap you've been trying to pound into my thick skull."

The rocking was back, unable to be prevented. "Ahh, so you finally believe I'm not here for the money."

"Yup."

"Or the excellent salary and benefits." Rocking, sweating, breathing shallow, quick breaths …

"Yeah."

"My, my, I should have ended up on my deathbed a lot sooner," Miles said as he managed a grimace in place of a smile and clicked the morphine pump. "If your voice is going, you can just put on the television or the stereo. That's what the nurse does if I ask."

"No, my voice is okay. Got something else you want me to read?"

"First Corinthians … thirteen …" Adam thought Miles had dozed off and began thumbing through his own Bible trying to find the book of Corinthians. He would underline this passage, or make a note or something. Miles' reedy voice continued, "… verse seven is my favorite, but …" Miles licked his dry lips, "… the whole chapter's pretty good."

Adam finally found the passage, and by the time he started to read Miles was quiet and murmuring again in his sleep. He decided to start with

Miles' favorite verse and had to swallow and take a deep breath before he could say it out loud, *"Love never gives up, never loses faith, is always hopeful, and endures through every circumstance.*[55]*"*

And then Adam began to cry.

---

[55] I Corinthians 13:7, New Living Translation

A foolish heart will call on you to toss your dreams away,
then turn around and blame you for the way you went astray.[56]

Chapter Eighteen

(Try to focus. Counting ... one, two, three, ... Thank You, God, for Your mercy and grace ... four. Try not to slur words.) "What is this? A party? Can't be. Much too glum."

"No, it's a meeting of your fan club, Dad."

"Pretty pitiful showing."

"No it's not. This is just the Executive Board."

"Ah, I see." *(Force self to not rock back and forth with pain. Does not help anyway.)* "I've been dreaming good dreams. Finally."

"Have you now?"

"About heaven. Lovely place ..." *(Fight the urge to go back to sleep to good dreams. Say what needs to be said. Try to remember what needs to be said ...)* "I ... am ... honored ... to ... be called ... your ... father." *(Stay. Awake. Stay. Still.)* James, ... Edward, ... April, ... Adam." *(Pump! Oh, God! The Pain! Where is*

[56] Grateful Dead, Foolish Heart Album, 1989

the pump?! Here it is ... hold on. Wait. Just a little bit longer ...) "Become a ... family, please?" *(Okay. Pump!)* "Love ... you ..."

The dog days of August had settled in with a vengeance and if Kathryn didn't get her run in before the sun was fully up she couldn't stand to do it. Which was why she was fully dressed at five-thirty on a Saturday morning getting ready to go jogging. There had to be a better way to stay healthy, she thought unenthusiastically to herself as she let herself out the front door. It was already hot, that muggy oppressive kind of heat that made you feel like you were breathing through a damp mask. She groaned as she stretched, already mentally deciding that perhaps she'd only run one mile instead of three. Now that's dedication for you, she thought with disgust.

Something made her look up and to her right and what she saw just about broke her heart.

"Adam?" He was slumped in one of the wicker chairs, clothes rumpled, hair sticking up all over his head, and a two-day's growth of beard on his face. Kathryn kneeled down beside him and touched his jean-clad thigh. "Adam?" Although he didn't respond, his eyes were open, red-rimmed, and looking at her. She reached up to smooth his hair and touch his cheek. "Been out here long, love?" she asked quietly. Still no response.

Instinctively she knew. Miles. It had to be Miles. All this past week, since their trip to the hospital, she'd known things were bad either from talking with Adam or April. Known there was very little time. The determination of that man to have persisted until he was finally bedridden and within a week of dying ... *Dear Lord, thank you for Miles' life. Thank you for his example, his persistence, and his patience. Be with those family members and friends he has left behind. Let them remember what was most important to him until the very end. Amen.*

There was only one reason why Adam would be here on her porch at this hour of the morning rather than at his home where all the ... turmoil ... was. There were no words that she could say. She thought of Gran and still, after all these years, the memory of the day she had died and those horrible weeks that followed was something she rarely allowed herself to linger over. The fact that Adam had brought himself here, to her, to her house, spoke volumes. She sat down against the side of the chair, laid her head against his warm thigh, and wrapped her arm around his leg. She would do exactly what she would want done; she would hold him and be there when he was ready to talk. As she sat beside him, he rested his hand against the top of her head and tangled his fingers in her hair. And still he was silent.

"I feel awkward about this, Adam. I have no business being here!" Kathryn was dressed professionally in a suit and heels while Adam looked neat and casual in dress pants and a casual shirt.

"Sorry, Katty-girl. The lawyer wants you here. Seems like Miles has mentioned you in his will. Aren't you lucky."

"I'm horrified! I have no business being mentioned in his will. He barely knew me."

Adam made a rude noise in the back of his throat. "I'll bet you he knew more about you than you do. Probably has a background file that details information about you all the way back to preschool."

"I never went to preschool."

"And Miles probably knew that, too."

That made her smile.

Things had been different between them since Miles' death four weeks ago, since the two of them had sat forever on her front porch drawing comfort and strength from each other. No words had ever been spoken between them that morning; she'd just continued to sit beside him and pray quietly while he stroked her hair and touched the side of her face. When Adam finally started to cry, it had been as natural as breathing to crawl into his lap and simply hold him. Three days later they'd stood side by side, hand in hand for Miles' small, intimate memorial service. They hadn't spoken of it directly, but from that moment on things were … well, set. Joined. Paired. Together. Solid. Unified. Kathryn sighed. No words really fit, but things were definitely different.

They now talked frequently over the course of each day and almost always had dinner together at his house or hers. If the day was too busy or exhausting to get together then they always ended with a long phone conversation full of the daily grind and anything else they saw fit to throw in.

Twice, he'd shown up at church unplanned and uninvited giving her his sardonic look of 'aren't you just thrilled to see me?' as he slid in next to her and whispered something inappropriate in her ear.

For all the time they spent together and talked, there were topics they hadn't broached such as the last days' with Miles, why Adam had begun to attend church with her, and finally, what exactly he felt for her. Kathryn suspected that these topics were all rolled up together in one, tight, complicated package.

Kathryn sighed. She knew what she felt: she was in love with him. Head-over-heels, 'never felt anything like it before' love. How could she not be? He had morphed before her eyes from the nightmare frog to the perfect prince. And the joke was, she wasn't quite sure which one of them had done the actual changing. He still had a wicked, irreverent sense of humor, only now she found she really liked his dry wit and off-kilter observations. She found his willingness never to take himself or his abilities too seriously endearing and, she was forced to admit, it was something that had been there all along. He had a genuine interest in her and her business, never contradicting her but occasionally offering a different perspective of a situation. And Adam continued to have a curiosity, albeit irreverent, about all things Biblical. She knew he was rereading the Bible for a third time, but this time much more slowly. He'd show up with take-out dinner at her house and ask something like, "Why was God so brutal with all of the non-Israelite tribes back in the Old Testament? Couldn't He have been more forgiving?" Or he'd open the front door of his house, grab her hand, drag her into the office and say, "You've got to explain this to me, it just doesn't make sense …" Or, the phone would ring at two fifteen in the morning and his sleep dulled voice would say, "Why did Christ say those things to the Pharisees, I just don't get it …"

He was still the same confident, cocky, brilliant man who had driven her crazy only two months ago, only now she couldn't seem to get enough of him.

The Bible study group had rallied around April and, surprisingly, suddenly had given Kathryn space. Quietly spoken questions like, "How are things?" and "Are you okay?" assured her that they were still praying, watching, and waiting. Again, perhaps it was she who was setting the tone and making things different. She preferred to keep all these new and special perceptions and feelings about Adam closely guarded. Was she afraid of what others would think? Did she fear that the reality of the situation was simply an illusion her own lonely heart had conjured up? They were terrifying thoughts.

But one thing was absolutely certain. She did not belong here at the reading of Miles' will. Never had she felt more awkward or out of place. Kathryn listened silently as the lawyer droned on and on with all the legalese needed to make the dissolution of Miles' estate final. April, dressed in blue velvet and wearing an orchid corsage, had given her a smile and a wave when they had first entered the office. Each of the children had been left money, stocks, bonds and a personal letter. Each of the sons was given the opportunity to choose one Corvette from the fleet of cars that Miles had collected over the years. The rest were to be sold and all proceeds donated to charity. April was given the *May's Flowers* with an admonition to remember that happy things always come in the 'wake' of the sad.

And Kathryn was given a cashier's check for $1,000,000 with it's express purpose to set up a trust fund to further the already "sound and admirable goals" of her company, Advancement Corporation. She was given liberal freedom concerning how to use the money, with the understanding that she would be "prudent and diligent" with the distribution and accounting of all funds expended. She was speechless.

James and Edward each gave her quiet smiles, neither showing any surprise. April had clapped and whooped, and Adam had given her a slow wink.

"Mr. Bishop added this codicil to his will approximately five weeks ago, Ms. McFadden. He had been thoroughly impressed with you when you presented your business aims and objectives. Since his health was not going to allow him to do what he wished in the long term, he felt this would suffice."

"I will do everything in my power to make the most of this gift," she choked out.

"As was expected," the lawyer smiled and nodded. "He also wished to give you this, to be opened privately at your leisure." He handed Kathryn a manila envelope, thick but not necessarily heavy.

Outside the lawyer's office, Kathryn had said to James, Edward, April, and Adam, "I'll provide you each with a yearly accounting of the fund - how I've dispersed and invested the money. And you are always welcome to see the books or ask any questions."

Edward smiled and chuckled. "Dad told us he was leaving you this money. He also told us that he suspected you would offer to give us an accounting." He looked intently at her. "Kathryn, this was something our father wanted to do. He spent the last ten years of his life trying to make atonement for things he did the first fifty. James and I decided long ago it was easier to just go with the flow that was "Miles Bishop" than try to go against it." He glanced at April, fishing for her car keys at the bottom of her enormous purse. "April knows what I'm talking about, too." Looking up at them she nodded and smiled. Edward glanced at Adam. "Our father was always dynamic, persuasive, and driven. Only the most obstinate of people ever failed to be swayed when he put his mind to something." He shrugged. "It's been my distinct pleasure to be on the receiving end of things these past years from my father. Whatever ... issues ... I -," he glanced again at James, "- *we* had with him have long been settled. We desired for him to have ..." he sighed and shrugged, "... 'peace' ... is the best way to describe it, in the end."

They separated, promising to try to get together as a group again soon. As April pulled away, Adam looked at Kathryn and said, "Why am I not surprised that she drives a bright yellow Volkswagen Beetle?" Kathryn smiled as Adam leaned over and murmured in her ear, "How about you take me out to lunch? You're the one who's got a check for a million dollars in your pocket."

"When are you going to look in the packet that Miles left you?" Adam asked Kathryn as they sat at a local deli enjoying the warm fall sunshine and eating sandwiches.

"When are you going to read your letter?"

He ate a potato chip. "Touché."

"Well?"

Adam shook his head. "Dunno. Probably after I take a stiff drink or two. Knowing Miles, it will be loaded with stuff that will piss me off to no end, and I'll have no way of getting even."

She smiled and nodded. "Knowing Miles he did need to have the last word." Taking a deep breath she said, "Did you ever talk? The two of you? At all?"

Adam squinted behind his sunglasses and looked off into the lunch rush business crowd going up and down the sidewalk. He looked debonair and handsome, casually slouched in the plastic patio chair, projecting wealth, confidence, and success. Perhaps that's what so endeared him to her. The reality that he so readily acknowledged that the real Adam was so drastically different from the perceived image. He blew out a sigh and said, "Yes, we ... talked. We didn't get all smarmy and lovey-dovey if that's what you're hoping, though. But we talked ... civilly. I ... acknowledged that I believed in his sincerity." He looked at Kathryn willing her to understand, to affirm. "It was ... the best I could offer at the time." He looked down at his feet.

Leaning forward, Kathryn touched his arm. "Miles told me that forgiveness wasn't necessarily what he was after. He was ... pragmatic. He wanted to try to right some wrongs, affirm things that needed to be affirmed. He didn't exactly say it that way but I got the feeling that he hoped to plant some positive seeds that would maybe grow and cover up the ... damage he had been a party to." She took one of Adam's hands, "Did he manage to plant some good seeds?"

Adam looked down at her hand holding his and then back up at the crowd and sighed. "Yeah, he planted some good seeds. I suppose he accomplished what he set out to do."

Padding into her living room, it was the first time Kathryn could ever remember wondering how a stiff drink would make her feel right now. Adam's plan, before reading his letter from Miles, suddenly didn't seem so far fetched. But she settled herself on the couch, curled her feet underneath her, and took a sip of her steaming tea instead. Bowing her head she prayed aloud, "Thank you for Miles' gift, Lord. Help me to use it wisely and to your pleasure. Let me make you smile."

Why was she hesitating? What could the envelope contain? Miles, with all of his maneuvering in her life had only brought about positive change. Right? Right.

Putting down her mug, she picked up the large manila envelope, tore it open and read the brief note clipped to the top:

My Dearest Kathryn,

Thank you for your shining brightness in my life these last few weeks. Truly you were the exact answer to my prayers.

Most of the information enclosed in this folder is part of the background check I routinely do on people I consider doing business with. I want to assure you that there are no copies - these are the originals. You may do with them as you see fit.

The album belongs to someone else. I thought perhaps you would know the best time to return it.

The CD is some interesting music to cook by. Promise me you'll listen to it at least once and take the time to listen to the words on some of the tracks, okay? I'll let you pick and choose which ones ...

With highest regards,

Miles Bishop

There were indeed three things in the envelope: a file folder labeled "McFadden, K.", a scrapbook of sorts, and a compact disc. She chose the file folder first, setting the scrapbook and the disc aside. Inside was a collection of detailed reports regarding Kathryn, all significantly startling due to the level of private information they contained: an accounting of her personal relationships, her financial background including an extensive credit check, a detail of her current net worth, and a profile of the last ten years of her investment portfolio for herself and her clients. Good grief. How had Miles managed to get hold of these things? Second was a copy of all the legal documentation regarding her abandonment and subsequent adoption by the McFaddens. Included were newspaper accounts of the fatal accident in which her adoptive parents had been killed. She had researched these herself as soon as she was old enough and was familiar with them all. But it was the last collection of papers in the file that made her breath become ragged and her heart race. All the other papers fell in scattered disarray at her feet as she picked up the final one, her hands shaking.

A note was attached to the paper and in Miles' handwriting he had written: *The Internet is a wonderful thing. Information, difficult to obtain in the 1980's is easy now. I tried a search for "Vincent" and "Alexandria (Lexy?)" for 1974, 1975, and 1976. I'm fairly certain this has to be you. What do you think?*

CITY OF SAN FRANCISCO
DIVISION OF HEALTH – VITAL STATISTICS
BIRTH CERTIFICATE

Name of Child: TIGER ROSE SHARON

Date of Birth: MARCH 23, 1975   Time: 5:01 p.m.

Gender: FEMALE

Father: VINCENT TORBETT

Mother: DANA ALEXANDRIA LESH

Place of Birth: ST. MARY'S MEDICAL CENTER

Kathryn sat, trying to breathe slowly and steadily as she processed the information that she held in her hand. Could this really be her? Could her real name be Tiger? The hours and hours she had tried to get herself to remember that simple slip of information had always been unfruitful … She shook her head and laughed bitterly at herself. She had even tried hypnosis once out of desperation. If her real name was Tiger Rose Sharon then she certainly had absolutely no memory of it.

There was a photocopy of a newspaper article. Again with an attached handwritten note from Miles: *You were picked up 10.22.80. In checking the papers after that date, I stumbled on this article. A little too coincidental not to be another accurate piece to your missing past, don't you think? Maybe, just maybe, it wasn't so much abandonment as just an unfortunate end to two very confused lives.*

Deceased Couple Identified

By Tomas Jankowski

NEW YORK CITY, Saturday, November 25, 1980 – Positive identification through dental records and a past missing person's report was received today regarding the identity of the man and woman found dead on East 13th Street early Wednesday morning from an apparent drug overdose. Vincent Michael Torbett, 34, and Dana Alexandria Lesh, 22, were pronounced dead on arrival at Queens Hospital.

Several residents had reported the presence of the two bodies in the alley adjoining 541 and 545 East 13th Street October 23rd. Both buildings have recently been in the news regarding the city's attempt to evict the squatters who have been in residence for more than three years. Arriving on the scene, police discovered the bodies of a Caucasian man and woman amidst the trash receptacles. No identification was found on the bodies.

According to Gordon Jackson, a long time resident of the neighborhood, the occupants of both 541 and 545 have been a 'constant problem' and he expressed 'no surprise' that the police were summoned once again.

Police, questioning some of the residents of both 541 and 545, were able to gain only scant information regarding the identity of the couple who apparently were part of large group of squatters following the current circuit tour of the rock group, The Grateful Dead. The Dead, as their followers call the group, performed Wednesday evening, October 22, at Radio City Music Hall to a sellout crowd. 'Dead-Heads', as the band's followers are known, have an almost mythical devotion to the rock group's lead singer, Jerry Garcia.

According to police, with the scant bit of evidence they were able to collect from the scene, as well as some information provided by a number of witnesses, they were able to trace Tesh's identity back to a missing person/runaway report filed over six years ago by her mother, Ms. Marylynn MacNamara of Tampa, Florida. It was through Ms. MacNamara's assistance that police were able to positively identify Torbett as well ...

Kathryn couldn't sit any longer. A feeling that she hadn't experienced in years was working its way up through the pit of her stomach, clawing up through her lungs making it difficult to catch a breath. Her heart was beating erratically and she felt waves of hot and cold. She pressed her forehead to the window, her pale face reflected in the glass. The loneliness ... The nothingness ... No home. No possessions. No *one*. Not even Gran anymore. Oh, God ...! A sob escaped from her tight chest.

Yes, God. *Fill the void, Lord. Fill the void* ... She took a deep shuddering breath and wiped the tears from her face. She was *not* a no one. She had a home and friends. God continued to bless her in a thousand ways. She would *not* slip down into that deep dark pit that had clawed at her and sucked her down for so many years.

Get back.

Get away.

"I am Kathryn McFadden." She had a thought and couldn't help it, hiccupping a laugh. "Formerly known as Tiger Rose Sharon, apparently." She took a deep shuddering breath. "Temporary daughter of Dana and Vincent." Kathryn closed her eyes and the image of Gran rose vividly before her, laughing and smiling. "Beloved adopted granddaughter of Laury McFadden and apparently the biological granddaughter of Marylynn MacNamara," she said suddenly full of pride. *"And always, a woman after God's own heart."*

The phone rang and she walked over to pick it up. "I read my letter," Adam said without preamble.

"I opened my package," Kathryn said back and was dismayed that her voice sounded unsteady.

"Are you okay?" She pictured Adam sitting up straight behind his big desk suddenly looking fierce.

"Mostly."

"I'm coming over."

"You can't. Not if you had a couple of stiff drinks before you read your letter."

He sighed. "Nah. I took it like a man. I did drink a Coke afterwards, though." Now his voice sounded unsteady.

"Are *you* okay?"

"Yeah. He left me a letter letting me know that he'd won in the end after all."

"He didn't!" Kathryn couldn't believe it.

"Well, he left me a letter saying what he'd hoped to accomplish before his death. Turned out, I gave it to him on a silver platter without even knowing it."

"What did he say he wanted?" Kathryn wandered over to the couch, picking up her birth certificate so she could sit down. Absently, she reached over to the photo album.

"Said all he wanted before he died was for me to realize that he was sincere. That he really, honestly meant what he was saying." Adam gave a short laugh. "Turns out that was about as much as I could offer him when we finally spoke. I told him *exactly that.* That I knew he was sincere. That I believed that he had really changed." He was quiet for a moment. "Do you remember how you said maybe it was possible that we could both win?"

"Um-hmm," she murmured into the mouthpiece.

"I think, once again, you might have been right." At her prolonged silence, Adam said, "Hey, you still there?"

"Maybe you should come over after all," Kathryn said rather abruptly.

"Ooo-kay. Be there in about twenty. You going to feed me?"

"Sure."

Hanging up, Kathryn stared at the first page of the scrapbook she had opened. Another one of Miles' notes was attached to the front inside cover. *Adam*, it read, *I may have been lousy at showing it, but I always cared.* 'CHILD GENIUS ACES ACADEMIC TESTS' with a picture of Adam at no more than age seven standing next to a man in a suit with his hand on Adam's shoulder. She flipped through the pages, reading quickly. 'SCHOOL DISTRICT RECIEVES STUNNING SCHOLARSHIP FOR CHILD GENIUS' with a photo of Adam, no more than ten, his hair slicked back and his shirttail hanging out. 'MIT ADMITS THIRTEEN-YEAR-OLD' with a picture of Adam standing next to a woman who Kathryn assumed to be his mother. 'FATAL CAR CRASH KILLS TWO' with a picture of a deadly highway crash scene. 'DELMONT GRAPHICS TAKES A CHANCE ON GENIUS TEENAGER' with a picture of a tall, gangly Adam in an ill fitting suit. 'HERE IS THE FUTURE OF BANKING' with Adam sitting in front of the computer grinning broadly into the camera. 'WALL STREET LOVES LEGRANDE, INC' with a shot of Adam as Kathryn knew him to be today - handsome and self-assured. There were pages and pages of clippings and photos. Toward the back were reports of private investigations done detailing Adam and whatever current state he was in physically, academically, and professionally.

When Adam arrived Kathryn was cooking up stir-fry vegetables and chicken in the kitchen with the stereo blasting. He wandered into the kitchen, hugged her from behind, and nuzzled her neck. "I didn't knock," he shouted, "because I didn't think you'd be able to hear me!" She turned in his arms and gave him a long kiss. "Hmmm," he yelled, "I should have gotten here sooner!" Adam cocked his head. "*What* are you listening to?"

Kathryn grinned, turned the flame off under the stir-fry, grabbed his hand and dragged him into the living room. Picking up the CD case she handed it to him and walked over to the stereo.

"*Tiger Rose?* The Grateful Dead? You're listening to the *Grateful Dead?*"

There was a momentary lull in the music as Kathryn selected a specific track. "Yup," she said. "And this is *my song*." She danced around him as he stood, bemused, watching her. Kathryn sang the first two stanzas aloud, *"What you gonna call that pretty baby? You must call it one thing or another. This one parted water, that one walked upon. Perhaps I'll call this child a Rose of Sharon. What's to be the ground that child walks upon? Will it be solid rock or shifting sand? Think I'll set him down on concrete highways. Think I'll bring him up to walk the land."* [57]

Adam caught her to him as she danced around him and they swayed to the blaring music. When the song ended, he let her reach over and turn down the volume, but the music still filled the room with its beat. "What's this all about?" he finally asked her once she came back into his arms.

"Miles left this for me."

"Miles left you a Grateful Dead CD?!"

Giggling, she nodded her head. "Apparently, my parents were huge Dead Heads. The *Tiger Rose* album came out the same month I was born, March, 1975."

Adam pulled back and frowned down at her. "How do you know all this?" When she gave him a look, he glanced over at the couch where the torn manila envelope still sat. "Don't tell me ... He didn't find ..."

"He did, Adam! He found my birth certificate and the name of my birthparents! Can you believe it?"

"Yeah, somehow I can," Adam said with little surprise.

She dragged him over to the couch and thrust a paper in his hand. Scanning it quickly he looked up with a crooked smile. *"Tiger Rose Sharon?* You're kidding me, right?"

Kathryn laughed. "The song I just played you is called "Rose of Sharon" from the Grateful Dead 'Tiger Rose' album. It's not too hard to figure out how my parents came up with my name, huh?" She handed him the newspaper article copy, and he began reading it.

Looking up at her, Adam reached over and cupped her cheek. "You okay?"

Eyes shining with unshed tears, she nodded.

"You want me to call you Tiger from now on?"

---

[57] "Rose of Sharon", Tiger Rose Album, Grateful Dead, March, 1975

She burst out laughing and shook her head 'no' vigorously. "Sit back. I have something for you, too."

"Uh-oh."

"No," Kathryn assured him. "It's good. I promise." And with that, she set the album in his lap and looked at him expectantly.

"This is for me?"

"Yup. Miles said in a note that it was up to me to decide when would be the right time to give it to you. Obviously he put all these things together a few months before his death. He had no way of knowing what state your relationship would be in. So he left me the album to give you when I decided." Adam stared at her for long moments before he finally looked down at the album in his lap and then slowly opened it.

He took a long time looking at it. Kathryn curled up next to him, her head leaning against his shoulder. He read every single article, scanned every single report, read each letter. When he finally closed the album he was quiet for a *long* time. At last he said, "He watched me my whole life," with something akin to wonder in his voice.

Adam rubbed his face and sighed a deep sigh that seemed to come all the way from his toes. "This whole forgiveness thing, Kathryn. I've been thinking about it. And you know, what you've said about changing, becoming a different person when you change your ... perspective on life?"

"Yeah ..."

"I think I *want* those changes. I ..." he turned to look at her, putting his arm around her. "I *love* the person you are, Kathryn. You're dream scenario on the outside but you're *so much more beautiful* on the inside. And what I love most about you is your spiritual side. I'm drawn to it. That peace, that willingness to try to see what's good and right in people and circumstances. It is so much more attractive than ... I ever thought something could be. *I want it, too.*"

He touched her face and murmured, "These past weeks and months haven't been easy, but they've been *good*, you know? I *feel* different and I like the changes. Suddenly, I get the feeling that I can have *it all*: happiness, peace, love, contentment ..." He leaned over and kissed her slowly and sweetly. "I want to be the good man you think I can be, Kathryn.

"I read that letter from Miles tonight and all I could think was 'I've got to get over to Kathryn's and talk to her about it.'" He reached up and smoothed her hair back from her face. "Am I saying this right? Are you getting what I'm telling to you? *I love you, Kathryn McFadden.* Big love. Full love. Can't-get-enough-of-you love. Want-to-grow-old-and-wrinkled-with-you love …"

He untangled himself from her and the papers on the couch and stood up and walked over to the fireplace, picking up a photo of Kathryn and a collection of laughing friends from the mantelpiece. Something told Kathryn to stay silent. Let him talk. Don't interrupt the flow.

"I don't want you to feel any pressure about saying that back, okay? I'm learning to be a very patient guy. I must get it from my …" he sighed and swallowed, "father. So, I don't want you to …" He didn't finish the sentence, just stood there looking rather lost and forlorn. "I never felt loved and I've never experienced love for another person, Katty-girl. You're making both suddenly very easy to do."

Kathryn came up behind him and wrapped her arms around his waist, resting her cheek against his solid back. She could feel his heart rhythmically beating and the tension that radiated through his body. She smoothed her hands up and down his sides and breathed in deeply his delicious scent of soap and subtle aftershave. "I've been thinking for quite awhile … that I love everything about you," she said softly. "I love your sense of humor and your ability to laugh at yourself. I love your curiosity about things in my life that you don't know about – my spiritual life in particular. I love talking and sharing," she chuckled, "and even sparring back and forth with wits and words. I love watching your *real self* come awake and grow more vibrant with each passing day. I've loved you for quite a while, Adam LeGrande." She laughed again. "Despite my best intentions not to."

He turned in her arms. "So I'm not messing this up?" he asked after a time, with real indecision in his voice.

Reaching up with both hands she cupped his serious face and drew him down so that their foreheads rested against each other. "No, you're not messing this up," she said quietly.

"Even though I always seem to …"

It had worked once before, so she used the same technique, kissing him to get him to be quiet. He wrapped his arms around her and just about squeezed the life out of her. When they finally broke the kiss she not only had both arms around his neck, she'd wrapped her left leg around his legs. *She would never get enough of this man.*

"So are things good enough for a name change?" he asked with a funny expression on his face.

Kathryn pulled back to get a good look at him, frowning, her heart pounding. "I don't get -,"

"I was thinking when we get married and you take on "LeGrande" we could slip in "Tiger" for your middle name. I like the sound of 'Kathryn Tiger LeGrande', don't you?"

"Don't joke …"

"I'm not joking."

"You don't have to …"

"Have you learned *nothing* about me in the time we've been together? Have I *ever* done or *proposed* anything that I didn't *want* to do?"

"No, but …"

"No 'buts', Kathryn Tiger, no 'buts' at all. We both know I'm a slow work in progress, and I've got loads and loads of work still ahead of me. It will probably take years," he chuckled, "heck, *decades* for me to get it all right. Normally, I wouldn't advise you to hook up with such a long term, fixer upper, but you have to admit -,"

"You *do* have a lot of potential," Kathryn finished for him with a huge smile.

"You took the words right out of my mouth, Tiger-Girl," he said, and then picked her up and spun her around while she laughed in the sheer joy of the moment.

Whoso loves believes the impossible.[58]

Epilogue

"Hello?"

"Hello. I'm trying to get in touch with a Ms. Marylynn MacNamara?"

"I'm Marylynn MacNamara. Who is this? If you're a sales person, I've asked to have my name put on the 'Do Not Call List' because -,"

"I'm not a sales person Ms. MacNamara. My name is Kathryn LeGrande and, um, ... I think I am your granddaughter.

(Shocked silence.)

"I, well, I am fairly certain that my mother's name was Dana Alexandria Lesh and my father's name -,"

(Voice high and shaky.) "D-Dana? Did you say Dana?"

"Yes. I'm sorry. I'm sure this is quite a shock for you and I've had quite a few months to think about all of this but ..."

"Dana was going to have a baby. That no account Michael Torbett got her pregnant when she was only sixteen years old! He was nigh onto thirty years old! I told him it wasn't right, tried to keep him away. Told him he was nothing but an abuser of

---

[58] Elizabeth Barrett Browning, 1806-1861

children … When I threatened to call the police he took my Dana away … I never ever got to see my grandchild. Not once." (Drift off into silence.)

"You filed a missing person's report."

(Deep sigh, voice filled with sorrow.) "Things didn't move too quickly back then over a runaway teen. No matter how much I pleaded and shouted." (Be lost, for long moments in the unhappy memories.) "I got a call only once from Dana. It was years after. That's when she told me that she had a little girl. Said she was very smart. Said she had long brown hair and big brown eyes. Told me that she wanted to bring the girl to me because things weren't going so well for her." (Swallow.) "I told her to bring herself back home, too. But she said it was … 'too late' … for her to come back home." (Said softly, almost in a whisper.) "I always wondered if I should have said something different …"

"Did Dana tell you what she named her little girl, Mrs. MacNamara?"

"You know, that was the oddest part of the conversation. I did ask her what the little girl's name was. And you know what she told me? She said — and I remember it just like it was yesterday — she said, 'Well, her most favorite of all her names is 'Katy'.' Isn't that an odd thing to say?"

"Well, yes, it is a bit odd when you don't know the whole story. Perhaps my husband and I could come down and visit you some time soon and we could talk and compare notes. I've had a private investigator looking into things for the past few months. That's how I was able to locate you."

"I never had the money for a private investigator. I just prayed. That's what I did. That's what I've been doing faithfully all these years. Praying."

"My husband, Adam, likes to say 'Prayer and Wheaties: The breakfast of champions'."

(Thoughtful silence followed by an amused chuckle.) "That's a clever one I've never heard. Who said that?"

(Sigh.) "Oh, Adam never quotes anyone. Thinks he's smart enough to come up with his own clever sayings."

About The Author

Susan McGeown is a wife, mother, daughter, sister, friend, aunt, uncle (don't ask), teacher, author ... but, most importantly, a "woman after God's own heart." Living in Bridgewater, New Jersey, with her husband of over fifteen years and their three children, writing stories is just about the best way she can imagine spending her free time. Each of Sue's stories champions those emotions nearest and dearest to her: faith, joy, hope and love.

Philippians 1:20-21

For I fully expect and hope that I will never be ashamed, but that I will continue to be bold for Christ, as I have been in the past. And I trust that my life will bring honor to Christ, whether I live or die. For to me, living means living for Christ, and dying is even better.